Totally Bound Publishing books by Jayce Carter

The Omega's Alphas
Owned by the Alphas
Shared by the Alphas
Saved by the Alphas
Protected by her Alphas

The Omega's Alphas

SAVED BY THE ALPHAS

JAYCE CARTER

Saved by the Alphas
ISBN # 978-1-83943-840-0
©Copyright Jayce Carter 2020
Cover Art by Erin Dameron-Hill ©Copyright January 2020
Interior text design by Claire Siemaszkiewicz
Totally Bound Publishing

Published in 2020 by Totally Bound Publishing, United Kingdom.

SAVED BY THE ALPHAS

Dedication

To all the people who will now giggle whenever
someone innocently mentions a knot.
I'm not sorry. Not even a little.

Chapter One

The monsters of Tracy's past clawed at her shoulders, never allowing her a moment of true peace. Her nightmares — the horrors her life had been for so long — did quiet as she watched her daughter, Karen, swinging on the playset in the back of the omega group home where they lived.

Sure, she'd never thought she'd end up living in a place like that. She hadn't grown up expecting to have a single room where she and her daughter slept in the same bed, where they ate their meals at a table full of other omegas and children who had no home.

And yet, she went to sleep without fear of one of her mate's mood shifts. She closed her eyes and knew Karen wouldn't waken to screaming, crying or the snap of flesh against flesh.

"Mom!" Karen rushed to the deck Tracy sat on, the little girl's red hair tangled from her games. "When's Sam coming?"

The question sent a lance of pain through Tracy's chest. Just the name sprang the alpha's face to her mind.

His black hair and tan skin, his lips always pulled into that reassuring smile. It haunted her sometimes, when she closed her eyes and recalled his sweet disposition.

She'd stayed with him for two weeks after the death of her mate, two weeks when she and Tracy had found some stability with the detective. He had gathered her into his arms when she'd cried as the ambulance had taken her mate's body away, had sat up with Karen when she'd woken from a bad dream that first night.

"I don't know." Tracy ran her pencil over the paper before her, sketching the landscaped backyard. "He's busy."

That, and she'd moved out, despite him asking her to stay. When they'd stood by his front door, Karen already in the waiting car, Tracy had struggled to put into words why she had to leave.

'Stay, Tracy.' Sam had leaned his shoulder against the wall with the same ease he always had. He never looked put out, never ruffled. Instead, a kind smile was always on his full lips and his brown eyes sparkled with charm. *'Karen's happy here, and I have more than enough space. You'll be cramped in one of those homes, and you won't have my charming smile.'*

'I can't.' She'd rubbed her palms on her thighs, nerves running rampant through her as they always did with Sam near. His presence and his scent made her want to crawl the walls. She wanted more and yet it sparked a fear inside her she couldn't ignore. She could never quite get a hold of herself around the alpha who had made it clear that he wanted her.

'Why not? Just help me understand the problem. I like you two here,' he'd admitted, voice low when she didn't answer right away.

'I'm not ready.'

'I'm not asking you for anything.'

8

'*You will. I don't have anything, and I need to take time for Karen and me.*'

'*Take the time here.*' Sam had reached toward her, as though he'd wanted to take her wrist, to touch her, to cross the threshold he was always careful to keep.

Tracy had jerked backward, fear winning out. It always won out. It wasn't Sam she was afraid of, but he was as good a stand-in as any for her demons.

He'd sighed and dropped his hand. A soft nod had ruffled his short hair, but he'd come no closer. '*Okay. Look, you've got a place here, and you can call me anytime. Spend some time, work on yourself, and come back.*' He'd stared at her, as though he'd wanted an answer. When none had come, he'd curled his lips up on one side. '*I can wait as long as you need me to.*'

Karen pulled on Tracy's hand, waking her from the memory, from the last time she'd seen Sam a month before.

"What?"

"Can we go see him? He said he'd take me for ice cream."

Tracy set her pencil down and tried to keep a steady face. Karen didn't need to see the longing there. "I don't know, sweetheart. It's getting late. Why don't you go play before we take you in and get you a bath, hmm?"

Karen gave her a sigh and a slight glare, one intended to say exactly what she thought about her mother's avoidance. The girl was too smart, a sad souvenir from being raised in a household with her father. She'd grown up having to be aware of every little thing, always afraid of setting off his temper, which meant she saw more than she should, knew more than she should have needed to.

She rushed off to the swing set again, and when she did that, when she played like any other eight-year-old, Tracy could almost pretend they were normal.

Karen was a regular kid who hadn't lived through hell. Tracy was an omega looking for love and a life and a mate, not the used-up, broken creature her mate had left after his death.

Sam's smile flashed in her mind again, and she returned her attention to her drawing. If only she could pretend things were different, that she was the sort of woman who could have a future with an alpha like that.

Instead of any of that, she hid herself in her art, in the care of her daughter, and shoved Sam's handsome face away.

* * * *

Sam sat across from Claire, the omega he'd come to know, her three mates moving around the house, prowling close as they always did. They were protective, as most alphas were, and even with people they knew and trusted, they never went far away.

Which made Sam laugh, because he'd damn well seen what Claire had done to the alpha who had threatened her weeks before. He'd seen the way the dead alpha's throat had been torn out, the teeth marks and chunks of flesh missing from him. In fact, he was likely in more danger than she was. Omegas weren't something to underestimate.

Even so, the sweetness of their worry charmed him. He'd always wanted that, the laughter of an omega and the playing of children filling his home.

It seemed less likely it would happen as the years passed, but that didn't stop him from wanting it.

"What about Alison?" Concern colored Claire's words.

"Without her coming in to talk to me, there isn't much I can do. I've added notes to files in case she gets picked up, but I've got limits, and helping an off-the-grid omega who won't come forward is one of them."

"She's missing," Claire said, drawing the words out as if that alone made her point.

"From what I saw, she can handle herself. She's vicious," Bryce chimed in, with a slight shudder.

"Vicious or not, I tried to call her two weeks ago, and I haven't heard anything. Tiffany hasn't heard anything. No one has been to her cabin in weeks."

Sam tapped his fingers against the edge of the kitchen counter, trying to act as though those things didn't get to him. He'd seen what happened to omegas when they disappeared, and it was never anything good. Still, Claire had been through enough. The woman didn't need to hear that if Alison was missing, she was probably dead. As a detective for an omega crimes division, he'd seen the worst. Sam knew exactly how many risks to omegas existed.

Instead, he shrugged. "I can't put a search out without any information, especially since she's staying off the radar on purpose. If I hear anything, I'll tell you."

Claire's shoulders sank, and immediately, Kaidan was there. He pressed a kiss to her temple. "She's fine, I'm sure. You can disappear when you want to, so I'd bet she can, too."

Claire tipped her head up and offered a sweet kiss to Kaidan, the exchange driving that ache deeper into Sam's chest, his envy of the life he wanted and couldn't manage to get.

So, instead, Sam dropped his gaze to the tile of the counter and gave them privacy, not wanting to intrude on the moment.

Claire's voice drew him back moments later. "She's doing well."

Sam's chuckle was soft, but he played dumb. "Who are we talking about, now?"

Claire's look said his attempt at humor didn't land. "Karen's been asking about you, too."

Sam even missed that little girl. He still had the picture she'd drawn him hung on his fridge, and damn if he didn't stare at that thing while he ate at his kitchen table alone. "She's a good kid. They're doing okay? Don't need anything?"

"They're good. I went to the house yesterday and checked in. Karen loves the big yard and the swing set, and Tracy is mostly just resting."

Sam leaned his elbow on the counter as he reminded himself that he was glad. He wanted her to be happy. He wanted Tracy to get her feet under her.

He remembered her black eye and injured hip after the last encounter with her mate, when her mate had found her after she'd run, after Claire had helped her run. The first night when he'd brought her to his house, as stupid as the choice had been, she'd woken from a nightmare. He'd pulled her against his chest and offered a gentle purr until she'd fallen back asleep. Her hip had healed fast, and he'd grown used to having her near.

Damn, she'd crawled beneath his skin fast.

It was good she was getting her bearings and working on herself, creating a life for them. He just wished he could be a part of it.

Not that he didn't understand her hesitation. The poor girl had gotten snatched up by that alpha of hers young, and he'd kept his claws in her for years. She'd never had the chance to be on her own.

So, he understood it, and if it was anyone else, he'd have said she should stay on her own for at least a year. He'd dealt with omegas in similar situations enough to know that rushing things wasn't the best choice.

The part of him that wanted her for his own, though, wasn't thrilled with the idea of waiting so long. The itch through him, the unease that never went away, demanded he go find her, that he sate himself with her scent and make sure she was okay.

He'd just denied it over the past month. Each time he'd craved her, when he'd wanted to call the house, wanted to show up no matter what a disaster he knew it would be, he'd just shoved it down. Of course, the more he denied it, the more it grew inside him. The thing was like a prowling dog on a chain, now.

He ground the heel of his palm against his chest as if it could break up the tension that had settled there.

"That's good," he said instead, hoping none of it showed.

Claire's eyes, sharp and far too smart, said she'd spotted it anyway. "You know, you can't go to the omega house, since they're not big on alphas, but maybe the next time I have her and Karen over, I could shoot you a text?"

Sam laughed at the ploy. "As sneaky as you are, that's probably not a good idea."

"Why not?"

"Because she was pretty clear about wanting space."

"Omegas don't always know what they want," Bryce offered from the other side of the counter. "Claire here wasn't easy to catch, and if I'd listened to her, it never would have happened."

Claire sent him a glare, and he only lifted an eyebrow in response. The affection between them, even with the subtle jabs, had Sam smiling.

"That's different. Tracy isn't wrong about this. She should have some time on her own, time to figure out what she wants." Sam offered Claire a smile. "Besides, I can wait. Thanks for letting me know they're doing well. If she needs anything, give me a call."

Joshua leaned against the counter, his shoulder pressed against Claire's as if he couldn't quite get close enough. "I helped her look over some of the financial paperwork last time she was here. Her mate's death certificate had come through, and she was given access to all the funds. That man had no shortage of money, so when she's ready to move out? She and the girl are set."

Sam hadn't expected that. Nothing in his interactions with Tracy had implied she came from money.

Claire spoke up as though she'd read the thought on Sam's face. "She didn't handle the finances, so I don't think she knew what they had. He was the sort to keep all that away from her."

"Probably afraid if she knew, if she had access, that she'd use it to run. Bastards like that enjoy cutting their mates off from any chance of help." Sam didn't bother to hide the anger in his voice at the idea of Tracy being trapped, of her being at that mate's mercy while trying to care for a young child.

Again, that tension rose in him, and try as he might, he knew he couldn't fully settle the powerful instinct. It wanted her. It wanted a shot at her mate, despite the fact the bastard was six feet under. It wanted to lock the doors and crawl into bed beside her, to know she was safe and that the child was safe, as well.

But that wasn't happening, at least no time soon.

He contented himself with giving in and giving up the pretenses. "Okay, fine. You've got me. Tell me everything about how they're doing."

* * * *

The breeze helped keep Tracy cool as she worked on a painting that had taken her two weeks. The mountain ranges surrounding her were lovely and frightening and reassuring all at once. They towered up on the edges of every direction, yet the few times she'd left the area, when she'd gone where the ground stretched out without anything to break it up, she'd felt exposed and uneasy.

Tracy had set up the old wooden easel the group home had on the outskirts of the property. A sketch the first day had quickly turned into a painting, with layers of acrylic overlapping to capture the brown of the mountains, the white of the rocks and the green patches in between.

Her skills had dwindled from years of disuse. She'd painted at first with Richard, during those initial years when things hadn't been terrible. She'd even sketched him, at times. The strong jaw, the jutting chin, the blues eyes that had turned gray with age. He'd even set up an art studio for her, bought her the things to create.

Those had been good years, and the idea never failed to unnerve her. People thought abuse happened right away, that a woman met a man and the first time they saw one another, he slugged her.

That wasn't the truth. It had started small, just red flags that she'd dismissed. Possessiveness, control, all things wrapped up in the lie of love. *I just worry about you, that's why you can't go out without me. I need to know where you are at all times so I can keep you safe*. It went from that to snapped insults, subtle and sharp.

Things grew, though. They always did. Whatever happened at the start of a relationship, it always picked up speed. By the time she'd stopped painting him, when the idea of sketching those hard eyes had made her hand tremble, she'd started to cower. *Why don't you draw me anymore?* She'd swallowed and tried, afraid to anger him, but the result had been lifeless, and he'd only grunted an unhappy sound and left her be.

Another year and she'd set down her paintbrush for good. Painting was about seeing the beauty in the world, and she couldn't manage that anymore.

The freedom she'd found since his death, the fleeting smile of her daughter as she played, those things brought back her desire.

Skill would take time to rebuild, the muscles having grown lazy, but it was the spark she'd found again.

It let her think maybe things might be okay.

The crunch of dry shrubs behind her had Tracy turning, the same panic that always rose in her when she was snuck up upon. *Will that ever go away?*

Behind her stood three men, all well-dressed. Two had the black suits and rigid stances of bodyguards, and the third, who rested between them, looked as if he'd never worked hard a day in his life. His black hair was slicked back, a fancy suit tailored perfectly to his thin form.

Clearly, he was in charge.

Tracy swallowed hard as she curled her shoulders in, as she tried to look smaller. She knew she looked foolish, like prey caught in headlights, but she couldn't do anything but freeze.

The man in the expensive suit spoke up first. "Tracy Pera?"

She nodded. Maybe they were police, coming to talk to her about what had happened, about her mate? Insurance?

"Hello. My name is Mario Navarro."

The name didn't ring any bells, but why would it? Tracy knew few people, had lived as little more than a prisoner over the past fifteen years.

Thankfully, Mario didn't seem to care what she had to say. "I knew your mate before his passing. We were business associates."

Tracy's unease lifted a little at that. "You worked at the financial group with him?"

Mario's smile nothing to reassure her. It radiated menace and condescension, like her question was almost adorable enough not to annoy him. "Is that what he said he did? I suppose it's as good a lie as any."

Tracy took a step backward and bumped into her easel, trying to keep a minimum distance between her and the men. They continued to advance in slow, purposeful steps.

Why did I go so far from the house? Karen was playing inside, out of the way, which was the only thing she found herself thankful for.

She should have never left the safety of the house. The few times she'd had to go out, she'd always gone with one of the beta males who volunteered to escort the omegas. They were kind and didn't set off her alarms the way alphas did.

These men weren't alphas, yet all her warning bells were screaming in her head.

Mario's smile twisted further. Did he like her fear? Was this the sort of man who got off on a woman's unease? On the power he felt from it? "I'm here because I need you to do something for me."

"I don't think I can help you."

"You sell yourself short, dear. Richard possessed files of some great importance. He enjoyed using them as an insurance policy to guarantee his safety and yours. This worked well enough while he was alive, but now that he is dead, I find myself feeling rather exposed. You see, the files he has do not look favorably upon me, and I would sleep much sounder at night if I were to have them back in my possession."

"I don't know about any files. Richard never talked about work with me."

"Of course he didn't. I didn't think he sat down and told you anything. I mean, why would he? You were…well, what you are. However, you lived with him. You have access to all he had. If anyone can find those files, it would be you."

"I can't. I don't know anything," she whispered, willing him to understand. Richard had told her nothing. He'd kept his work away from her, never confided in her or treated her as an equal.

His teeth flashed in the bright sun, and the action was odd on his face, as if he'd practiced it from alphas but couldn't quite get it right. "You will. I'll give you one month to locate the files and return them to me. And don't think about involving the police, because you will not like my response."

Tracy froze until Mario nodded, the gesture polite, as if they'd had a lovely conversation and he was then taking his leave. He walked away with the two hulking bodyguards, and the roar of an engine said they'd started their car. They must have parked near the back road of the property. She didn't dare move until the noise had died away, telling her they'd left.

Tracy gathered her art supplies, tucking the painting beneath one arm and the easel beneath the other. She rushed for the safety of the house, with its impressive security system and massive locks.

The moment she got inside, she took a deep breath. *Everything is okay.* She had no idea what that man was talking about, but she was safe inside the house, right? Nothing could get her there. Even so, she called out Karen's name.

Karen came out from the theater, the noises of a kids' movie following her as she squinted, her eyes not adjusting from the dark movie room. "What, Mom?"

Tracy dropped her things and gathered the girl in her arms. She pressed a kiss to her red hair, a tremble inside her she hadn't realized had grown so strong.

Relax. People make things up all the time. No one can get to either of us. He was bluffing.

Tracy ushered Karen back off to finish her movie. No need to burden the young girl. The rush inside had meant Tracy had pressed a still wet painting to her side, and along with ruining the piece, she'd smeared all manner of grays and blues on her clothing.

She closed the door to her room, trying to laugh off the encounter, to make the entire thing into a joke where she'd overreacted and let fear get the best of her.

A letter on the bed stopped her short. The folded piece of paper had her name on the front in perfect calligraphy.

With a shaking hand, Tracy lifted the paper and unfolded it.

Tracy,
In case you thought you were safe, rest assured, you are not outside my grasp. What I asked of you is not difficult and complying is your best option. However, if you thought about betraying me, if you thought about denying me, I would suggest you rethink it.

No signature rested at the bottom, but it didn't need one. Mario's face, his arrogant, threatening smirk, mocked her in her mind.

He was bluffing, right? Just because someone snuck a letter inside didn't mean she wasn't safe. The walls of the home had become her fortress, her shelter against a dangerous storm.

That's what she thought until the first bullet shattered not only her window but also the safety she'd thought she'd found.

Chapter Two

Sam paced the long hallway outside the conference rooms.

"Just go in already." Bran leaned against the wall, watching Sam refuse to stand still.

"She didn't ask for me."

"So? You're here, ain't you?" Bran twisted a paperclip in his hands, a nervous habit that came from his endless attempts to quit smoking. While he didn't work closely with Bran all that often, the other officer was a good one, despite being far too nosy.

"If she wanted me, she could have asked." Sam shoved his hands into his pockets, trying to stay out of the way.

People rushed from room to room, taking statements, running background checks. The attack on the omega house wasn't the sort of thing that happened by accident. Six bedroom windows and no injuries? *Either a miracle, or someone meant it to be a warning.*

"People don't always ask for what they want." Bran gave a not-too-subtle nod in Sam's direction.

Point taken.

"She doesn't need to see me like this anyway."

"Yeah, sure, omegas hate when men get all protective." The eye-roll Bran offered would have made a teenage girl proud.

Still, he knew he was right. An omega with a past like Tracy's didn't need to see the sort of rare violence Sam had going on in his head. It meant he'd resigned himself to the background, to the details and the evident and the things that left him out of sight and it seemed, out of mind.

She should have asked for me.

Just as the petty, sullen thought crossed his mind, a familiar face appeared when he turned the corner into the break room.

Karen stood, staring at the vending machine with the sort of empty expression he'd seen before.

Poor girl had been through too much, seen too much. She didn't need this on top of it all.

Should I turn around? Her mother didn't want to see me. Maybe I shouldn't get involved.

As he convinced himself to back away, Karen turned and met his gaze. The little girl's bottom lip trembled, the subtle show of upset before she tried to bury it.

Sam couldn't walk away, not after that, not after Karen tried to be so damn brave. She shouldn't have to do that.

He waved off Bran and crossed the hallway, then pulled a dollar from his pocket and slid it into the machine. "I like the chocolate the best."

"Mom said I should get something healthy."

He laughed, popped in the C-6 for the chocolate bar, then slid another dollar into the machine before getting one of the apples at the top. "There. Now you did what she said but you get some chocolate, too. I think you've earned some chocolate."

Karen reached into the area at the bottom where the food rested. "Mom's scared," she whispered.

"I know. We're going to figure it out though, don't you worry."

She bit at her bottom lip, her gaze down. "She's packing."

Sam crouched so Karen would look at him. "What do you mean, she's packing?"

Karen shifted her food to one hand, then reached into her pocket. She withdrew a piece of paper but didn't turn it over. "Just afterward, she threw all our stuff into bags."

Sam tried to keep the frown from his face, but he doubted it worked. *A startle like that is sure to make anyone want to run, right? Especially with Tracy's past.* "What happened probably just freaked her out. She'll settle down, and everything will be fine."

Karen fiddled with the paper, twisting it as if she wanted to give it to him but was afraid to. Finally, she shoved the note into his hand.

Sam took it, opening the paper until he could make out the words. Each word, every hardly-veiled threat, had his temper rising.

Temper wasn't something he normally had a problem with. Things just slid off him, never getting him angry, never getting below his calm, cheerful exterior.

The idea that someone had threatened Tracy, that they'd taken a shot at her, that they'd frightened her in a place that should have been a sanctuary had him wanting to bare his teeth.

"Where did you get this?"

Karen scraped her foot against the tile floor. "Mom hid it under her mattress, where she always hid things

23

from Dad. She doesn't know I took it." Karen lifted her head to meet his gaze. "I don't want to run again."

Sam set his hand on the girl's shoulder and squeezed. "You won't have to run again, I promise."

"What about that?" She gestured toward the paper.

"Don't you worry about this." Sam tucked it into his pocket. "Whoever wrote this? They can't get you."

"You promise?"

Sam nodded, his words suddenly mattering like they never had before. He wasn't a liar by nature, but lying to Karen was just wrong. "Yeah, kid, I promise. I'll take care of it."

When Sam entered the conference room, Karen having stayed in the chair just outside, Tracy didn't even turn her head at first.

She looked exhausted. How long had she been there? Five hours? Sam fought the desire to just haul her out, over his shoulder if needed, and deposit her into his bed to sleep. It was where she should have been from the start. They could talk about the attack and the threat later. None of it mattered more than her well-being.

But she wouldn't give in to that, and even trying it would send her running, so Sam tamped down the desire. Instead, he inhaled so her scent filled his nostrils.

Tracy must have done the same, because she spun toward him, knocking over the chair she'd been sitting in, her eyes as wild as her red hair.

Sam lifted his hands, palms out, and stayed by the door to give her space.

He'd seen her have this fight before, watched her warring between wanting to trust him and fearing him. His alpha side, that terrified her. But the man? Him, she knew. Hell, he was pretty sure that part of him she even liked.

So, Sam waited for her gather her courage, for her to let the knee-jerk reaction fade and think through the fear.

It happened, slower than he'd have liked, slower than it had when she'd stayed at his place. Was it the attack? The distance? He'd hoped the month apart would let her feel more secure, but that wasn't how it seemed.

She's just been through a lot. At the reminder, he tried to let go of the tension inside him. That tension seemed odd. Sam wasn't a tense man. At thirty-seven, he'd found little would bother him.

This bothered him.

Tracy's shoulders slumped and she dropped her gaze to his feet, as though she couldn't not watch him but couldn't bring herself to look him in the eye, either. "Sorry," she whispered.

The shame in those words tugged at him.

"Nothing to be sorry about." He meant it about more than that moment. She didn't have a damned thing to be sorry about, and he wished she believed him.

Instead of acknowledging that, she wrapped her arms around herself, her thick red hair braided and hanging over one shoulder. She wore a sweater, thick and baggy and unassuming. It was how she'd dressed since he'd first met her, as if she tried to attract as little notice as possible. A stupid plan, because the woman was breathtaking no matter how much she tried not to be. The freckles that stood out on her face made her look sweet, especially when paired with those bright amber eyes, too big and innocent to be fair.

Tracy took a step backward, and that woke him up. *Right, don't leer at her, you idiot.*

"What are you doing here?" she asked with a hesitation, a nervousness that said she wasn't sure she was even allowed to ask.

"I work here," he reminded her, instead of admitting to the truth.

"Right."

He fought a smile at the way she said that, as if she'd forgotten. She hadn't forgotten, just hoped to avoid him, he'd bet, especially if she planned to run.

The last thing she'd want was to get back on his radar if she was going to up and disappear. Of course, how the silly woman could think she'd ever gotten off his radar, he didn't understand.

Then again, understanding women was something no man — alpha or otherwise — was any good at.

"I'm fine." She took her seat again after picking it back up. "You don't need to worry."

Like hell I don't.

Once he was sure she wasn't going to head straight into a panic attack, Sam fully entered the room and took the seat across from her, using the table as a barrier for her comfort. He wanted to grab her, to pull her into his arms, to feel all those subtle curves beneath the baggy clothes she wore and explore each one, to promise he'd let nothing happen to her, not ever. Except, he knew damned well that wouldn't happen, not with how flighty she was.

Hell, with how covered up she stayed, he had no idea what was even beneath those far-too-big clothes she wore. She was thin — too thin really — given her neck and hands. She'd put on weight over the time since her mate's passing, over her weeks with him. Still, he yearned to discover her hip-to-waist ratio, to see if she had dimples on her ass, to see how far down those mass of freckles went.

Her eyes widened and her cheeks reddened. The start of something that could almost be interest sprang in her eyes before fear overtook it.

Knock it off. It's not as if you're going to sleep with her here, anyway.

Sam called on his easy-going nature before tipping his lips into his normal, charming smile. Better to not address all that lust she must have scented from him. Talking about it wouldn't make her feel safer. She'd just have to learn he wouldn't hurt her, and that would take time.

Thankfully, time he had. Sam had never been afraid to play the long game, to wait for what he wanted, and there was no doubt in his mind that he wanted this omega. It all came down to if he could convince her of that.

"I saw Karen down the hall."

Tracy toyed with the hem of the sweater as she sat. "She's afraid. She's been through enough, and she shouldn't have to be afraid anymore."

"She's a tough kid, like her mom. She'll be fine."

Tracy's soft nod and hard eyes screamed her thoughts. *She'll be fine because we won't be here anymore.* Poor woman thought she could just skip town like that? That no one would know or care?

Still, he approached things carefully. Conversations were minefields with flighty omegas, and he didn't need this one blowing up in his face. "What's your plan?"

"Plan?" A tinge of hysteria colored the word. "They said the windows would be fixed by night, and they've already put in extra security."

"No. What are you going to do? Running won't help."

Her face paled. "I don't know what you're —"

Sam pushed the piece of paper across the table, and she didn't even reach for it. She didn't need to, did she? Instead, she watched the note as if it were a spider, slinking around and waiting to strike. "Where did you get that?"

"Does it matter?"

A pause. "Karen found it. I should have known she'd figure out my hiding spot."

"She asked me to keep you guys safe."

"She shouldn't have asked you." The tremble in Tracy's voice showed she wasn't as dead-set on going as she seemed.

"Come on, honey. You don't want to pick up and take off again, not when you two are finally getting your feet under you. Let me help." *Let me take care of you.*

She dragged her tongue against her bottom lip, shifting in the chair. He could almost see each thought that crossed her mind, each objection, each fear. She didn't want to be a burden, she was afraid he couldn't help her, she was afraid of him.

Finally, Tracy met his gaze, the fight gone from her tired, amber eyes. "This isn't your responsibility." Even as she said it, he heard beneath the words. She wanted him to help, she just didn't know how to ask for it.

"It is now. I swore to her I would, and I don't make promising I won't keep. Until we've figured this out, you're stuck with me, honey."

* * * *

Walking into Sam's house conflicted Tracy. Being there again made her uneasy, yet the warm decor, the lived-in furniture and the atmosphere made her feel safe.

It's not the house, you coward. It's the alpha.

Karen rushed past her, her colorful backpack slung over her shoulder as she ran for her room.

Tracy went to tell the little girl to wait, but Sam waved off her concern. "Room is still set up for her, don't worry. Never changed a thing in it."

After a month? "Why not?"

Sam carried Tracy's bags himself, having snorted softly when she'd attempted to help. The sight of him hefting the bags over his broad shoulder had managed to make Tracy's stomach flip, to some strange place between desire and fear.

"I was hoping you'd come back. What can I say? I'm a hopeless romantic," he said.

Tracy opened her mouth to refute the whole 'romantic' part of his statement, but he didn't wait around long enough for her to. Instead, he passed her, heading in the same direction as Karen, to the spare room he'd given to her. Not more than a minute later, she heard the hushed whispers of Sam and Karen, up to no good, she was sure. When she and Karen had stayed with Sam before, he Sam and Karen had worked sneakily together to get whatever they wanted. Desserts, special dinners, time at the park. Tracy constantly felt outnumbered, which should have annoyed her.

Instead, it had been strange to have someone who listened to Karen, someone she could play that 'us against them' game with the way she did with Sam. She deserved that sort of foundation, that stability.

Sure enough, Karen walked out with a grin that said they'd come up with an idea Tracy wouldn't like.

"What are you up to?" Tracy asked.

"I want to spend the night with Claire."

The idea seized her chest. She didn't let Karen go places often, and after the fright at the group home? The thought of Karen out of her sight had terror freezing her.

Sam spoke up from behind Karen. "Claire's place is a fortress, you know that. I think she could use a night away, and you and I could talk." When she was ready to argue, Sam added, "I don't think you want her overhearing our conversation, do you?"

At that, Tracy paused. Sam meant their talk about who had left that note, about what had happened. He hadn't pushed at the station, only explaining how running wouldn't work. Whoever had orchestrated that message had done so with no less than four highly trained snipers, given the simultaneous shots fired and the distance from where they'd shot from. Not to mention, they had to have watched her for a while since they knew where the bedrooms were and had gotten a note inside.

A person like that wouldn't let her run off, not until they got what they wanted. Karen didn't need to be there, didn't need to hear those details. She deserved a night away, a night to just be a kid, and she trusted Claire like no other.

Tracy forced herself to nod. "Okay. I'll call her."

Two hours later, Claire and the three alphas she lived with had picked up Karen. The idea of her being in a house with alphas put Tracy on edge, but she knew Claire, and the three alphas had proven themselves.

As trustworthy as any alpha could, at least. Alphas weren't all bad, weren't all like Richard, but Tracy had dealt with enough that she struggled to remember it.

It left Sam and her alone, with him seated in the recliner he tended to use during the evenings and her perched on the edge of the couch in case she needed to bolt.

It again reminded her of how different they were. He was large, quiet, steady. He smiled easily, talked to others easily, had all the confidence in the world. A slight five-o'clock shadow had sprung up on his strong jawline, but it did nothing to dull his sweet-natured look.

"Talk to me, honey. I just want to help."

Tracy took a deep breath before spilling the details, her gaze down on her hands where she twisted them. Sam asked questions, and she answered them as best she could. The main point, though? She knew nothing about what Richard had done for a living. He'd left her out of that part of his life, and she had no idea who he knew, where he might have kept any files or even what he did.

Sam remained silent for most of the story, letting her pour it out. At the end, he remained quiet, a slight twitch in his eyes the only sign he'd heard her, that he still thought about it. Finally, he nodded. "I know Mario Navarro. He's involved in things most of the police force doesn't acknowledge. He's paid off a lot of people to keep his nose clean, or at least keep it looking that way, and he's more than capable of doing what he said he could."

"What do we do, then?"

"I'll go talk to him."

Tracy sat up straight, an instant no on her lips. "You can't do that."

Sam offered her that smile that melted parts of her she'd thought were frozen solid. "You worried about me?"

"No," she said, afraid of Sam seeing too much, of him expecting something, of him mistaking her worry for affection. "He said if I went to the police, I'd be sorry."

"Trust me, I'll handle it. Nothing will happen to you or Karen."

She didn't push as much as she wanted to. She'd learned a long time before not to argue with an alpha once they'd made up their mind. It never ended well for her. Her best bet had always been to keep her head down and just try to survive. The only choices she'd made in her life had been disastrous, so leaving it to others had always proved safer.

She left the subject be and tried to gather courage to broach another topic. "I can't do this," she whispered.

"Do what? Talk to me?"

Tracy risked a glance up to meet his lovely dark brown eyes, so many shades deeper than her own amber. "I know you want something from me that I can't give you."

"How would you know if you haven't asked me?"

"Because I can see it. I can smell it. You want things from me, things I'm not capable of. I appreciate what you've done for Karen and me, I can't ever thank you enough for that, but, Sam—"

"I heard you weren't sleeping in the group home. I can see the bags under your eyes."

"So?"

"So, you were sleeping here. Are you really going to say you didn't like being here? That Karen didn't like it?"

"I needed to stand on my own."

"Did I hobble you? Did I keep you from doing anything?"

No, he hadn't. If anything, he'd pushed her to try new things, to regain that footing she'd lost. He'd given her space, freedom and a safe place to be when the world and her past overwhelmed her. He'd been the one to suggest counseling, to offer self-defense class information, to wait in the car as she'd run errands, telling her she could handle them even as fear had pricked at her.

Tracy took her bottom lip between her teeth and stopped hiding. "Eventually you were going to get tired of what I can't give you. You wouldn't have been happy with me not wanting anything physical. Everything has a price, and I can't pay what you want from me." Admitting it hurt. Even though she couldn't be what Sam was looking for, she hated having to say it out loud, having to put her shortcomings and flaws on display, even to a man who knew them. She hated it more because she wanted what he did but wasn't capable of it.

Sam reached out, moving slowly enough, she could have pulled away.

She didn't.

He set his large, warm palm on her hand, the weight reassuring. "I'm not asking for anything you won't give me yet."

"Yet?" The word came out rough when she caught the promise there, the certainty.

His lips curled up into a smile that had her lower stomach tightening, a flash of desire so quick and subtle that she almost missed it. "Yeah, honey, yet. I'll wait as long as it takes, but you're going to give in."

"How can you be so sure?"

Sam traced her knuckles with his thumb, the touch teasing and coaxing. "Because I've seen you look at me, too, and even if you try to hide it, you want me. You've just got to realize it."

Tracy wanted to argue, but the gentle sweep of his thumb against her skin said differently.

No matter how it frightened her, she did want him.

* * * *

Sam didn't like to walk into situations without a plan. Some things couldn't be helped, though, and this wasn't the sort of thing he could bring back-up to.

Mario sat at a table in the Italian restaurant Sam's contacts had tipped him off about.

Maybe this was a terrible idea. *There's no 'maybe' about it. Walking up to a known criminal and telling them to knock it off? Always a brilliant plan.*

Still, Sam didn't have many options. He figured one good scare and Mario would back off. He couldn't consider whatever Richard had worth it to get on the radar of a cop. People like Mario were about risk vs reward. Sam needed to show him that the risk was too great to bother.

He took a seat across from Mario, who raised his hand when his hulking guards came forward.

"And who might you be?"

Sam lifted his badge, flashing it to Mario before tucking it away again.

Mario cocked up an eyebrow, then took a sip of the wine in front of him. "And to what do I owe a visit from the city's finest?"

"I'm here on behalf of a woman you sent a message to yesterday."

Mario set the glass down slowly, his gaze hard but giving no other sign of surprise or concern. "Yet you're not here with anyone else. You aren't here in an official manner, are you?"

"Does it matter? I can make life very difficult for you."

Mario laughed. "I have the FBI watching me, and the local police and another handful of organizations who would all like to see me brought down. I doubt you can cause me any additional trouble. If you could, you wouldn't be sitting here like this." He leaned back, staring at Sam. "Tracy wouldn't have gone to the police on her own. She's a broken coward."

A rumble in Sam's chest told him he'd growled. He cut it short, cursing himself for the mistake.

Mario caught it, a vicious smile on his thin lips. "That explains it, doesn't it? This little show of dominance you're doing, it isn't about your job. That means it must be personal. Well, well, didn't she move on fast? I would have thought of her as an omega who took things slower, but then again, what else do they really do?"

Sam unlocked his jaw when his molars started to ache. *Relax. Don't let it get to you.* "If anything happens to her, you won't like what I do."

"You won't do a thing. If you take this to your boss, they'll tell you to lay off. If you push, I'll push harder. Tell your whore that the only way she and that child of hers get out of this in one piece is to do what I'm asking. If she gets me what I want, everyone walks away. It's not so bad a deal."

"Call her a whore again and see what happens."

At that, Mario straightened. "I've given you far more understanding than I normally allow. Threaten me again, insult me again, and you can see what happens."

Sam narrowed his eyes, frustration simmering inside him. He wanted to slug the man for the insult to Tracy, for frightening her, but he kept his head. Mario wasn't kidding. He had far more power than any criminal should, and Sam's plan was to make this go away. Hitting the asshole would only make things worse. "She doesn't have what you want, anyway."

"She can get it. She will if she wants to keep breathing."

The threat slipped his temper free. He lifted his lip in a snarl, his voice dropping an octave. "You're going to want to stop threatening her."

Mario leaned in closer, over the table. "You alphas think you are something special, something above everyone else. You aren't. You are animals, driven by hormones and instincts, and you think you can do whatever you want, say whatever you want, and there will be no consequences. You think you are at the top of the food chain, but I assure you, you are not. Do not forget it."

Before Sam could speak again, Mario waved forward the guards. One hauled Sam out of the booth, grip hard and sure.

Mario gave his parting shot with a bite in his voice. "Tell Tracy to hurry. I tend to grow impatient."

The two guards hustled Sam from the restaurant, and no one looked up. If that didn't tell him the sort of place the business was, nothing did. They all minded their own business, not willing to get involved or risk their own necks.

Fine by him. He didn't like the idea of civilian casualties.

The bodyguards all but threw him into the alleyway, hard enough he caught himself on the opposite wall.

He fought the desire to turn and spit a snarky insult at them.

"One more thing," one said.

Sam did turn, then. "Oh yeah? And what is that?"

"Mr. Navarro wanted to ensure you fully understood where you were on the food chain."

Sam huffed a dark laugh at the stupid statement. "And how does he plan to do that?"

The answer came when one of the brutes nailed him in the jaw with a sucker punch, and one that was clearly not going to be the last.

Chapter Three

"Tell me what's wrong," Tracy said for what had to have been the fifth time since Kaidan had picked her up at Sam's house.

He'd asked her to go with him, and a call from Claire had settled her nerves. If there was any alpha, besides Sam, she might have gone with, it would have been Kaidan. He was the quiet, sweet one of Claire's alphas.

Claire said she would have come but had to stay with Karen. Whatever was going on, they didn't want the girl to see.

"Try to relax," Kaidan said as he opened the car door on her side, his voice mild.

They were at the hospital. She'd recognized the route quickly, and each turn that took them closer had only made it harder to breathe. Tracy stood but didn't move away from the car, terror making her feet heavy.

Why was she there? What was she supposed to see?

"Is it Sam?" Her voice cracked. She hated hospitals, always had.

Ever since the first time Richard had broken her arm and she'd had to spend a night there, when she'd had to lie to the nurses and doctors about how it had happened, she'd always hated the place.

Now? The idea of Sam there made her stomach sink.

A weight came to rest on her shoulder, and she flinched from it.

Kaidan lifted his hand away, but he didn't look insulted. Then again, Claire had been jumpy, too. Kaidan had to understand. "He's alive," he said.

The words alone let her breathe. At least she wasn't identifying a body.

"What happened?"

"Why don't we get you inside, and you can talk to the doctor yourself. She'll answer any questions you have."

Tracy couldn't get her feet to move, but when Kaidan set a hand on her back, when he applied pressure, she followed the silent demand. Fighting an alpha, even one who had treated her well, wasn't something Tracy did, so she numbly walked, following Kaidan's cues.

They went into the hospital and took the elevator. The flashes of each time Richard had put her there rushed her, the times she had lain in the bed, her mate beside her, when they'd walked out of there and she'd known she was headed back to that house.

"Breathe," Kaidan said.

Tracy lifted her head, realizing they'd come to stop in front of a door. Her lightheaded sensation said Kaidan was right, and she pulled in a gasping breath. Drywall bit into her palm as she grasped the wall to steady herself.

"You'll feel better once you go inside." Kaidan didn't open the door, turning toward her instead. "Look at me, Tracy."

She held on to his steady voice and lifted her gaze to his. He didn't turn away, didn't do anything but give her something steady. After a moment, he nodded as though he could see she'd gathered some sense of strength.

It fled from her, however, when he opened the door. Sam lay on the bed, his eyes closed, an IV from the crook of his elbow, bruises and discoloration marring his familiar face.

Her stomach sank at the sight of Sam hurt, and she knew then he meant more to her than she'd ever admitted.

Please don't let me lose him already.

* * * *

Tracy pressed the button of the vending machine. She hadn't eaten all night, having spent it sitting beside an unconscious Sam.

Him silent seemed wrong. A few of his fellow cops had come by, taken one look at her and treated her with an odd sort of reverence that surprised her. No one knew who had attacked him.

Well, I know. It was Mario. It had to be. She'd said nothing, though. Tracy wasn't the sort to speak out of turn, to make decisions like that on her own. Maybe telling anyone would put them all in more danger. It left her sitting there, useless and helpless until Sam woke. Then again, that was what she was used to, letting others make choices, deal with her problems. *Coward.*

The doctor had insisted he'd recover, that he was unconscious due to the sedatives rather than injury. Alphas required specialized medication to put them out, much like omegas. The heightened hormone levels inside both made them unpredictable and dangerous.

Still, a night of the constant beeping of machines, the stench of bleach warping the comforting scent of Sam, left her on edge.

The metal of the vending machine twisted, but the package of crackers caught before they fell, dangling just out of reach.

Really?

Tracy stared in silence as the bag hung, some cosmic joke about the rest of her life, about things that were snatched away, always just out of reach and her helpless to do anything but watch.

Frustration grew inside her, sparked by the bag of crackers but fueled by everything else. By Sam being in a hospital bed because he'd tried to help her, by her past, by her lack of a future. It exploded inside her as she hit her palm against the plexiglass front of the machine.

It was a weak strike, yet more than she'd done before.

A huffed sound behind her reminded Tracy of exactly who and what she was and she twisted to face the newcomer, a wave of panic setting in.

A man stood behind her. *No, not a man, an alpha.* He was tall and wider than any man had a right to be. His hair was long, brushing just past his shoulders, and had an almost strawberry tint to the dark blond. In addition, facial hair covered his face, neatly groomed but spread over his chin, his jaw and his top lip. It all made him look wild, like some man who belonged in the middle of a jungle, not a brightly lit hospital. "You sure showed it."

Tracy frowned at what seemed like a non sequitur, until the man nodded at the machine.

Right, the crackers.

41

Still, she said nothing. It was safer to say nothing, to give an alpha no reason to become angry.

The man laughed before reaching past her and kicking his booted foot against the vending machine. Sure enough, the crackers fell to the bottom, and he reached inside to grab the snack.

Tracy took them when offered, the response automatic. *Do what alphas demand but give them nothing to use against you.*

He leaned a shoulder against the vending machine, his gaze working over her in a slow, careful perusal. His eyes mirrored hers, a light brown but with flecks of green that lit up from the fluorescent. It didn't seem fair that anyone should look good under fluorescent lights. "Are you here visiting someone?"

"Yes," Tracy whispered.

"Your mate?"

The word had the color drain from her cheeks and her chest tighten. *Mate?* That word held so much more than just letters. It held her past, and pain, and fear, and a multitude of things she didn't want to unbox with a strange alpha studying her far too closely.

She shook her head. "No, not my mate."

He released a sound that wasn't quite belief, his gaze never straying from her. "I see. Well, my name is Mason."

Mason. She rolled the name on her tongue, testing it even as he watched her with unnerving intensity.

When she didn't respond, didn't offer him anything else, he tilted his head and gave a crooked smile. "Interesting," he said so quietly, it was as though he spoke to himself. "Well, I think I'll see you around."

The strange man said nothing else before pushing off the machine and strolling away, Tracy's gaze locking to his broad shoulders and wide back.

* * * *

"That's nice." Sam's voice was rough from disuse, but he couldn't not respond to the gentle way Tracy dragged her thumb over his hand. He'd woken to pain, dulled as it was, through his body, but damn if he noticed much beyond Tracy's scent and that soft, chaste stroke.

Tracy yanked backward so fast he ached from the loss. He would have sworn he'd felt her while he'd been out, that sweet touch of her hands to his seeping past even the medication used to knock him out.

Was there anything better to wake up to?

"Are you okay? Doctor, he's awake." She rose from her spot to flag down a short doctor who stood on the other side of the room.

The woman came over, black hair pulled back in a ponytail, no makeup on, a no-nonsense attitude that made Sam suspect she made a terrible conversationalist but a great doctor.

Well, she'd kept him alive, so she had to be okay.

"How are you feeling?" The doctor leaned over him and flashed a light into his eyes.

"Fine." Even though he didn't always behave like a typical alpha, showing weakness was something even he didn't care to do. Those instincts in him, the ones that made alphas far more animalistic than the betas, hated showing weakness. Weakness got people killed. Still, Sam reined in the desire to snap. Just because something was instinctual didn't mean he couldn't control it, couldn't think through it.

The doctor snorted and finished her quick exam, though Sam's gaze rarely strayed from Tracy, who stood back, her arms crossed, her body tense.

She still wore those clothes three sizes too large that hid her figure, but damn, he'd missed it.

"When can I get out of here?"

The doctor stood back, her lips thinning. "You shouldn't leave for at least a week. Your arm is broken, a rib is cracked and you've sustained many contusions."

Sam maneuvered himself to sitting, hiding just how much work that took. "I've had broken bones before and a cracked rib just takes time and rest. There's no reason for me to stay here."

"You'll need help, and I understand you live alone."

Sam waved her off with the arm not in a cast. *Huh, look at that, it really is broken.* "It's fine."

"I won't release you if you're going home alone, Mr. Franklin. Without help, you will need to remain here for at least a week."

"I'll help him." Tracy didn't come closer, and her voice was so soft it nearly didn't carry over the argument between Sam and the doctor.

The doctor turned to face her. "I didn't think anyone lived with him."

Tracy's gulp was loud, but she pressed on. "I'll stay with him and help him."

"Do you have experience with injuries?"

Shadows haunted her eyes, and Sam wanted to catch her hand, to pull her closer and press a kiss to her temple.

She'd never allow it, though, and she'd hate for him to do so in front of a stranger. Instead, he remained still, let her answer for herself.

As fast as those horrors crossed her eyes, she leashed them. "Yes, I know how to take care of injuries like this."

The doctor didn't seem entirely convinced, but she agreed to gather instructions for her and said they'd release him by nightfall.

Whenever that is. What time is it? What day is it?

When the doctor left, Sam and Tracy remained awkwardly, the entire hospital room between them.

"You shouldn't have gone," she said.

Even her chiding made him smile. Sure, he didn't care for her seeing him beaten up. He wanted to be her hero, and yet he'd gotten his ass handed to him instead.

Doesn't matter, I'll keep her safe.

"This is just a scratch. Don't worry about it."

"It's not a scratch. You were unconscious for over twenty-four hours. Your arm is broken." Tears swam in her voice, and they broke Sam's heart.

"Hey, no," he said, voice gentle. "Come here."

Her feet moved automatically, bringing her to his side in a moment. When he patted the side of the bed, she leaned her hip against it. "Don't you dare cry."

"What happened?"

He didn't want to say anything because it would only make her worry. Unfortunately, that trembling bottom lip had him picking his words carefully. "Talked to Mario, and he's not too inclined to just forget about this."

Fear sparked in her amber eyes. "I told you. After you're on your feet, I'll run—"

He reached up with his good hand and cupped her cheek, risking the touch, hoping emotions ran high enough she wouldn't flinch. "Not a chance. This doesn't mean we're done, it just means we figure out a different plan."

"What plan?"

"Don't worry about it right now." Telling her the truth, that they'd have to find the files to use them as leverage, would only further frighten her. That was the last thing he wanted. "Have you been here the whole time?"

Tracy pushed her hair behind her ear, and the action caught his focus. Her hair, red and wild, haunted his dreams. He wanted to slip his fingers into the strands and hold her still as he kissed her breath away.

Instead, he contented himself with the thought and kept speaking when she didn't answer. "You need sleep," he said.

Tracy offered him a tired smile. "We'll be going home in a few hours."

Home. The way she called his house *home* had him feeling like the injuries didn't matter. He liked the sound of that, the idea of them picking up Karen, of them all heading back to the home they shared. Hell, he liked the idea that she thought of it as safe.

As quickly as she said it, she seemed to notice the gravity. "I didn't mean —"

Before he could wave her off, the doctor returned, a file in her hands. "Your emergency contacts were here earlier, and I need them to sign this."

"What emergency contacts?"

The doctor lifted her gaze. "We called those on your file when you were brought in in case someone needed to make decisions for you."

"I never filled out paperwork for that."

"You did, but it was quite a while ago."

"Who's my emergency contact, then?"

A voice from the doorway caught his attention, answering before the doctor could. "Well, it's been a while."

Something flashed inside Sam, between happiness and anger, like a kick to the stomach when he laid eyes on Mason, his old friend. Wait, the doctor had said contacts, as in more than one.

Yep, there he is. Dylan strolled in next, his dark eyes full of menace and annoyance, his short hair still the same familiar light brown that almost made him look youthful. *Almost.* "Well, isn't this cozy?"

"Fuck," Sam muttered.

The two men he'd wanted nowhere near Tracy.

Chapter Four

Dylan doubted Sam had changed a bit in five years. He looked the same smug asshole he'd been before, even busted up as he was. Too handsome, too charming and too damned aware of both things.

A quick excuse to the female sent her rushing off, the timid thing at least good at playing innocent.

Then again, omegas always were.

And he knew she was an omega. It was easy to tell with how Sam looked at her, and he'd always fallen for omegas.

The moment the door shut, once the omega had left the room, Sam's easy-going smile stripped from his features. "What are you doing here?" He asked the question of both Dylan and Mason, as if the two alphas had intruded.

Like fuck, Dylan hadn't asked to get a call at three in the morning. Sam didn't get to act pissy over this. If anyone got to have a temper tantrum, is was Dylan.

"The hospital called. It seems you haven't updated your emergency contacts in a while," Mason said.

"So you should have ignored the call."

Mason's laugh held no real humor, but no malice either. Then again, Mason had never given into their feud with his heart. He'd walked out because the other two had, but he'd never held on to the hurt or anger. That wasn't Mason's way. "You should have known better than to think that. We owe too many favors to ignore each other. Doesn't matter how much bad blood there is, we don't ignore calls for help."

"This isn't a call for help. It was a mistake."

Dylan made an ugly sound at the bullshit. A mistake? Lots of things were mistakes, like the shit Sam had pulled, but this? This was just karma, really. It was fate reminding him that at the end of the day, he was never going to quite escape the other two alphas or their past.

"Mason has an annoying streak of nobility. What are you doing here?" Sam held the arm in a cast tight against his side, and the bruises on his face stole away some of those boyish good looks he had.

Maybe Sam's words should have bothered him. Sam had basically called him someone without scruples. *Too bad for him I don't care what he thinks.*

Dylan crossed his arms. "I don't really care what you do, but your mom would castrate me if I let anything happen to you. I saw what she did to that stray dog she took in."

Sam narrowed his eyes, his gaze hard. "Well, as you can tell, I'm not going to die any time soon. Sorry to have wasted your time." He paused, then shook his head. "Actually, I'm not."

Dylan couldn't help the dark chuckle at the barb, didn't bother to hide it. Better Sam know he was amused by the little show than think he could get under Dylan's skin.

No one got under Dylan's skin.

Mason, forever the one in the middle of them, tried like always to fix things. "So, that your mate?" Mason nodded toward the door.

The skittish little omega, too thin for Dylan's taste and with a mass of wild red hair, stuck in his head. *Because she's dangerous. They all are, just females who twist alphas up, who take what they want and leave husks behind.*

He'd seen it enough times.

"She's not up for discussion," was Sam's reply, and no bigger verbal 'do not cross line' could be made.

And Dylan tramped right on through it because that was what he did. "Really? Because I got to wonder what she's hiding under that baggy sweater."

Sam's snarl was hard and fast, low and dangerous in the small room. Fuck, it was fun riling him. Too bad Sam was too hurt to do more than snarl.

"Knock it off, Dylan," Mason snapped, tone exhausted as though he'd been herding kittens all day and was sick of their shit. "Sam, stop snarling for fuck's sake. You know he's just needling you. And before you start trying to kick us out again, it seems you not only didn't tell the hospital we didn't talk anymore, but you didn't tell your buddies at the station, either. As soon as I showed up, they sure did spill everything. About Tracy, about the attack on the omega group home, about the attack on you."

Sam's gaze fell to the window. "So? None of that is your problem."

"Well, we're here, aren't we? Those calls we got and the plane rides we took made it our problem. I don't know what exactly you and that female have gotten yourselves into, but judging from the way she flinches and the number someone did on you, I'd say whatever it is seems way more than you can handle."

"We're fine."

Dylan's laugh was mocking as he jammed a finger into the rib Sam was favoring, to be rewarded with a gasp from the other alpha. "Yeah, real fine. You telling me you think you can protect that girl? Because from where I'm looking, you can barely stand."

After Sam drew in a few deep breaths, pain washing over his features, he lifted his gaze to them again. "So? What are you suggesting?"

Mason answered fast enough to keep Dylan quiet. "We're already here, so let us help with whatever this is. I'm pretty afraid of your mom, too, and I don't want to explain to her why you ended up six feet under."

"And you, Dylan? You're wanting to help out of the goodness of your heart?"

Dylan let a full laugh out, then, one he hoped showed Sam just how stupid that idea was. Dylan did nothing out of the goodness of his heart, and he sure as hell wouldn't for Sam, not anymore. "Not a chance."

"Then why help? Why risk yourself?"

Dylan smiled, a flash of teeth that lacked any warmth. "I saw that omega, the one who has you all tied up in knots. I can't wait to see her break you into little tiny shards, and I want a front row seat to it. Besides, maybe I'll get some payback, and you'll see how it feels when your best friend fucks the woman you love."

* * * *

Mason laughed softly as he stood before Sam's house. *That alpha never changes, does he?* It had been five years since their big falling out, and yet the house looked the same. Same stone walkway, same glass windchime making prism designs below the front window. It was as if no time had passed at all, and Sam had kept everything the same.

Then again, Sam had never cared for change. He'd always been the one to cling to the familiar, to want things to just stop moving.

Dylan's car pulled beside his, and the other man was out of it so fast Mason felt like lecturing him about it. Not that lecturing Dylan had ever worked. He was as stubborn as a feral cat and about as friendly.

He'd never have called himself good-looking, but Dylan was. He had those dark features that, coupled with his constant brooding, made him the sort of asshole women loved to try to change. He wasn't as large as Sam or Mason, his body thinner, his muscles lean and cut. Still, between the slight facial hair across his jawline and the permanent 'fuck you' expression that never left his face, Dylan never failed to make people look twice.

Just not always for a good reason.

Who'd have figured we'd be here again?

Mason slung a bag from his trunk over his shoulder. He hadn't figured so much as hoped. The fight between the three had never sat right. In the end, despite him not having a problem with either of the other men, he'd been forced out of their family as well. If he'd stayed in contract with either, mended bridges with either, it would have been impossible to get the two other alphas together again. They'd have seen his involvement as picking a side.

So, Mason had waited. He'd kept on with his life and pretended there hadn't been a huge chunk missing without the brothers he'd found.

"You aren't really going to try and sleep with that female," Mason said, knowing exactly what Dylan was thinking.

Dylan slid an almost identical bag over his own shoulder. "Are you telling me you don't think Sam deserves it?"

"I don't think the omega deserves it."

Dylan's dark gaze narrowed, that temper of his slipping. "You and Sam always think the best of omegas, like they're innocent. They aren't, you know. They act innocent so someone will take care of them."

"They're not all like Nora was, like your mom was."

Dylan skimmed over the comment, even as tension threaded through his body at the mention of the omega who had torn them apart, at his mother who had screwed him over. "And Sam's no better. Sure, she might have used her skills to seduce him, but he went along with it."

"So did I."

"No, you accepted it as the only choice, that's not the same. I wouldn't have walked in on her in *your* bed."

Mason carded his fingers through his hair and pushed the long mess from his face. *What's the point? Five years and this hasn't gotten better. I won't fix it in a ten-minute pep talk.*

The bigger issue than Sam and Dylan, because they'd been doing this for years, was Tracy. Sam had given them a run-down, both of her past and the current issue. It made him understand how she'd acted when he'd seen her at the vending machine.

An omega with a past like that wasn't going to be welcoming to two new alphas moving into her house, especially with her young.

It didn't change that it was still the only choice. Sam was in no condition to keep her safe, and the way he stared at her made it clear he'd started to bond with her. Losing her would be a pain none of them wanted him to experience.

Dylan had thought he'd loved Nora, had thought they were bonding, but he just hadn't known better. Mason was sure of it, knew Dylan had been more worried about her being his than about her, which was a pretty good sign. *All this anger over an omega he didn't even really love?*

Tracy would have to adjust to having them around, for her own good.

And there was a part of Mason—a not insignificant part—that held hope. He'd always known what he wanted, and years of chasing omegas on his own had only proven it was what he needed. It was why he'd tried to make a relationship work with Nora, despite his own feelings, because he'd wanted the family. It hadn't worked with her, but then again, none of them had loved her, and she hadn't loved them.

Could Tracy be different? Could she be the perfect fit for all three alphas?

And if she was, if they could even get her to give them a chance, would she just break their hearts?

* * * *

Tracy had hardly acknowledged the two new alphas in the house. Even when the one she'd met, Mason, had smiled, she'd just hidden behind Sam like a coward.

Which was funny, since Sam was hardly able to do anything to keep her safe.

Still, she'd wanted nothing to do with either man. Mason was larger than any man should have been, standing taller than Sam or Dylan, and far wider. He didn't scowl, having a similar jovial attitude to Sam, only with more cursing. If she wasn't so afraid, she might have dared to call him handsome, in an untamed, primal sort of way.

Dylan, however, was not at all the same. He seemed all hard lines and harshness. He'd scowled, lip pulled up in an almost constant snarl that made him appear large despite being smaller than both other alphas. He reminded her of a Doberman, all sleek lines that perhaps didn't carry the bulk of a Rottweiler but was just as lethal.

"Talk to me." Sam sat on the closed toilet lid in his bathroom, Tracy having been sorting his medications and putting them away.

She didn't respond quickly. She liked to think about things before she spoke, to weigh the words. All words had a cost, or so she'd learned, and she didn't like saying anything without being willing to pay the price. Sam had told her about the two alphas, had explained he knew them well, that they'd help keep her safe, but she'd said nothing back.

I'm so tired of being afraid all the time.

"I don't like new alphas," she admitted, voice soft.

"I know, and if there was another way, I'd go with it."

"You don't seem to like them, so how can you trust them?"

Sam fidgeted, though the movement had him wincing when it jostled his cracked rib. "I trust them with your safety. How's that?"

"Vague."

He smiled, a glimpse of who he was beneath the bruises and broken skin that marred his handsome features. "I admit, we didn't end on a good note. There was a fight, and none of us are willing to get over it. The thing is, even with that, it doesn't change that I trust them. They're more than friends, more than blood. We grew up together, and there's no one I trust more. They won't let anything happen to you."

"Yeah, I've heard that before. It's been my experience that you can't trust people."

"Do you trust me?"

I want to. The thought surprised her. She'd never trusted anyone, not really. She did what they said because it was safer, but she'd never trusted them. She might not trust Sam yet, but the fact she wanted to was new.

When she didn't answer his question, he continued, "We'll get there. What if I tell you about them? Will that help?"

"Maybe."

Sam patted the side of the bathtub, and Tracy sat there when she'd finished putting the pills away.

"Mason is the one with long hair."

That brought forward his face, the wild look to him achieved by that hair, by the beard, by the fact he was the largest of all three by quite a margin. Even so, he held an oddly gentle nature, like a huge beast happy to curl up at someone's feet. *Not that you can trust that. Even gentle alphas are alphas at the end of the day.*

"He owns a construction company out in Arizona doing commercial remodels. No mate, no children. He's straightforward, says what he thinks, doesn't sugar-coat much, but he's easy-going. Dylan is the quiet one. He works as a private investigator, usually on custody or divorce cases. He tails people, does surveillance, that sort of thing."

Dylan hadn't spoken to her, hadn't even tried. If anything, he'd only gotten more tense and angry-looking each time he'd spotted her, giving a look just this side of glowering.

"He doesn't seem nice."

"He's not." Sam straightened, as if he'd realized how bad his words sounded. "I mean, he's safe for you, but he isn't friendly. Don't expect him to want to be buddies, but he'd never hurt you. You're as safe with him as you'd be with Mason or me. Just don't try to make small talk with him, because you'll never win him over."

Tracy sighed and leaned forward. How did things always end up complicated for her? She'd been happy at the group home. She'd been happy at Sam's before. Every time she found happiness, the world was determined to tear it from her.

Sam set his hand on top of hers and offered a gentle squeeze, the touch already easier to accept. "You should lie down. You were up all night. When will Karen get here?"

"Tomorrow morning. Claire thought it would be best if she stayed the night there again, got a full night's sleep."

"Makes sense. No reason to uproot her early, plus I'm sure she's having a great time. If I know Joshua, he's spoiled her with every type of ice cream and candy possible." He shifted again, as though he couldn't get comfortable. Then again, between his rib, the bruises on his face, and his arm, how could he be comfortable? Still, in typical alpha fashion, he tried to hide it. "I hope they have a kid, soon. They need one, and I know they've all been waiting too long."

Tracy nodded as she thought about a child in that household. Each time she went there with Karen, the girl would get spoiled rotten by not only her 'Auntie Claire' but each of her uncles, too. And she ate it up, milking every last thing out of the alphas she could. Even Bryce, the strict one who didn't smile much, still snuck her treats and let her get up late to watch TV long after she was supposed to be asleep. Yes, Tracy wanted them to find that sort of happiness, and yet, a part of her was jealous.

Jealous that she'd had the child but none of the rest. She loved Karen without end, but she that didn't stop her from wishing she was the omega with a loving mate, that Karen had a father who would dote on her the way each of those alphas would their child.

But she wasn't Claire, was she? Claire had picked herself up after her abusive past, had forged a new life for herself. Tracy had hidden away in a group home and let the world pass her by. She hadn't even dealt with the legal or financial issues after Richard's death. Instead, she'd hired a lawyer and just tried to put everything on hold.

As if she'd ever figure it out. As though she'd ever be one of those strong women who could deal with things on their own, who didn't need to hide behind someone else.

A touch to her cheek had her jerking back so quickly she nearly toppled into the tub.

Sam sighed but pulled back. The look on his face said he'd been talking to her, but she'd missed it. "Sorry," he said. "I didn't mean to startle you. You should get some sleep."

Tracy stood and ignored her still racing heart. "Come on, I'll get you settled, first. You need rest, too."

It took nearly forty-five minutes to get Sam into bed. He took another dose of painkillers and rested in the sweats and shirt he'd gotten from the hospital. They were loose enough to not highlight much of his body.

That helped. As terrible as it might make her, Tracy preferred dealing with Sam like this, when he was hurt and not nearly so handsome. When he woke those uncomfortable desires inside her, when she had to face them, it complicated matters. This was easier.

The scents of alphas filled the house. Sam's was strongest, familiar and less threatening. Each hour that passed, however, the other two's scents occupied more and more territory.

After three hours in bed, sleep wouldn't come. Even as exhaustion tugged at her, she couldn't settle. Instead, she ventured from the safety of her room, needing to see the sky, to not feel walls closing in around her.

No one moved in the house, no sound or signs of life. Sam was far gone in a drugged sleep, no doubt, and the other two alphas must be sleeping as well.

The large deck outside, the one that overlooked a rolling hill, putting them up high, had fascinated Tracy the first time she'd seen it.

In fact, the entire house amazed her. It was huge yet modest. It had a bunch of rooms and bathrooms, as though made for a huge family, but the fixtures and decor weren't over the top or fancy. Instead, it was painted in warm beige tones, with an almost cabin appeal. It fit with Sam. He'd never live somewhere fancy, somewhere with stainless steel finishes where he'd have to worry about fingerprints. No, Sam was the sort to choose ease and comfort over anything else.

And Tracy had clung to that style. It had made the large home safe and cozy despite the size.

But that view from the back deck, the way the sky stretched to the mountains that surrounded the house, the way the bright stars stood out against the endless dark sky filled her with a strange sense of freedom. She breathed in, filling her lungs with the crisp air.

"You're up late."

Tracy spun at the voice, finding Mason behind her, no shirt, and larger in the darkness than he had been in the light.

All those old fears crashed over her. She didn't have a hospital of people around, she didn't have Sam — she had nothing. It was her and an alpha she didn't know in the dark, alone.

Why did I leave my room? What was I this stupid?

The air thinned until despite how quickly she gasped, nothing helped.

A creaking drew her attention, and she expected to find Mason looming, to find him just in front of her, reaching for her.

Instead, he had taken a seat on the couch positioned in a U-shape. It made him look smaller, and she got the point he was making.

I'm not going to do anything.

It gave Tracy the chanced to lean against the railing, sliding down until her ass hit the ground. Even still, she didn't close her eyes, didn't take her gaze from the alpha who watched her with unnerving silence.

After another minute — or maybe ten, she really couldn't tell — Tracy shuddered out the last of her energy.

Mason must have noticed, because he spoke up. "I'm going to get Sam."

"No." Tracy almost shouted. She didn't ever speak without thinking, yet she'd nearly snapped the denial. A slow inhalation and she spoke more carefully. "He needs sleep to get better."

"You think he wouldn't happily get up for you?"

Of course, he would. Tracy didn't even need to question that. Sam would wake without a complaint if he thought she needed him.

That wasn't the point, though. The fact that he would didn't mean he should.

"He needs to sleep. I'm fine."

Mason didn't move, not a muscle twitching as he stared at her. "I should have realized sneaking up on you was a bad idea. Just ain't used to other people being up late."

She didn't respond, focusing all her energy on calming her racing heart.

Her lack of response didn't silence the alpha. "Sam sleeps like the dead even without the party-sized amount of opioids in him. Dylan isn't a deep sleeper, but he gets up early, so he's pretty religious about his bedtime. Me, though? I'm always the one who can't sleep."

The conversation distracted Tracy, the fondness with which Mason talked about the other two. Sam hadn't spoken like that—his words had been clipped and full of tension. Whatever fallout had happened between them all, Mason must have gotten over it.

A smile tugged at Mason's features, softening his expression in the darkness. "You normally not a great sleeper, or is this just my lucky night?"

The fact Mason hadn't pushed his luck, hadn't come closer let Tracy risk stepping into the conversation. "I don't sleep well," she admitted.

"Anything I can do to help?"

"No. I just can't help it. I always wake up at every sound, need to check them. I've been like this a long time."

"Hypervigilance."

"What?"

"It's called hypervigilance when a person is always on guard for danger after a traumatic event. They tend to check locks, have to know what time it is, have to know where everyone around them is." He spoke like it was just information, but the words chafed.

It wasn't just information — it was her life. It was the scars she carried that she didn't like people to see. She'd rather he think her some girl who didn't sleep well, not a broken thing after an unnamed traumatic experience.

She rose, anger replacing her nerves for a split second. "It was nice talking to you," she said, her old self, the one afraid to upset an alpha, the one she hated, speaking before she could stop it.

Mason didn't stand, but his gaze still followed her, that focus of his unnerving. "No, it wasn't. You don't have to lie to protect my feelings. I didn't mean to pry, but I have a habit of saying whatever's in my head. Sorry for upsetting you. Last thing I want is for my fellow night-owl to ignore me."

His apology came with no sense of deceit. He seemed honestly sorry for upsetting her, and in that, she had to admit, it wasn't entirely fair to be angry.

Or maybe that was the part of her still afraid.

Part of me? It's all of me. Just a coward.

Exhausted by the day, by her fear and her constant put-downs and her entire life, Tracy wrapped her arms around herself and let her thin shoulders drop. "I appreciate that you're here to help Sam and I, but whatever you're doing right now? It's not worth the effort. If you think you want me as a friend, I can assure you, you don't. If you're hoping for more, it won't happen. I'm not" — she gulped softly — "normal. Don't waste your time trying to make some friendship between us. Think of me like a cat who doesn't come out from beneath the bed when you come over. It's not going to change." As she spoke, her voice dropped to a whisper. She forced the words out, risked his wrath. Sam had assured her he was safe, but with Sam asleep, with the darkness looming, with Mason's body so large and male, she struggled to believe anything.

Mason made a soft sound in the back of his throat, one that said he didn't believe a word she said. She kept walking away, and his voice followed as she reached the door. "You might be surprised — felines tend to like me. Goodnight, kitten."

Chapter Five

Normally, Sam enjoyed being taken care of. He'd never been a man who disliked some sweetness, when a female would bring him things to dote on him.

Then again, during those times in the past, he'd been able to do it himself, as well.

And he hadn't had a flighty omega in danger whom he couldn't protect.

What used to give him pleasure now annoyed him. The way he had to lean against her, the fact he'd brushed his teeth in front of her, in the bed. All of it burned at his pride, especially when he wanted her to think well of him.

Tracy stared at him, an expectant look on her face. *Great, I wasn't paying attention. Must have asked me something.*

"What was that?"

"I asked if you wanted a shower."

The idea of hot water washing away the bits of dried blood still on him sounded amazing. The hospital had cleaned what they needed to clean, but nothing else, and the man who had done the cleaning had had as much charm as a rattlesnake.

Then the reality hit him, as it liked to do. A shower would require a not-so-sexy bag over his cast and a lot of help from a certain skittish omega.

Not like I'm about to go ask Dylan for help. He'd drown me.

"Probably not a great idea."

"Why not?" Even though she asked, the look on her face said she knew why.

If she needed him to spell it out, he would. "I'll be naked, honey, and I don't think that's what you want to be anywhere near."

Her gulp came out loud and nervous. Even so, she pressed, and Tracy never pressed anything. "I'm here to help you, Sam. This happened because of me, and I saw the look on your face when I asked. You want a shower."

"Think about it. I'm going to be naked, and while getting you naked and wet is a goal of mine, this isn't how I saw it happening." He tried for the joke, as though it could slice through the tension and make things better.

She didn't laugh. "I can do it. I trust you, Sam, and I want to take care of you."

He sighed. When she dug in her heels like that, he knew better than to argue. Hell, he knew better than to argue with any omega who had her shoulders set like Tracy did. They could out-stubborn even him. "Why don't you grab one of those plastic cast covers the hospital sent home, then start the water?"

Fifteen minutes later, Sam realized he'd never outgrown feeling like an idiot. At least, he hadn't when faced with a woman he wanted desperately while he wore a bag over his damned arm. *Not the way I pictured our first time getting naked, that's for sure.*

His medication had kicked in, so he could move with more energy, the painful tugging inside him lessening to a dull ache. He'd still leaned on Tracy during the walk, but maybe that had more to do with the feel of her body against his.

The removal of his clothes had proven problematic. The shirt he'd needed help with, since his arm couldn't bend enough to get over his head. Tracy had averted her gaze as she helped take the fabric off. At the sweats, he'd leaned against the counter and had her turn her back.

Not like she isn't going to see everything in a minute.

The push of the sweats off his hips and down his long legs was easy enough, and he used his feet for the bottoms so he didn't have to bend. It left him naked and in the room with the female he'd fantasized about since the moment he'd met her. *Keep it together.*

"Ready," he said with a voice that was nowhere near controlled.

Tracy turned, her gaze pinned to his eyes, as if she was being damn careful not to risk a look farther down.

Go on, look, please.

"I should probably take some of this off." She gestured to herself.

His turn to gulp. "Probably. Only as much as you want, though. You don't need to be naked, but I'd imagine a sweater that thick will get soaked fast."

She nodded, and with trembling hands, caught the bottom hem of the sweater to pull it free.

It was the first time he'd gotten a look at her outside of those three-sizes-too-big clothes, and it stole his breath.

He'd known she wasn't very large, but he'd failed to realize just how pixie-like her body was. Her shoulders were small and light freckles showed all over her skin, though the parts hidden by the clothing nearer matched the tone of her skin. They all matched the light honey of her wide eyes. She didn't have much of a chest, but that didn't stop Sam's brain from taking a detour into filth as he imagined how it would feel to take one of her pert little nipples past his lips and tease it until she was a moaning mess. Her waist was narrow, and her hips didn't spread out too far. Stretch marks showed like silver stripes on her stomach from where her short tank top had ridden up, the marks from carrying a child to term when she was already so small. She didn't have a porn star body, with huge fake breasts and a perfect hourglass figure, and yet her body didn't fail to get a rise out of him.

He yearned to drop to his knees and worship her, to slip his tongue along the slit he knew was tucked away between her thighs, covered with the loose leggings she wore.

His gaze moved up to her eyes, and the fear there forced him to leash his wants.

It wasn't all fear, though. Or, maybe it was, but not fear of him. He could tell with the way her scent had strengthened and the tentative response of her body that the fear had more to do with her own reaction. She didn't want to want him, and she didn't know how to handle it.

Still, even if they both wanted anything, even if they'd both been on board and horny, he was too damned injured to live up to it. Wild sex was off the table. "World's most boring strip-tease, huh? Maybe we shouldn't put dancing as a back-up plan for us."

The joke forced a smile across Tracy's tense lips, and didn't that help him even more? It was a stupid joke, but it did what he needed it to. It broke that hold they'd been stuck in, turned the situation from sexual to something else.

They were naked, and they had attraction between them, so it wouldn't ever be totally platonic, but at least it had shifted to something easier to handle.

Tracy leaned into the shower to feel the spray once more, and the caution charmed him. She was a caretaker at heart, wasn't she? A deep breath, then she stripped off the leggings as well and set the folded pile of her clothes on the counter. It left her in the tank top and a pair of boy short panties that showed off long, lean legs.

Fuck, I'm in trouble.

Tracy slipped an arm around Sam, trying to ignore how good all his heated skin felt pressed tight against her. She knew how dangerous alphas were, yet she craved him. It never failed to make her want to shout at the injustice of it all.

Though, it was hard to fear Sam. In fact, when he'd watched her with such intensity, with a hardly-hidden lust, a warm flutter in her stomach had shocked her.

His gaze had traced her body, and the heat behind his eyes had said he didn't find it lacking. He'd paused at her chest, at her hips, at the length of legs. Richard's harsh words, when he'd criticized her lack of a larger bra size, when he'd called her boy-shaped, those

Jayce Carter

hurtful words couldn't find a foothold inside her when Sam watched her with open admiration.

And that terrified her. More than she feared the man himself, how quickly she'd fallen for him did the trick. Was it just that she needed someone? That she'd take anyone if they weren't as bad as Richard?

The idea cooled some of the lust as she helped him into the shower. A large built-in bench inside offered the perfect place for him to sit, and she ignored the clingy sensation of her clothing as water soaked it.

I'm helping. It's a professional obligation, nothing more. Even as she said it, she knew it wasn't true. Excitement and fear of touching him fought for purchase inside her, and none of it had anything to do with a professional obligation.

It had a lot to do with an ache that had started between her legs, however, with the way her nipples had tightened to erect peaks beneath his sinful gaze.

Tracy rubbed the soap on a washcloth, then smiled at the scent. *So much like him.* Something masculine and simple, like sandalwood. She worked it into a lather, then started at his neck.

His thick muscles twitched and tensed beneath her light touch, but the action so engrossed her she didn't notice much else.

Instead, she worked the cloth over his shoulders, which were wide and covered in more muscle. She avoided the line of the bag that kept his cast dry and skimmed away from any of the bad bruising or cuts.

His body enthralled her. Hard, solid, strong. And yet, each brush of her cloth over it got a reaction, as if it wasn't as impenetrable as it seemed.

His first deep groan was cut short, as though he didn't want to startle her, yet the erotic sound only

69

tantalized her senses. She wanted to hear more like it. She wanted to draw out those sounds he couldn't keep in, so bone-deep that they escaped from his soft lips no matter how hard he fought it.

It made her feel powerful.

The word didn't feel right, not when used about her, yet that was how she felt.

"You okay?" His voice had dipped rougher, deeper.

She nodded as she moved to his firm chest, teasing over his flat nipples, rewarded with a full-body shudder and a sound that lived somewhere between a groan and a growl.

And even with that, she couldn't find the ever-present fear.

Was it because he was hurt? Did she somehow feel safer? A strong wind could blow him over which made her feel less like prey.

When she went for the next pass over his chest, the washcloth dropped to the tile floor. It left her inquisitive hands, already soapy from the bodywash, to finish the job.

His skin burned her, making the water spray on her back feel lukewarm in contrast. He didn't complain about the change, didn't say a word about how her fingers now skimmed over his bare flesh, her touches only a cheap mimic of cleaning anymore.

If he was happy to play dumb and ignore her behavior, so was she.

She could hear heart beat even over the steady rhythm of the falling water. Steam filled the tile surround, and it caused sweat to run down her forehead. It made her heart speed, too.

That's not the water.

Tracy kept going, down over his pecs, over his stomach. She followed the dark hair that became sparse over his abs, and when she dared to dip lower, he wrapped his strong grip around her thin wrists.

She lifted her gaze to his, arousal clouding her thoughts until she couldn't understand why he'd stopped her. For the first time in so many long years, she'd enjoyed touching another. She wanted to keep touching.

"Maybe that's enough," he said, voice more gravel than sugar.

"Why?"

His large hand hung loosely around both her wrists, a showcase in their size difference. "I might be injured, but I'm still a man, and I don't think you're going to like the effect this is having on me."

The comment drew her gaze down to his lap without any conscious thought from her. Sure enough, his cock was hard, jutting away from his body, pre-cum beading at the thick head. The sight brought on an initial burst of fear, but that fear couldn't gain a foothold.

Her lust made it slip away, so she didn't leap from the shower and run crying like they had both expected.

She tugged her wrists until he released her, until she could return her seeking fingertips to the hard expanse of his stomach. This time, she didn't bother to avert her gaze. She openly stared, her body having already decided it liked what she saw before her mind could butt in.

His cock pressed against his lower stomach, long and thick and curved up slightly. A line of dark hair ran from his navel to his groin, the same dark hair that started up again on his thick, muscular thighs.

What would it feel like to sleep with him? Sam had never given her a reason to fear him. He'd been nothing but careful, restrained. Was that what sex would be like with him? Could she actually enjoy it?

Before she'd had sex, she'd thought about it, like any young girl did. She'd scoffed at the whole idea of women being proper, of how they were expected to hate sex. She hadn't known she was an omega at the time, had assumed she'd grow up like any beta, find some handsome boy, get her heart broken, break a few of her own.

A soft sigh left her at the naïve girl she'd been. She hadn't been afraid of her own shadow back then, hadn't run from anything, hadn't put up with anyone's nonsense. No, she'd expected to go out and do things in her life, important things. And sex had been one of them.

And at the start, sex had been good. That was one of the things she'd learned at the group home, that abuse didn't start off bad. It hadn't for her and Richard. The first few years, Richard had been everything she'd thought she'd wanted. She'd enjoyed toying with him, teasing him until they spent all day wrapped up in bed together.

That had changed, though, and by the end, by the time Karen was born, she'd loathed his touch. She'd flinched each time his looming hands would brush against her, and no matter what he'd tried, he hadn't been able to make her want him anymore. That part of her had withered, but perhaps not died.

"What are you thinking about?"

Tracy slipped her hands down his sides until she stroked her thumbs against his lower stomach on each side of where his dick rested without touching it. "That I always wanted to like sex."

It was the privacy, the thundering of the shower droplets as they splashed against the tile and the heat of his skin that coaxed her into answering.

A rough chuckle left him and vibrated through her hands. "Well, when we get there, you will."

"When?" She brushed his cock with her thumb, the touch so soft she only knew she'd done it for sure by the growl that left his lips, fast and hard and all instinct.

When he spoke again, that growl might have stopped, but it still vibrated in his words. "I'd never force you, but I'm pretty sure we both want this. I don't care how long it takes, but yeah, I'm thinking it's a when, not an if."

"Why?" This time, she stroked a thumb down each side of his scorching length in a blatant stroke. The conversation made it easier to not focus on what she was doing, on just how close his dick was, on how she teased him. Even so, the twitch of his cock at the touch, the way the heat of his shaft made his skin seem cool all made her bold. "You can't tell me there aren't less complicated omegas out there."

"Less complicated? Maybe. Complicated hasn't ever mattered to me much, though. I took one look at you that first night I met you, and I knew you were meant for me."

A humorless laugh left her as she recalled the night. Her leg had been torn up, and Claire had been injured because of her. If Tracy had been stronger, smarter, braver, none of that would have happened. And when Sam had shown up? As she'd sat in the back of an ambulance and Sam had spoken from the door, outside the tight space, not crowding her, she'd hardly said a word. *Some catch.* "You have a thing for cowards?"

Strong fingers at her chin lifted her gaze to his. "Coward?"

"I was hiding in the back of that ambulance and not talking. No one even came in because they knew I was too scared."

"Then you don't remember what I do. You were in that ambulance, yeah, but I didn't stay out of it because you were afraid. You had Karen tucked behind you and your teeth bared. You were a hair from going into a rage. That's why none of the EMTs were in there."

Tracy frowned, the event hazy. Only, then she recalled a rough vibration in her throat and the way a few of the EMTs and other police had backed away.

Sam stroked her jaw with his thumb. "The way you protected Karen, the flash in your eyes, that wasn't something I'd be likely to forget."

Tracy frowned as she trailed her fingers down the length of his cock, this time a purposeful stroke rather than an accidental brush.

His fingers tightened. "As much as I'm enjoying this, and as much as I've thought about it, you should probably stop."

"And if I don't want to stop?" She swiped her thumb over the head of his dick, the thick stickiness of his precum so different from the water and steam that surrounded them. "Will you make me?"

With that, Sam leaned his head back against the tile, as if he'd lost some internal fight, and his voice came out thicker than the steam in the shower. "No. It might just kill me, but no, I won't stop you."

And nothing had ever looked quite as good as Sam sitting there, naked, like a sacrifice.

Sam feared his ribs might break again with how his heart pounded against them. The meds took the edge off, so the pain had receded to manageable.

In fact, that he could even get hard amazed him. It must have been Tracy herself, her scent reaching down past the pain and the meds and the injuries, and if she wanted him, his body would damn well give her anything. *Bonding hormones are incredible.*

She dropped her gaze in a slow perusal, and when her scent thickened in the room, he knew she liked what she saw.

Even with him banged up, even with a bag over his broken arm, she still liked how he looked. It made want to puff out his chest and stand taller, something that stroked that old primal part of him that wanted his female's approval.

His female? Yeah, she was. It didn't matter how uncertain it was, how new, how complicated – she was his. He knew it with everything inside him, and he'd do whatever he had to so she felt safe, protected and wanted.

And right then, that meant keeping himself still even when what he wanted was to taste her.

He'd dreamed about her taste, woken in the middle of the night sweat-soaked and panting after a dream where he'd feasted between her thighs.

Worse, her nipples had pulled to tight little tips beneath her drenched shirt, and with no bra to obstruct his view, he saw it all. It would be so easy to reach out and cup one, to thumb the hard peak until she moaned for him. *I want to hear her moan. I want to make her moan.*

The tension through her said she'd bolt if he so much as tried, so he stayed put. He rested in surrender for her, even when she wrapped fingers around his thick shaft.

Well, he stayed still, but couldn't help the grunt when she stroked him, the strangled sound at the searing touch that went so much deeper than heated flesh.

Her hands were hesitant, unsure. She touched him as if deciding if she even liked it, if she was interested at all.

Of course, he could smell her interest. It hung in the air, thick and tantalizing. She liked it, but she walked a thin line, something between who she'd been and who she wanted to be.

She dropped to her knees, and he parted his legs to make room for her. If he'd been controlling this, he'd have never put her below him like that. Still, she didn't seem afraid.

Her full bottom lip was trapped between her teeth when she lifted her gaze. "What do you want me to do?"

The question made his lips tip down. "Whatever you want."

Tension thrummed through her, and he could see the anxiety rising. She might not trust him, but she didn't trust herself, either. Selfish, maybe, but he didn't want to lose the moment. "Stroke me, Tracy," he said, like a plea.

A breath of relief from her, then she followed the direction. She made her small hand into a tight fist for him, and stroked up his full shaft.

He followed the motion with his ravenous gaze, fascinated by the sight she made. "That feels good, even better than I thought it would. Just like that. Tighter, honey."

She obeyed each direction, relaxing into the situation, into his orders. It was as if she could turn her mind off, switch off that fearful part of herself and only obey.

We'll have to work on that later. For now? I need this.

He neared his release too fast, but who would blame him? He'd pictured this too many times and having her sweet hand on him felt too good. Hell, it wasn't like he had to hold out because she hadn't come. There was no way she'd let him touch her, not yet.

"Faster," he growled out, not bothering to hide the desire that saturated his rough voice. Let her see it, let her realize the depths of how badly he needed this. "Keep that up and I'll come, honey, so you need to decide fast if you want that."

She didn't hesitate. If anything, her hand sped even more, jerking him off with rough strokes that were clumsy and yet hotter than anything he'd felt or seen before.

Sure enough, moments later, he lost it. He dropped his head back so it smacked the hard wall as the sensations rolled over him. His legs, his ass, his lower back all tightened before he came, seed leaving his shaft to coat his stomach and her fist.

She didn't stop, and the feeling of her hand turned uncomfortable on his softening and sensitive cock. "Stop," he croaked, body so tired he could have slept right there in the shower.

She stilled, but she didn't release him, didn't break the connection.

He forced his eyes open to stare down at her. She still knelt, stroking him almost lovingly in something like reverence, an odd situation seeing as she'd gotten him off, as she'd done him a favor.

"I…"

When she didn't continue, he stroked his hand across her cheek despite his lack of energy. "What?"

Her lips pressed together, and it was clear she wouldn't say.

Fine. He'd said he'd wait, and he would.

He'd wait just as long as she needed, because the longer he spent with her, the surer Sam was that he couldn't let her go.

Chapter Six

Sitting at a dinner table felt strange. Dylan had grown accustomed to eating on the couch with the TV on. The noise made his apartment feel less empty, and it did well to cover all his negative thoughts.

Instead, they all sat at a table together, like some twisted family. The omega, her offspring from another alpha, Sam, the love-struck idiot, Mason, the eternal optimist, and Dylan.

Tracy had cooked, and the moment the scent of sautéing onions and peppers had hit his nose, he'd known it would be good. The first bite of chili confirmed it.

She'd avoided them most of the day, staying out of sight after the shower she'd helped Sam with.

And doesn't Sam look relaxed? Clearly, she isn't the wilting flower she pretends to be. Typical omega, playing a part.

The kid had been dropped off later, in the early afternoon. Dylan had stayed out of the way when an omega and three alphas had shown up, the omega going into Tracy's room to visit while the alphas had headed into Sam's.

It reminded Dylan again how long he'd been gone. Sam had developed new friendships, a new life in the absence of he and Mason.

Whatever. I made a new life, too.

An empty life, that consisted of more work and alcohol than was healthy.

"This is delicious," Mason said.

Tracy cast a tentative look his way, the start of pleasure growing across her cheeks. So, she enjoyed praise, huh?

Dylan filed that away, like he did everything else. He wasn't as talkative as the other two, but he saw everything, heard everything. He kept note of each weakness he saw, each detail that could get him closer to whatever he wanted.

He wanted the omega.

Not forever, not for real. He wasn't a sappy fool like Mason and Sam, content to be led around by the dick by some omega. However, he wasn't dead, either, and the scent of an omega would draw in any alpha with a working nose and a cock. The idea of taking a taste of her, of pissing off Sam, of getting to prove again he was right, those things sounded pretty fucking good to him.

The past that had caused the divide between them bit at him like it always did. He saw Nora's face, her lying smile that he'd believed no matter what. He remembered walking in to find Sam and her in bed, the lance of pain as he'd realized one of his best friends had slept with the women — the omega — he loved.

Loved? Maybe. It's not like I have a lot of experience.

Jayce Carter

Now that Sam had someone he was smitten with, Dylan saw no reason to let the slight pass. He'd sweet talk the omega, tempt her into bed and show Sam how it felt.

Maybe he should feel guilty for using her like that, but hell, from what he'd seen, omegas hadn't exactly been pillars of model behavior.

She'd only end up betraying Sam in the end, and the sooner he realized it, the better.

Besides, Dylan wouldn't force her. Tracy would fall for him because, in the end, that was what omegas did. He wouldn't promise her anything, wouldn't lie to her, and he'd make sure he showed her a hell of a good time.

And Sam would realize that omegas weren't worth the trouble they caused.

Hell, maybe it would take some of the piss out of the friendship. Maybe they'd be able to put the Nora situation behind them once they were even.

A part of Dylan he didn't like to acknowledge wanted that. While he liked to play the 'I don't need anyone' part, shit was always more complicated than that. He'd missed Sam and Mason, missed having them around, missed the grounding effect the two had on him. He was negative, and he was short-tempered, and they'd never failed to pull him back to level ground.

Too bad omegas ruined everything.

It had started with his mother, who had only been too happy to run off and leave him with his piece-of-shit stepfather, had continued to Nora and now this newest one — *Tracy* — seemed poised to keep that shit going. Some things never changed.

Later, after the food was finished, when they'd filled the meal with idle chatter — mostly from Karen — Tracy nodded toward the other room. "Why don't you get an ice cream and watch something in the living room?"

Karen took her empty bowl into the kitchen and set it beside the sink before getting into the freezer. She found the ice-cream cones easily, as if she'd gotten used to where Sam kept them.

Then again, Sam was a man of routine. Even after five years, Dylan knew they'd be on the bottom shelf in the freezer, near the back, behind the frozen burger patties.

When the girl left the room, some of the ease went with her.

"She's a good kid," Mason said.

Tracy nodded, her gaze on her empty bowl instead of any of them. It was as though without her daughter, she just melted into a puddle, like keeping an eye on Karen was all that gave her spirit.

"Should she really be in the middle of this?"

And there it went. She shot Mason a look that had enough bite to take an inch or two off his dick. "My daughter isn't going anywhere."

See? The whole scared-omega thing is bullshit, just a part she plays to get what she wants.

Sam responded, probably smart since he already had something going on with the woman. "She doesn't need to go right now, honey, but it's worth thinking about. This situation could get ugly, and I know you don't want Karen in the middle of it."

Tracy's eyes softened, but she didn't seem ready to give in. "You promised you'd keep her safe. I haven't run, because you promised. If you can't do that, if you don't want to, just tell me. I'll take her and skip town."

Yep, omegas were always ready to cause problems and run. She'd gotten Sam hurt, fucked up Mason and

Dylan's schedules and now she'd take off and leave that shit on their doorsteps to deal with. *Typical.*

"I know I promised that, and that's what I'm planning to do. I'm a realist, though, and she'd be safest with Claire or Tiffany. No one will force you to do anything, but just think about it. She doesn't really need to be around any of this, does she?"

Tracy dropped her gaze from the intense stare, her body seeming to shrink before their eyes — it wasn't like she was big to start with — and all that spirt drained from her. Or had she hidden it? *Hard to know with omegas.*

When Tracy seemed to have ended the conversation, Sam rose from the table, movements slow. A pang of guilt streaked through Dylan. No matter how much he and Sam weren't getting along, he'd never want the other alpha hurt. That was like breaking one of his own bones.

"I've got to check in with the station." Tracy's panicked expression had Sam setting a hand on her shoulder. "It's fine. Why don't you stay put and relax?" He leaned down and whispered more into her ear.

Dylan couldn't hear it, but he could guess what he'd said. The omega was high-maintenance and required a hell of a lot of handholding and reassurances, it seemed.

How exhausting.

Whatever Sam said worked, because she stayed put as he limped into the kitchen, asked who wanted ice cream and tossed one to Mason. Dylan and Tracy had declined.

Mason spoke up as he tore open the wrapper on the ice-cream cone. "You're a hell of a cook. Can't recall the last time I ate that good."

"Thank you," she said, voice soft, eyes wary. So, she liked praise, but without Sam, she didn't accept it so easily.

That fear in her eyes pricked at him. He told himself it was annoyance. She had no reason to be afraid of him, or Mason or Sam. It pissed him off that she looked at him with those big, nervous eyes like some doe in front of a hunter.

That was the easy thing to think. Under that, he knew damned well it pricked at him because he didn't want her afraid. The fear of a female, of an omega especially, didn't fail to set him on edge. He wanted to coax a smile from her, to soothe those fears.

No. Don't let her play you like that. Instincts were shit, and he refused to let them control him.

Dylan took a sip of the coffee before him, never a man for sweets.

Mason looked over his shoulder in the direction Sam had gone. He rose, then nodded that way. "I'm going to go check in. You two play nicely." He turned a hard look on Dylan, pointing a finger at him. "Mostly, I mean you."

Once alone, Dylan looked over at Tracy, then lifted his warm cup of coffee to his lips, ensuring his face showed just how not impressed he was with her. She might be an omega, and she might be pretty as fuck, but she wasn't anything a million other omegas couldn't be.

She hadn't had any of the dessert Mason had offered up, which had him frowning. "Why didn't you have any ice cream?"

She flinched at his voice, an almost invisible twitch of her shoulders. "I can't care for desserts."

Dylan's lips tipped down. Females of any sort were a mystery to him, and he tended to blunder right past good sense when it came to dealing with them. Maybe it came from having a shitty stepfather and no mom he could remember, but he'd never known how to talk to women without pissing them off. "Why not? Afraid of the calories? Because if anything, you could use putting on a few pounds."

Tracy straightened her back, and a whole lot of nothing washed across her features. They were carefully blanked, and it made Dylan lifted his lip in an almost-there snarl. She was hiding.

He hated that. Hiding was the first trick of omega deceit.

Before he could say a word about it, she rose to her feet. The movement was graceful, careful, soundless. She took her dishes, then spoke without meeting his gaze. "I should start on the kitchen."

Dylan watched her leave, her steps so soft she moved like a ghost through the room. Before she passed the corner, she reached back and pulled down the hem of her already huge sweater, tugging it down even farther past the curve of her ass, as if embarrassed.

Dylan released a soft growl at the ache in his chest when he realized he'd hurt her.

No matter how much he told himself he didn't care, that ache didn't stop.

I don't care, damn it.

But, fuck it, he did care.

* * * *

85

Mason sat outside on the deck, the cool breeze on his back. He'd worn only his sweatpants—even his feet were bare.

He'd never liked clothing. It was one of the few perks of his job. Working in construction meant no one batted an eyelid when men decided it was just too damned hot to work in the Arizona sun with a shirt on. Nothing felt better than the sun on his skin, than that strange sense of freedom. Even now, back in his home state of California, he couldn't shake the habit.

Hell, he'd probably have forgone clothing entirely if it wasn't for the timid omega who he was currently sharing living space with. Well, that and the kid. He knew his days of nudity would end once he had young of his own.

And, if he were honest, he'd sat out there for the past hour hoping she'd be tempted to visit.

He'd made it clear he didn't sleep well, that he was often up late. It seemed she was as well. He'd thought she might take the hint and come talk. Maybe it was a useless hope, and maybe he shouldn't have been talking to her, but Mason tended to go with his gut. His gut was that the omega was pretty and sweet and he wanted to know more.

As the moon crawled higher in the sky, and as the minutes ticked by, he started to doubt she'd show.

At least, he did until the grumble of the sliding glass door announced his visitor.

Tracy came out, two cups in her hand.

"Little late for coffee, don't you think?"

Her smile was soft, unsure, but she still stretched out to hand him a warm glass. "It's tea. No caffeine."

He inhaled the tendrils of heat. *Mint. Chamomile. Lavender.* Soft, sweet, calm, that was just like her, wasn't it? "Thanks."

Tracy held her own mug and took a seat on the chair perpendicular to him. Not quite right beside him, but much closer than she'd been the night before.

That was something, right?

"So, how bad was Dylan while we were gone?"

A spark of something unhappy simmered behind her eyes, but she pushed it away. "He was fine."

If that ain't a lie, I don't know what is. Why's she lying?

Then it hit him.

"Dylan won't do shit to you, kitten. If he, or any of us, hurt you or piss you off, you just speak up."

She didn't respond, but her leg bounced as though she could rid herself of the nervous energy that way.

Mason pushed again, gentling his voice. "I get it, I do. You don't know us, and you don't trust us, but I can tell you that we won't go off on you just because you tell us you didn't like something we did."

She opened her mouth, closed it, then sipped the tea. Was she collecting her thoughts?

He expected her to talk about Dylan.

Instead, when she set her cup on her knees, she sighed. "Richard didn't appreciate criticism."

Richard. Sam had growled that name out. The asshole had terrorized her for years, and he could see the scars clear as day when she crept through a room, afraid of drawing attention.

Mason tried to stay loose, relaxed, to not show any reaction. "We ain't Richard. I can't say you'll always get what you want from us, but we won't ever be mad that you told us the truth." He laughed, a rough sound in the dim light. "Hell, with the way you smile? You'll probably get what you want, too."

Ah, there is was, that smile. She offered it like a prize, tentative and unsure and fucking brilliant. "What happened between the three of you?"

"Ugly history, that's it."

"Sam doesn't seem like the type to hold grudges for just anything. I want to understand what happened."

Mason rubbed his fingers over his chin, then through his beard. He wasn't all for sharing the nitty-gritty details, but hell, she deserved some understanding, didn't she? Especially if anything went anywhere, she should have an idea of how shit had gone bad. "Oldest story there is, kitten. We were best friends from childhood, grew up together, did everything together. Hell, before it all went to shit, we lived right here in this house together."

She twisted, gaze on the slider, eyebrows inching toward one another. Could she see it? The way they'd fit there, the sense of family?

She turned back toward him and nodded. "I guess that explains why the house has so many rooms."

"Exactly. Well, that didn't last. There are some specifics that aren't my place to share, but basically? A woman happened. Three of us fell for same omega."

Her gaze dropped and he let the words percolate, let her mull them over. Would she panic at the idea of being in a similar situation? Would she like that idea?

Her voice was steady when she responded. "So, you shared her?"

Mason recalled the three alphas who had brought her daughter over, the ones who walked around their single omega as if she made up their entire world. Seemed Tracy had some experience with the idea of that sort of relationship. *Least she didn't run off screaming.*

"Not exactly. It was more like we figured we could ignore one another enough to make it work. It didn't, though, and she wasn't really in it for all of us anyway. I think she went from one to another to see what she could get, and she enjoyed the attention, the jealousy." Mason tried to shrug off the frustration the memory created in him.

They could have had something great, but she'd never wanted it, not really. He still remembered the way she'd press her lips to his ear and whisper about something Sam had said, because she liked that flash of anger. She liked to stoke the drama.

Though, hell, had they been ready for that shit either? They'd gone into it as the only chance to fix the fracture made by Sam's actions, not as something they all wanted. They'd been jealous assholes, and she'd enjoyed every second of fanning those flames. Nothing but idiots yanking one another in every direction.

He guessed he could understand why Dylan and Sam might be hesitant to think about that. Hadn't turned out so well for them, had it?

Still, staring at Tracy, at the way the moonlight lit up those sweet little freckles on her cheeks, he had to wonder if maybe the issue the entire time hadn't been the wrong girl.

Would this omega fit better? Could he see that sort of family working this time?

Could she be the piece that fit them back together?

Something brushed his knee, and he peered down to find her fingers hesitating in the air.

"I asked how long ago that was."

Mason shook off the strange way his heart sped at the touch. He wasn't fifteen anymore, when his heart did that stupid racing thing every time a pretty girl smiled at him. "Five years. Thing is, there's a reason Sam never took our names off his list. I don't care what he says about being busy, don't care what we fight about, we're family. He left our names on those forms because he knew damned well we'd come. Didn't matter what happened, if any of us called, the other two would drop everything to show up. It'll be like that until we're six feet under."

"That seems nice, having someone always there."

"Heard Sam talk about your mom, so you aren't totally alone, right?"

She brought her legs up to cross on the chair, the position possible only because of how damned small she was. "I love my mom, but I couldn't see her much, not after Richard."

"Yeah, bet she wouldn't have been too happy about what that bastard did."

"Nope. She hadn't wanted me to get mated, but I was determined and young and at the start, Richard hadn't seemed so bad."

"How old were you?"

"Met him at fifteen."

"Did he know you were an omega?"

She shifted in the chair as if the conversation were unpleasant. It wasn't hiding, but rather seemed she didn't like the memories. "Yeah. I was an early bloomer and went into a heat at fourteen. They put me on suppressants to help with any risks until I got older."

"Fifteen?" Mason whistled low at the young age. Fifteen-year-olds should be out breaking hearts, not settling down with alphas. "How old was he?"

"Thirty-five. By the end of my sophomore year, I'd dropped out of school, and as soon as I turned eighteen, we got married. I thought having a guy that age interested in me showed just how mature I was." Her shoulders rose in an 'it doesn't matter' gestured that seemed far too dismissive of how wrong the entire situation had been. Still, she pushed forward. "Karen came a few years later, an accident. I'd tried to take birth control, but it doesn't work well for omegas. The last thing I wanted was to risk bringing a child into that mess. Richard was thrilled—he'd always wanted kids. And—don't get me wrong—I love her. I'm not sorry I had her. I'm just sorry I had her the way I did. She shouldn't have been in the middle of any of that."

Mason risked the question he knew he had no right to ask, the one that had plagued him since seeing her. "What finally made you leave?"

Tracy lifted her gaze to his, and he saw a spark of fire there. Seemed Richard and the world hadn't totally doused it. "I was putting on makeup to cover a black eye and Karen walked in. I remembered being seven and watching my mom put eyeliner on, how I learned it from her, and I realized Karen was learning from me. I thought about her future, about what lessons I was teaching her, about the life she was going to go out and find. For the first time, I knew I had to show her better, show her that what I was doing wasn't the life she should accept. Even if it killed me, I was going to give her a good role model." Tracy's gaze dropped to her hands, to where she spread them wide, then closed them. After a long sigh, she seemed to curl into herself. "Some role model, huh?"

Mason shook his head and leaned forward, chancing the risk to take her small hands in his, to capture her gaze with the motion. "You risked a lot, Tracy. You taught her freedom doesn't have a cost that ain't worth paying. At the end of the day, you did everything you could to give that girl a good life, and I've seen the way she looks at you. I've seen her spark and her bite and her sweetness. You've done pretty well by her, I'd say."

Tracy froze, going still enough to impress one of those living statues.

Would she run? Would she yank away? Hell, he wouldn't blame her for either.

"You want me to let you go?" He asked the question softly, without inflection.

Instead of answering, she closed the distance, leaning forward and brushing her soft, warm lips to his. The touch was so gentle it almost tickled.

Mint clung to her kiss, deceptively sweet at first, just like her, but stronger than it seemed. It left a tingle on his lips as he remained still, as he let her have the kiss at whatever speed she wanted.

He'd let her have anything. She could have done whatever she wanted right then, and he'd have let her with a smile. The tentative kisses were a drug he'd not been prepared for. They weren't meant to be passionate. Instead, they were almost like a thank you, but that didn't stop his body from getting all its own ideas. His cock hardened, pressing against his sweatpants and making him regret not having wrangled himself into something a little less obvious. He'd be sporting a hell of a tent when he stood up, and he doubted she'd be all that happy about it.

And, after Sam and Dylan, maybe he should have been guilty. It was clear Sam was head over heels for her, but Mason just didn't care. The more he sat and talked to her, the more he saw her between the three of them, the surer he was that something simmered between all of them, something that could be what they needed if they got out of their own ways.

Something he wanted to set ablaze and burn with.

The kiss deepened, and the blossoming of her scent, the way it grew and caught on the breeze, made his balls ache with desire. The knot at the base of his cock stung with want to fill her, as if her scent alone called it to action. How she affected him so quickly, he didn't know. Sure, alphas could get a whiff of something and spring an erection for no damned reason, but this was different. This had an intensity, a need that his normal 'hey, I'm here, anything for us to fuck' erections lacked.

Not happening tonight, buddy. Settle down.

Tracy placed her hands on his knees as she leaned closer, using the position so she touched him nowhere but their kiss and where she braced herself. Her soft, hot tongue burned a path across his lips, and he risked returning the kiss. He parted, his own tongue skimming hers, his first taste of her.

Divine.

As quickly as it happened, she pulled back. She wasn't frightened...but unnerved? Definitely.

Is it the kiss? Too fast?

The shame clued him in. Ah, she didn't think she should be kissing him, not with whatever was going on with Sam.

He could have reassured her, could have told her it wasn't so uncommon, but it wouldn't help. She needed to trust him before she'd believe shit he had to say. Instead, he caressed her wrist with his thumb, with the hands still loosely around hers. "That was nice."

The way her teeth pressed into her full bottom lip made him groan as she tugged away from his hold.

What else could those lips do? "I should get some sleep."

"Sure, kitten. Goodnight."

When she left, and he found himself sitting alone with her scent still strong and the taste of her toothpaste and tea still on his tongue, he couldn't wipe the smile off his face.

Coming back had for sure been the right choice.

Chapter Seven

Sam sat across from the detective he hardly knew. That was how it worked with special groups, though they didn't interact much. He knew the omega crimes area folks, but vice was a different matter.

Detective Grayson Harper was a hardass, but honest, if Sam had learned anything. Still, departments didn't like to share their information or cases, always afraid someone would one-up them.

Mason sat in the hallway, the detective unwilling to talk in front of a stranger, and a civilian at that. Not that Mason minded. He tended to be happy about anywhere.

"I can't say anything about ongoing investigations to anyone outside our department. You know the rules, Sam."

Sam shifted to ease the pain in his side. He'd dialed way back on his medication so he could come in this evening, so he could be clear-headed enough to ask the right questions. It meant the pain, which had been just an inkling before, was now a full-sized presence knocking against his skull.

"I'm not trying to take your case. I'm just trying to keep someone important to me safe."

Grayson sighed and suddenly looked every day of his hard fought forty-five years. "I can't tell you much, Sam. I can tell you that Mario Navarro is bad news, but given your stay in the hospital, I'd guess you know that. It means I don't need to tell you to stay out of his way, either."

"That isn't possible anymore. This isn't a 'tend to my own garden' situation. He's pissed in my yard, and now I have to deal with it."

Grayson sat back and rubbed his fingers against the bridge of his crooked nose. "You're with Richard Pera's mate, right? Yeah, you've stepped in some shit, there."

"I noticed. No one will say anything, won't do anything. I've put in requests with all my favors, and I'm getting a whole lot of nothing back."

"Not surprising. Richard dealt with money transfers between a lot of very bad people. I'm talking omega trafficking, drugs, guns. Navarro is only one of the people he dealt with, and really, he's small time compared to a few others we've linked Richard to. Tracy should really go into hiding, because if Richard did leave files behind, if he wasn't just bluffing, I doubt Navarro will be the only one looking."

"She has a kid, a life. That asshole tore everything apart for her once, and I'll be damned if he does it to her again. She can't just pick up and leave." Especially because doing so would mean leaving Sam, and he just couldn't get behind that idea.

"I've looked at what I can find on Navarro, on Richard, on whoever else we've linked them to. There's a reason no one has gone after Richard or what he has, why nothing sticks, and it's because there are too many bought and paid-for politicians and cops in this. I have no idea who is keeping everything quiet, but someone with a lot of clout is. If you push this, if you get any files, I doubt you'll live long enough to use them. Hell, she barely survived Richard, and keep at this? He might still get her in the end."

Sam curled his hand around the cane he'd used to help him walk, fury replacing the pain. He wouldn't let anything happen to Tracy.

It didn't matter how many ant hills he had to kick over, how much tigers he had to poke or just how many wounds he got from it, they'd get to the bottom of this.

He swore it right then, that no matter what it took, Tracy and Karen would be safe.

* * * *

Dylan hated staying up late, but sometimes there weren't other options. With Mason and Sam meeting with that cop, Dylan had to keep an eye on Tracy, Karen and the house. The place was wired like a fortress, but nothing beat a good old-fashioned watch.

It meant when he'd have rather been curled up in his warm bed, he was sitting in the living room with the television playing, volume almost all the way off.

Karen had gone to sleep a few hours before, after sitting beside him and watching a nature show on predators. Seemed she liked lions. Funny, since Dylan had always liked lions. Maybe it was some male fantasy, the whole ultimate manly symbol being a lion, but Dylan had always favored them.

The kid was sweet. Too sweet to have gone through what she had. Still, she hadn't batted an eyelid at sitting beside him and watching the show. She'd even spoken up a few times, asking questions about why the lionesses did all the hunting, about if they were stronger than the males. Not that Dylan had been able to answer too many of them, because zoology wasn't exactly his specialty.

Still, she'd listened to what he could say, enraptured like he was way smarter than he was.

Tracy, for her part, had remained on the sidelines, like a lioness from the show, watching over her cub. She hadn't spoken to him, casting him only a blank look when Sam had explained he had to leave.

Fine by me. I don't need to talk to her.

She'd headed off to sleep herself just after Karen, and Dylan found he didn't care for the silence. He should — he was used to it after all. He lived alone, which meant silence was sort of his constant companion. Now though? Without Karen's questions and Sam and Mason's conversations, Dylan felt unsettled.

A sound had him rising, and when he hit the hallway, a creak came from the floor of Tracy's room.

Was she awake? Couldn't sleep? Mason had mentioned she'd woken up each night and ended up sitting outside with him.

Maybe that's what this was? *Well, I'm not sitting outside, so she's on her own.*

Which wasn't true, because Dylan wouldn't let her outside without a set of eyes on her. His declarations didn't ever seem to stick.

Another sound, soft and cut short, like someone trying and failing to be quiet. The green blinking and silent state of the security panel in the hallway said nothing had tripped the alarm.

He didn't go for his pistol, safely tucked away in the gun safe in his room. It would take too long, and he was still sure no danger lurked inside the room.

In fact, he wanted to turn around. He wanted to go back to his spot on the couch. As long as no one was inside her room, as long as she and the kid were safe, anything else just wasn't his business.

Except, a broken gasp tugged at him.

Dylan snarled to himself, low and angry, as his feet moved without him thinking about it. Before he knew it, he stood in the doorway of her room.

His eyes adjusted slowly, the darkness taking form from nothing. The bed remained made and empty, so his gaze followed the hitching of breath.

Sure enough, cowering in the corner, Tracy sat with her back to the wall, her knees to her chest.

He froze, indecision tugging at him. *I should turn around and go. I'm here to make sure she doesn't get herself killed, but dealing with this? Not my job.* Even as he told himself that, his feet wouldn't budge.

No matter how much he said he needed to go, that he had no business getting involved with female hysterics, instinct kept him rooted. An omega was crying, afraid, and his instinct drew him to look after her, to fix it.

He kept in the growl that threatened to leave him when he realized there was no chance of him walking away so long as she poured tears like that. A sound like that would just make her cry harder, make it take longer for him to get the hell away.

With Karen's room just beside them, Dylan used the dimmer to turn the lights on low as he shut the door.

She might not like the door shut, but she'd like her daughter waking up even less.

Her gaze jumped to his, a moment of panic before she blanked it.

She did that a lot, didn't she? Hid whatever was there, whatever she thought or felt. As someone who was constantly showing shit on his face, he envied that sort of control.

"What do you —" She broke off the snapped question, then tried again in a mild voice lacking the attitude. "How can I help you?"

Dylan crossed his arms, trying for annoyed. Annoyed with being bothered, of course, not annoyed because the red that rimmed her eyes and the wetness still on her cheeks tore at him. "You were making enough noise, I could hear you from the living room."

She ran her tongue along her teeth, as if she wanted to say something sharp but couldn't bring herself to do so. "I'll stay quiet," she said instead.

And, fuck, that riled up his temper. "Didn't ask you to keep it down."

"What are you asking for, then?"

It was his turn to open his mouth and say nothing.

Why pretend? Truth was getting more and more obvious. Even though it was just fucking hormones and pheromones and biochemical bullshit, he wasn't going to get a step away from this fucking omega until he calmed her down, until he'd settled her into bed, and she was relaxed.

Sometimes being an alpha sucks.

"Come on," he grated out. When she didn't move, Dylan gestured at the bed. "Let's go. Get in."

She swallowed so loudly, it had to hurt her throat. Still, she rose, using the wall for balance as she got to her feet. It was the first time he'd gotten a full, good look at her. He almost thought she wore those huge, baggy clothes to bed. Nope, seemed she dressed down to sleep. A T-shirt that was form-fitted highlighted her small breasts and narrow waist. Pajama bottoms with polka dots wrapped around her legs, the entire ensemble practical rather than seductive. Still, he wanted to groan at what it did to him.

He'd said she could use eating more, because in his experience women were always looking for compliments, always thinking they were too fat. She didn't have an ounce of stray fat on her, but none of that detracted from her beauty.

And he hated her more for that, for the fact he wanted her, that the want and desire thrummed inside him like a living thing needing out and at her. He didn't like feeling out of control.

She moved with slow, careful steps, her bare feet padding against the carpet. She cringed slightly as she slipped past him, and he'd swear she didn't breathe.

Dylan pulled the blanket out, and she took the spot without complaint. Even with the tension through her, the masked fear, she crawled into the bed where he'd indicated.

Which, honestly, surprised the hell out of him. He'd expected a fight. He'd expected arguing. While he wasn't an alpha who wanted to spend his time reassuring some flighty omega, he had fucking expected it to happen.

Why hadn't she? Clearly, she wasn't interested in doing as told.

Lines appeared in her lids as she squeezed her eyes shut, not looking at him, not saying or doing anything.

Again, he stared at her, his brows furrowed. She looked so small there, her hands fisted tight, her body stiff.

A tremble in her bottom lip and it all became far too clear.

She expects me to demand sex. A growl left him at the idea, at the thought of anyone forcing her to do anything.

Worse? At the idea that if it happened, if he were that sort of asshole, that she'd just lie there.

Then again, a scar on her cheek, probably from catching a ring when backhanded, showed the price she'd paid in the past.

Guess I can understand how giving in can be easier.

His growl made matters worse, and the tenuous hold on her emotions snapped. The tremble of her lip grew, and her breathing sped until he worried she'd pass out or throw up.

Neither seemed good.

"Oh, fuck," he snapped without trying to soften his voice at all. This was him, and it was best she knew it now. He sat on the bed, above the covers, and slid his fingers into her hair. He grasped those wavy strands tight enough, her eyes snapped open. "I'm not going to fuck you, Red."

Red. The nickname slid off his lips with more than a little venom in it.

The name fit her, with that wild mess of fiery hair and those freckles on her nose that he absolutely refused to think of as cute.

She blinked, eyes clearing before a deep inhalation from her said she'd drawn his scent into her lungs.

And look at those pupils blown wide. They sat like saucers in her eyes, obscuring the amber. It wasn't lust, not yet, but damn if his snapped voice didn't shake loose that fainting-goat shit she was doing.

"You're not?" she asked so softly he strained to hear it.

"No, I'm not. You think, what? The second Sam turns his back, I'm going to be in here on top of you? I'm not a fucking monster. Better question is why the fuck you were gonna let me?"

Her tongue, pink and soft-looking and able to conjure up far too many filthy thoughts, slid across her bottom lip. "I learned a long time ago it's safest not to fight alphas. I always lose."

And there went that punch to the gut feeling he was really resenting her for. He didn't want to feel shit for her, but she kept drawing it out of him.

Dylan softened his grip in her hair, though he didn't pull his hand away. Why not? He refused to think too deeply about it, choosing to grasp the soft red strands in a gentle touch. "That's not true. You may suffer a little less at the start, but you'll have it way worse for longer. You've got fight in you, whether or not you see it."

A lot of doubt spread across her face, and that didn't shock him. Still, she didn't argue.

Funny that a female *not* arguing would annoy him.

"Now that you aren't crying anymore, go to sleep."

He pulled back, but her eyes did that wide shit again. *Fucking wonderful.*

Dylan let out a long sigh, one he made sure sounded just as annoyed as he felt, and scrubbed his face with his hands. "Fine," he muttered. He didn't crawl beneath the covers, sure that wasn't what she wanted, and instead lay on top of the blankets on the bed. Neither of them needed any skin-on-skin contact.

Sure, he wanted to fuck her, but when that happened it would be hard and fast, just bodies. Lying in bed, comforting her, that shit wasn't him and it sure as hell wasn't what he wanted between them.

Despite the tension in her, she relaxed slowly, as though each second he didn't pounce helped her to ease.

An ache he couldn't ignore forced him to speak. "Sorry about dinner last night."

Tracy rolled to her side to face him, a good swath of space between them. She pillowed her head on her hands, strands of her hair obscuring her pretty eyes. "It's fine."

"No, it isn't. No idea what I said to hurt your feelings so much, but you hadn't done anything to deserve it. I can be an asshole a lot of the time."

He waited for her to explain, but when she didn't, a wave of his hand encouraged her.

"I eat plenty. Richard liked to point out that I was scrawny, that I looked more like a boy, that I wasn't *womanly*." Didn't that last word hold a wealth of weight?

That nearly made him choke on his own spit at the absurdity. Had her old alpha been blind? As much as he didn't want to admit it, no matter how hard he fought it, Tracy was a knock-out. She had that innocent-pixie thing that just wasn't fair. Hell, she looked like some fairy creature, too fucking ethereal for their world, and the red hair? Made her look like trouble.

"Well, he was an idiot, Red. There isn't a thing wrong with your body."

"I'm not—"

He lifted an eyebrow to shut her up. "Not a thing. And trust me, I'd have no issue telling you if there were. "

She waited a moment, lips pressed together as if deciding if she'd say anything at all. Finally, she went for it. "You don't like me, do you?"

"Not really, no. Isn't exactly your fault, I'm just not a fan of omegas. I've seen the shit they can do too many times to want to be anywhere around it. Seeing as you don't care for alphas, I'm thinking that should suit us both just fine, right?"

She nodded, though hesitation made the reaction slow, and the word sure didn't sound all that confident. "Right."

Dylan relaxed back on the bed, ignoring the way she stared at him, letting her look her fill. This whole lying next to her thing? That was him being selfish. He was just trying to keep her quiet so he could have some peace.

It isn't about her, not a bit.

He let the lie remain even as he closed his eyes and drifted off to the sound of her even breathing.

* * * *

Tracy woke to an alpha's scent all over her. All over the bed. All over everything.

It sparked a deep panic as her brain sorted through the night before. She recalled the breakdown, when her life had seemed too big, too out of control. She'd slid down in the corner of her room as she'd realized how much she had resting on her shoulders and how ill-equipped she was to handle any of it. Mario. Richard's affairs. Living with three alphas. It had all been too much.

Dylan had come in, and not being sweet, he'd managed to pull her free of the panic attack before it had fully taken hold.

Sam would have been sweet. Mason, too, she suspected. They'd have offered kind words and soft caresses, if she'd let them. They'd have told her it would be fine, that they'd protect her. She wouldn't have believed them, of course, but the attempt would have been nice. She'd have considered offloading those worries to them.

Not Dylan, though. Instead, he'd all but snapped at her. In fact, he had. Still, his no-nonsense tone and his lack of interest had helped.

Instead of someone else picking up the pieces, she'd done it.

Somehow, with him there, she'd realized she *could* pick up the pieces herself, that she didn't need someone else to put her back together. She'd done it, and afterward? The rest of the problems had seemed manageable.

And funny enough, he still lay in the bed beside her, stretched out on top of the blankets. His eyes were shut, hiding the dark brown of them, the light of the rising sun just peeking in through the window. He had unhappy lines carved deep into his expression, as if he wanted to complain even when asleep.

Why is he so unhappy? She'd thought at first he was just a jerk. Perhaps even like Richard.

Though, Richard had been sweet, hadn't he? He'd been good at playing the game, at seeming like the perfect mate. He'd doted on her in the hospital when the doctors were there, played the part of the loving, worried mate.

He'd hidden his monster so well, few caught a glimpse of it beyond the evidence it left on her.

Dylan had seemed like that monster on the front, like someone who would backhand her for talking out of turn. Then, when she'd been ready to accept whatever he'd do to her, he'd been the one to bolster her, to tell her she didn't need to accept what any alpha did, even him.

He'd not taken advantage of what she'd have given without a fight, then stayed when he'd seen it in her face that she'd wanted him to remain.

He'd even spent all night in her bed and hadn't so much as touched her.

It made Tracy brave in a way she hadn't much in her life. She sat up to look at him, to really study at him for the first time. He had a light ghosting of dark hair on his jaw, and she knew without touching it that it would be rough against her skin. He wasn't as dark as Sam, and his hair was a light brown that almost made him seem young. Lines sat between his eyebrows and in his forehead, creases that said he frowned. *A lot.*

Then again, had she seen his smile? Dylan's only two moods seemed to be pissed off and indifferent.

Though, the way he called her Red made her heart flutter. It wasn't with any particular fondness, at least on the surface, but each time he rumbled it out in an almost growl, she melted a bit.

What is wrong with me? I've been down this road, and I know where it leads.

Even still, she watched him, fascinated by the strength he carried, by how different he was from her, from Sam or Mason.

Her quiet contemplation shattered when his dark eyes snapped open, his face setting in the hard lines of annoyance he always wore.

His gaze darted around, then settled on her. "It's late," he snapped like an accusation before sitting up.

It forced her to lean back to not risk getting too close. If she'd stayed put, their lips might have brushed.

Or slammed together, with how quickly he moved.

"Thank you," Tracy said. "You didn't have to stay last night, so thank you. It helped." The words stuck in her throat, so used to remaining silent. Still, he'd done something for her, a small act of kindness — no matter how grudgingly given — and Tracy appreciated it.

Dylan turned to cast her a withering glare, as if any of the sweetness from the night before had evaporated and left an angry, different man in its place. "Don't get used to it. I'm not going to waste my time whenever you decide to have a breakdown. I'm not Sam. I don't get off on omegas with victim complexes."

The words came out so flat and angry, Tracy drew back as though to fend off a blow. The words themselves were sharp, each syllable serrated and deadly. The harshness on his face said he'd meant them to cut.

Tracy opened her mouth to say something, anything about his terrible attitude and sharp words, but she hated herself a little more when she only squeaked out a soft "Sorry."

Would she always be like that? The shadow Richard made her into?

His face softened, the action so fleeting she'd have missed it if she'd blinked. As quickly as it happened, it was gone. "No reason to get up right now. Give yourself another hour, Red."

The door shut with a decisive click, and in the moments afterward, when she ached from the cutting edge and truth of his words, only one thing soothed the sting.

He'd called her Red, and that damn nickname had been spoken gently, almost affectionately, like an apology.

And in that, she worried. Richard had drawn her in with sweetness, but how much more dangerous could a man like Dylan be, who lashed out with such ease?

And why did she want to hear him call her Red again so badly?

Chapter Eight

Mason leaned back in the chair at the dining room table, grinning at the way Sam fumed over him balancing on two legs. Sam always was the mother hen of them, wanting shit to be perfect. He'd taken after his mother, no doubt.

Sam's mom was a saint, putting up with all of them, no matter how often they made her life more difficult. Sam had taken over the role when they'd grown up, never shying away from threatening to call his mom over if they didn't listen.

And Betsy sure as hell could put them to shame if she wanted to.

It made Mason groan as he thought about Betsy, about the way she'd walk in and grab him by the ear, despite her being a tiny spit of a woman. Hell, he'd lean down just so she could do it if he'd gone and done something he knew was wrong. At sixteen, when he'd gotten drunk at some shady party, it had been Betsy who had shown up and hauled his ass back, despite him already having a foot in height over her. Her mates had come with her, but they'd stood back and watched, letting her drag him out from the party like the misbehaving pup he'd been.

Damn, he shouldn't have stayed away so long. They exchanged cards for holidays, and she called him every second Tuesday of the month to check in. She was a whirlwind, that omega, and he'd never have made anything of himself without her.

Mason, being the forgotten middle child in a huge family, had been largely ignored in his own household. Too many kids, not enough time. Betsy, though, had been an omega who had only had one kid, who hadn't managed to get pregnant again, and who had always wanted a bigger family than that. It meant she'd taken in her son's riffraff friends, treating Mason and Dylan like cubs she'd claimed. From kindergarten, she'd acted more a mother than his own. She'd attended more of Mason's school functions than his own mom every had.

Dylan had woken early, as usual, and come storming out of Tracy's room. That had surprised the hell out of Mason. The hard set of his face hadn't implied he'd had much fun, but hell, when did Dylan ever look like he'd had fun?

Tracy's face when she left the room later said that whatever had happened hadn't gone well for her, either. Not fear, just a quiet discomfort.

She'd retreated with Karen outside, a bag of chalk in the young girl's hands. Tucked beneath Tracy's arm had been a pad of paper with a pencil pressed in the spiral binding.

Once she'd exited, Mason twisted his head to look at Sam, chair still poised perilously on the two legs. "Should I punch him, or do you want to?"

Sam pressed his cane into the tile floor as he came over, then sat gingerly across from Mason. "I think you'll have to. I'm more likely to fall over than land the hit he deserves."

"Hey, maybe if I let you and he go at it for a few rounds, you'll get over this bullshit."

Sam winced, face tight. He wasn't taking enough pain meds, and that sure didn't surprise Mason. While Sam took care of those around him, he always ignored his own needs.

Mason shoved himself to his feet, walking to the back room and grabbing the pain meds off the counter. When he returned, he dropped the bottle on the table.

"I don't need them."

"Sure. You're wincing when you move for shits and giggles."

Sam muttered beneath his breath, but he opened the lid and dry-swallowed two of the white pills. A grimace said he didn't enjoy it before he kept talking like there hadn't been a break. "I know you want us to get over this, Mason, but I don't think it's happening."

"Why not?"

Sam released a long sigh, and damn if Mason couldn't hear all the regret in it. "I can't change what happened, and I can't even expect him to forgive me. I betrayed him. You know it, I know it, he knows it. Nowhere to go from there."

"And you know what we all know now, too? That Nora was only in it for the fun of running the three of us around. I'm not saying you were right, but damn it, aren't you sick of letting it screw up everything? How long are you going to keep paying for one mistake?"

Sam tapped the fingers of his good hand on the table, then traced the label of the pill bottle. "It's been nice having the house full again. I never built this house expecting to live in it alone."

Yeah, Sam never did alone well. He might have grown up the only child, but he'd spent his childhood with Mason and Dylan. Not that Mason cared for it, either. He'd grown used to having people to lean on, having others to share the general daily struggles of life. As the middle child of eight, quiet freaked Mason out. First it was his own flesh and blood family, then from the age of five, when they'd met in kindergarten, Dylan, Sam and Mason had been inseparable.

At least they were until the disaster that had been Nora had swept through their lives.

"About Tracy," Mason started. What would he get for the change in topic? A punch to the jaw? The silent treatment? Worse, would Sam call up his mother? Nah, that was more Mason's move.

"Are we really doing this again?" Sam dragged his good hand across his face as if he could wipe away the frustration with the conversation.

"Nah, it's not the same. Are you really going to tell me that what you had with Nora is anything like what you're feeling with Tracy?"

"No," Sam admitted. "Whatever I've got with Tracy, whatever I want with her, it's different. It's, I don't know, it's more."

That's exactly how it felt. It had been puppy-love jealousy before. It had been alphas more interested in owning than keeping. It had been about their own selfish egos. With Tracy? Fuck, it was like something inside him grew up, like it wanted so much more than he'd ever wanted before.

And how did that happen so fast? How could he want something like that and barely know the girl?

Sam made sense, he'd known her longer. Mason didn't know shit, yet that kiss? Fuck, it had been sweet beyond belief.

"She's not like Nora," Sam said. "She isn't going to be happy about this. If you think she's flighty with one alpha, imagine her trying to deal with two."

"Three."

"Like hell, Mason. Dylan is about as sweet as mud. Do you really think he has any business around an omega with Tracy's past? She needs steady people, people who will go slow and be careful. Dylan doesn't have that in him, and that's not even counting our past."

That was anger talking. Dylan was a good man. He might not be sweet, but Tracy wasn't as fragile as she looked, either. Or, at least, she didn't have to be. Dylan wouldn't have stayed in her room the night before if Tracy hadn't wanted him, which meant the omega had some tie there too.

Sometimes Mason wondered how such bonding worked. When omegas settled down with more than one alpha, the alphas ended up just as close. Was the bond more than just omega to alpha? Did the males connect in a way he didn't understand? Something that bonded the omega not just to each alpha but the alphas to one another, too? Did it create a family unit?

It would explain the pull between her and Dylan, wouldn't it? Maybe the bond between the alphas caught her in its wake, too.

And, really, if Mason were entirely honest, he couldn't picture trying to cultivate something with Tracy and Sam without Dylan. He was as important to the group as any other, as vital as an organ to the trio of alphas. It meant he had to get Sam and Dylan working together and past their issues.

How, he had no idea, but hell, if Sam hadn't thrown a punch, it meant there was a chance, and a chance was enough.

* * * *

Sam had done everything he knew how to do. He'd knocked on every door, made every call, pulled in every favor he had. None of it had gotten him any closer to a solution that didn't include putting Tracy in danger.

Well, in more danger. The truth was that she had a barn-sized target on her back and him pussy-footing around wasn't going to change that.

They had to go after the files Mario wanted. It was the only chance to keep her safe. If they found the files, they could turn them over and put Mario away. Hell, if they were as incriminating as people thought, it should have helped to keep her safe from anyone who thought about coming after her or Karen.

Of course, then she might decide to leave. She'd stayed because she needed Sam, but if she didn't anymore? She wouldn't want to put up with Sam, with Mason or Dylan.

And that was the future he'd started to see. It was true, since the other alphas had gotten back, since they'd filled the house with life again, he'd stopped seeing his future as his alone. Maybe Mason was right. Maybe it was time to let go of the old angers, but how?

What he'd done to Dylan wasn't right, and he wouldn't pretend otherwise. When Nora had looked at him, when she'd smiled and all he'd been able to scent was aroused omega, he'd lost his damned mind. He'd been stupid, thinking with his dick and nothing else.

He couldn't blame Dylan for being pissed. He'd betrayed his best friend, and for what? For an omega who had ended up cheating on him and leaving him only months after destroying the friendships that had built up his life?

Knowing that wouldn't appease Dylan's anger, though. The other alpha would hold tight the grudge, like he always did, just more proof that he should have that chip on his shoulder he loved to cling to.

But, if they could fix it, if he and Dylan could form some new friendship in the wake of their old one, what would that mean?

Would he be any good for Tracy? Would she even want him?

Sam rested in his home office that sat off his bedroom, frustration coloring his vision. He wanted to pace, to go for a run, to do something to burn off the energy inside him that grew with the realization that he had so few choices. Unfortunately, his body wasn't about to let him do that. It made him even antsier.

I hate being feeble, needing people.

He wanted Tracy to lean on him, to be strong for her, not to need her to fetch things for him, to not need her to do simple tasks he should be capable of completing himself.

A body appeared in the doorway. Or, it didn't appear, but he'd been so distracted, and his meds made him so unaware, that he'd missed it until he looked up to find Dylan there.

How could the other man's face be as familiar as his own, yet so distant?

"What do you want?"

Dylan leaned his shoulder against the doorway. "When are we going to stop hiding and fucking do something?"

"We aren't hiding. I've been trying to find good options."

"We both know there's only one option. Find the fucking files. That's it."

"Do you want her in the middle of this? To send her back into her old life to face that again?"

At least Dylan had the decency to scowl. "Believe it or not, I want her safe. I just know it won't happen as long as she has this price on her head. It's pretty fucking simple. Find the files. Take down the asshole. That's it, Sam, and all your thinking won't find another way out of this." Dylan's gaze traced the pictures on the walls, most of them with him in them as well. "She's tougher than you think, anyway. She outlasted that fucker, she'll outlast the shit he's causing her now."

Sam wanted that confidence. Then again, Dylan hadn't been there, he hadn't seen her that night. He could still recall the way she'd protected Karen, but also later, once the girl had been asleep and Tracy had sat outside on the deck with Sam. She'd crumbled, like the numbness had shattered her into a million pieces.

No, he didn't like the idea of her going back into that pain again. The last thing Sam wanted was to see her slide back, to have the horror of her past anywhere near her again.

But Dylan wasn't wrong, either. It was the only choice, and waiting until Sam was better, waiting on some distant hope that they could figure out a better option wasn't realistic.

"You spent the night in her room," Sam said.

Dylan crossed his arms, but at least he didn't gloat. "Yeah, I did."

"Are you just trying to get back at me? A taste of my own medicine?"

Dylan let out a dismissive grunt. "You aren't that important, Sam. I wouldn't waste my time with some omega just to piss you off."

"So, what are you doing?"

Finally, Dylan met Sam's gaze. "She was crying, okay? I'm an asshole, but even I have my limits. Trust me, whatever you and Mason are doing, however stupid you two are for trying to get involved in this shit again, I'm not. I remember the last time, and I know how it turned out, and I'm not looking to repeat that. You two want to stick your dicks inside that trap, go for it, but as for me? No thanks."

Sam listened to the anger there, the fear, and maybe he should have been pissed. He should have been annoyed that Dylan spoke about Tracy like she mattered so little. He couldn't find it, though.

Instead, he focused on the quiver in Dylan's voice, a spark of hesitation, as if he wasn't sure he believed what he'd said.

"So, you aren't interested in her?"

Dylan cast a withering glare in Sam's direction. "I wouldn't fuck that omega if you paid me to, Sam, and take a little advice from the one without amnesia. She's going to cost us all way more than we're wanting to pay. But you want to do that? You want to throw shit away, that's your choice. As for me? I'm getting nowhere near that omega. Too damned costly."

Even as Dylan proclaimed it, even as he said there was no chance, Sam heard what he didn't say.

Jayce Carter

Just like when Dylan had made those sweeping statements in the past, when his stubbornness had him digging his heels in and refusing to go a single step, he usually gave in. He was stubborn, sure, but when it came to what he wanted?

Sam doubted Dylan's stubbornness would outlast the omega for long, and where would that leave them all?

* * * *

Tracy dragged the pencil over the paper, distracted as she sketched, her mind miles from the image. Drawing allowed her hands to work and her mind to clear. She'd come up with her best ideas when drawing, during the years when she did draw. Having it back was like finding a piece of herself that had been lost along the way.

She would draw and paint landscapes, portraits, all sorts of things that followed her. Lately, a few risqué images had come to mind no matter how she chided herself. She'd pictured Sam, his charming smile and his sweet eyes and not a stitch of clothing obscuring her view. It had appeared in her mind so crisp, she couldn't shake it. The same had happened with Mason, though that wasn't hard to see why.

Mason was masculine perfection, and who wouldn't want to draw those intense eyes and his long hair? She had to take some liberties with Mason's anatomy, since she'd only seen him shirtless. Still, she couldn't imagine he was small, and the slight curve to his length, the veins, the heavy sac, she'd spent more time than she'd ever admit adding the details to his drawing.

The most surprising, and the subject of her quick sketch that morning? Dylan.

Despite him rejecting her as he had that morning, she'd been unable to push away the sight in her mind, and in her experience, the only way to rid herself of it was to give it form on paper.

She'd roughly sketched his basic features. The stern eyebrows, the intense eyes, the thin lips perched in a happy line he never lost. She thought for a moment, if he every smiled, if he ever relaxed, he might actually be the most handsome of the three. His hair, short and wavy and messy, made him look young. It was only all the attitude that aged him.

His picture, given she was outside near Tracy, had remained innocent. She'd left him in a shirt and only drawn his face and chest. While Mason's picture had been intense but kind, like a loyal German Shepherd, and Sam more like a Lab, Dylan's drawing had been all hard edges. He reminded her of a junkyard dog, and it showed in the lines she'd laid down on the paper.

Why did that call to her? *Because I know what I'm getting with him. At least I won't be disappointed.*

But, no, that wasn't it. At least, it wasn't the whole truth. So, why?

Her attraction, no matter how unwise, made sense with Sam. She knew him, and he'd protected her time and time again. Now it was even easier given his physical state. Mason? He wanted her, but he was slow. He was also unfairly handsome, like pulled right from the covers of one of those trashy books Claire sold in her shop.

But Dylan? He wasn't suave. He wasn't sweet or kind. Well, he had stayed with her when he hadn't needed to. He hadn't hurt her.

Is my bar really that low? So long as someone didn't hit her, they were worth being infatuated with?

And why the hell was she thinking about any of them? The last thing she needed was the complications of alphas making her life even more difficult. Hadn't Karen gone through enough with her father?

A low whistle caught her attention, and Tracy twisted to find Mason taking a seat beside her. He nodded at her picture. "So cooking ain't your only talent?"

Tracy flipped the cover down, wanting to hide the image. Would he get jealous? Angry? It had been foolish to do something so stupid, to risk his ire. In her experience, alphas didn't do well sharing. They preferred to tear at what they wanted until they destroyed it.

"It's nothing," she tried to say.

Mason reached out and caught the notepad. He pulled it from her grip with a gentle tug, one she wanted to resist but couldn't bring herself to.

He flipped open the cover and first found the page she'd been working on. "You've got talent, kitten. How long have you been drawing?"

Tracy sensed no anger in his voice, no immediate danger. "All my life," she said, but frowned. That wasn't entirely true, was it? "I stopped for a few years."

"Because of that asshole?"

She nodded but didn't offer more. What more was there to say about it?

"Well, you captured his scowl pretty damned well. Even Dylan would be impressed. You made him look almost human." Mason chuckled as he flipped pages, commenting on the mountains, on the sketch of Karen when she'd fallen asleep, of the dog that liked to show up at the group home.

She recalled what sat on one page, but he flipped to it before she had the chance to stop him. His light brown eyebrow lifted, and amusement danced in his eyes.

Tracy reached for the paper, her cheeks so hot she knew she sported a brilliant shade of red. Her pale skin always showed blushes, and it made her think about how Dylan called her Red.

"Well, well, well," Mason said, holding the pad away from her but still angled toward him. "Ain't this interesting?"

"It's not what you think."

Mason sent her a mocking grin that lacked any real sting. Instead, he seemed pleased. "Ain't it? Seems to me you've been doing a little imagining in here, kitten. Is the good detective aware you've been making some guesses as to how he might look under his clothing?" His smile split wider at the look on her face. "So not imagination, huh? He let you study him up close? Because to get this detailed you had to be *studying* him for quite a while."

"Please don't tell him."

Mason gave her a wink before handing back the sketchbook. "Why not? With the way he looks at you, it ain't like he isn't hoping for that."

"It wouldn't be right." She tucked the sketchbook under her hands as if that could erase that he'd seen her nude sketch of the other alpha.

"Why not?"

She bit softly at her bottom lip. "This is just for me. I don't want him thinking something will happen, that I want more, that I can give him more. It wouldn't be fair to lead him on like that."

Mason leaned back, and the sun brought out light freckles she hadn't noticed on his face. His hair had a touch of red to it, as well, that almost glowed in the light. "It would only be leading him on if you didn't mean it."

"I don't mean it. The picture was just drawing. It was esthetics."

"Esthetics?"

"Something pretty."

"Well, I can't wait to see Sam's face when he knows you think his cock is pretty."

That conversation had her flushing worse, especially the way he said *cock* as though it was no big deal. He didn't understand, wasn't listening. Tracy caught Mason's hand in a tight grasp, willing him to hear her. "I can't give that to him. I don't want him thinking I can."

Mason glanced down at where she touched him. "You can kid yourself all you want, but, kitten, you want him. It's clear in the drawing, and it's clear in your scent."

Tracy went to argue, but Mason tapped his nose. He would know, wouldn't he? When she couldn't outright dispute his claim, she tried yet again to explain the nuances. "Maybe I am attracted, but wanting something is different than being able to follow through."

"Why?"

"Because I've been down that path. I've seen where it leads. Things seem okay at the start, and they're fun...then they stop being fun. I can't go through that again, and I can't put Karen through it."

"So, you'll just draw dirty pictures and fantasize?"

"It's all I can have."

"You can have more, kitten, you just have to be brave enough to give it a try."

"Mom!" Karen's voice shattered the quiet moment.

Tracy yanked back, startled by her daughter's appearance, not wanting her anywhere near the conversation.

Karen stopped just before the table and dropped a pine cone in front of them. "Look, it's the biggest one yet."

Tracy slid on her practiced impressed smile. "That's amazing, sweetheart."

"That's a nice pine cone. You ever turn them into bird feeders?" Mason asked.

"You can do that?"

"Sure, kid. We slather that in some peanut butter and stick on birdseed."

Karen's smile fell, her eyebrows inching in toward one another. "Sam probably wouldn't want me to hang them up, though."

Pain lanced through Tracy's chest at the sound of her daughter's worries. Richard had never wanted them to hang anything, to put childish things anywhere in their home. No drawing on the sidewalks outside, no pictures on the fridge and certainly no homemade bird feeders. He'd had an image to uphold, after all.

Mason didn't crumble at all, though his eyes darkened a hair. "Of course he would, kid. Any damn place you wanted them, and I'll make sure we've got the hooks. Sound good?"

Excitement filled Karen's face, something Tracy hadn't seen nearly enough of. Karen gathered the pine cone up and rushed inside.

Tracy went to thank Mason, though she doubted she had words to accurately explain what that exchange had meant to both.

Before she could, Mason turned a sidelong look on her and smiled. "You see, kitten, even though things have been one way before, doesn't mean they always have to be that way. They can change, if you want them to." He didn't sit around to further explain his little gem of advice, instead leaving her to ponder it on her own.

Things changed. But did they ever? Could she trust them to?

While she didn't know the answer, she knew she wanted to believe it.

That's a start.

Chapter Nine

Tracy took a deep breath as she stared down her old house. She'd spent most of her years with Richard in the thing, his picture-perfect vision of a life he'd forced her into. The shrubs were still immaculately trimmed, the lawn mowed, the entire place like something out of a 1950s movie.

It made her stomach churn.

Karen wasn't there, thankfully. She'd gone with Claire for the day, the two going for manicures. The thought of whichever alpha got guard duty for the day being forced to participate helped shake the crushing sense of oppression that settled on her. In fact, she'd bet Joshua would happily sit and have his nails done along with them.

Though Bryce scowling and joining in grudgingly when Karen insisted would have been more amusing.

A hand set on her lower back, and Tracy jerked away from it, waking up from her musing.

"You sure you're up for this?" Sam's voice was soft, no hint of upset that she'd pulled away.

Dylan chimed in as he walked past them, not bothering to even give her a second glance. Sunlight caught on his hair, made it look almost blond. "She doesn't really have a choice, does she? She'll be fine. Come on, Red."

While Dylan's lack of concern grated, it also got her moving. She nodded toward Sam, her best 'I've got this' expression she could manage without lying.

"Who takes care of this place?" Mason asked.

Tracy slid her keys into the lock, the click of it like the warning of a landmine. "I hire a company. My lawyer gave me all my options, but I couldn't make any decisions right then. It didn't seem right to sell it, but I sure wasn't going to live here. So, I'm just letting someone take care of it for now."

"That lawyer didn't work for Richard, right?" Dylan asked from her right side.

"No. I met her through the group home. Why?"

Dylan didn't answer, but Sam piped in. "Anyone Richard hired might have his best interest in mind, or those he worked with. It's good you went with someone new, someone you can trust."

The conversation drifted off as they entered the house, as the memories threatened to pull her under.

They weren't all bad, either. That was the hardest thing to understand and explain and come to terms with. Richard had been bad, there was no doubt about that, but no one was all bad or all good. Tracy remembered carrying Karen in as a newborn, the way Richard had set up her room, the way he'd stared down at their newborn in awe.

She recalled the time Richard had brought her home a gift. The large easel stored in the upper closet, and a new pack of the finest paints he could find her. She'd already stopped drawing, and he'd taken notice, wanting her to start again.

That was the thing, though, Richard had loved her, she supposed, in his own way. He'd been broken and bad and selfish, but that didn't mean every moment was terrible.

She'd lived in this house for almost fifteen years, and yet she still couldn't decide what to do with it. It was set back on five acres, a huge eight-thousand-square-foot monstrosity with far more rooms than were needed.

She'd always wanted a smaller place, something cozy and warm and safe, but Richard cared more about what strangers thought than what his mate wanted.

"I don't think anything is here," Tracy admitted as she put her code into the security panel by the door. "I'd bet his office if it was."

"He'd never keep this sort of thing there. That's the first place any of those associates would look." Dylan walked around the large living room, his face all business. Then again, Sam had said he was a private detective, right?

Tracy gestured to the house with a wide sweep of her hand. "Well, I don't know what to tell you. Before I ran, I spent a lot of time here, and there isn't anything like what you're talking about that I've seen. Besides, he had cleaners in here all the time, and if he had something that important hidden, wouldn't he have been more careful about it?"

Dylan nodded. "Probably. When you deal with people like he did, you get paranoid. Still, it's all we've got to go on right now. Even if they aren't here, we might get a clue to where he stashed them. First things first, give us a tour, show us what the rooms are. It'll make a search quicker."

Tracy did as requested, holding it together as she went room by room. Many of them weren't used, just his hopes for future children that Tracy had managed to avoid. Still, they saw his office, Karen's room, the living spaces and the guest rooms. She gestured at the door to the room she'd shared with Richard, but no one had taken a step toward it.

After the tour, the alphas went their own ways to search the different areas of the house, and Tracy gathered her courage to look in the one room she didn't want to.

Her first step into her old bedroom felt like walking into a crypt. Something she knew was empty, but still full of ghosts. That was what lived there, now. Not her, not her family, but the ghosts of who they'd been.

She could see the screaming fights with Richard, when he'd start out trying to stay calm, but the red would grow across his face. She'd see how, at first, she'd argue back. She'd fight with him, demand he be less controlling.

She saw her bags by the door when she'd threatened to leave that first and only time, when he'd put her in the hospital as a lesson.

She'd never forgotten that lesson.

It had been the start of her learning to shut up, to stay quiet and obey, to play it safe. She'd discovered that alphas were so much stronger than she was, and that fighting them never ended well.

All those lessons prowled the room. Her past, the one she'd run from, the one she couldn't run far enough away from.

But he was dead, and he'd left her a mess that she had to get out of. She had to keep moving, keep searching. She owed it to Karen, to herself. Tracy pushed aside the worries, the memories, and focused on her task at hand.

Sifting through the ruble of her old life to try to save her new one.

* * * *

Sam sighed as he limped down the hall. He'd helped check every place he could think of in the huge house — office, storage rooms, gym — but they'd found nothing. Richard hadn't left so much as a work receipt. The papers in his office were all fakes. They were information about clients that didn't exist, just dead ends in case someone did break in. The more Sam had dug, the more he'd realized that nothing of Richard's life had been honest.

His job had been completely under the table, dealing with people that were beyond dangerous. His marriage had been a sham, where he'd hurt the omega he was supposed to love and care for. Everything in his life had been a fake picture, something he wanted to portray but without substance.

They'd spent a few hours at the house, and Sam wanted to check on Tracy. Mason and Dylan had both done so, peeking into the large double doors that went to the bedroom she'd shared with the alpha. She'd been searching each time. Slower than they were, but then again, they had no personal connection to the house.

He crossed the threshold to find her seated on the carpeted floor, items strewn about in front of her. "Hey, honey, you okay?"

She didn't turn her head toward him, her gaze locked on the items. "I miss him sometimes."

Sam wished he could sit on the floor, but there was no way his leg would go for that. Instead, he pulled the stool from her vanity over so he could sit across from her. "That happens. I've dealt with omegas who have been abused. It's not uncommon."

"I shouldn't miss him. I know what he did, what he was. I know better than anyone else all the things he did to me, but sometimes all I can think of is that I miss him."

"There's no one right way to get better, no one road that leads there."

She spoke again like she hadn't heard him. Maybe she hadn't. Maybe this was one of those times when she just needed to talk. "I hate him, too. I hate what he turned me into, what he did to Karen. I hate that I have any fond thoughts of him at all, that I think about the good times." She hopped to her feet and picked up one of the things in front of her—a music box. When she opened it, a ballerina spun and a sweet song played. "He got me this for our last anniversary. He said he had to scour the city for something like this, to always be very careful with it. I thought he'd done something so sweet for me, that he'd really tried hard. I'd even thought maybe it was a new start, that he was trying to say sorry."

"Maybe he was," Sam offered, not sure what to say. Was it better to put Richard down, to remind her he was a monster? Or did she need those good moments with him, something to make her past important? He wished he could read her mind, that he knew what she needed, how best to help her.

Tracy let out a hollow laugh. "No. I was sitting here thinking about it, about how he warned me to be careful with it, that it was fragile and expensive. He didn't normally care about money, so why did he this time?" She flipped the box over, pushed clasps on the bottom out of the way and pried up the black wooden board that made up the base of the music box. She shook her head as she pulled out a key hidden inside. "He didn't care about me or the gift at all. It was just another way to use me."

Sam's heart ached at the pain in her voice, and she tossed the key to him. Mason and Dylan stood in the doorway of the room, spectators to the truth, to her realizing she had meant even less than she'd thought to the alpha to whom she'd given so many years of her life.

Her hands trembled as she held the box, whites showing on her knuckles. The desire shone bright in her eyes. She wanted to destroy it.

"Wait," he said. "Don't make any decisions when you're this mad, huh? Wait until you feel better."

Her lips pressed into a thin line, but she nodded. "Right."

Dylan's voice broke into the conversation. "Go for it, Red."

They all turned to face him, and the shadows on his face matched Tracy.

He kept going. "Throw that shit against the wall and stomp it until it's a thousand pieces, yeah?"

Sam went to argue, to remind them all that a steady head would help the most. Except...maybe Dylan and Tracy understood something he didn't.

"I shouldn't," she whispered.

"So? Fuck shouldn't. That asshole used you again, and that shitty little music box? That's just proof. You don't have to be proper or calm or restrained. You don't owe that to anyone, especially not him. Fuck that."

She stood for another moment, staring at Dylan so intently, it was like an entire conversation passed in the silence between them. One quick nod and Tracy turned, grasped the box by the thin leg and swung it down against the solid wood vanity behind her. She didn't stop there, though. The thing probably had been expensive, because it took more than a few swings before it started to come apart. The music played, skipping with each hit and clicking as it broke. The tune slowed until it stopped, when the music box was in pieces that no longer looked like the beautiful thing it had been. The vanity hadn't done much better, with scratches along the front and the perfume and makeup bottles from the top knocked over.

Sam waited for the breakdown, for her to collapse into tears. He waited for the inevitable crash where he needed to help her pick up the pieces again.

Instead, she pulled in a breath, panting from the exhaustion and emotions of the blow-up, then nodded. "Let's figure out what that key goes to." She walked out of the room, past Sam, past Mason and Dylan, as if the entire thing hadn't happened.

Mason only huffed a soft laugh and followed, but before Dylan could, Sam spoke up. "How did you know?"

Dylan paused, his back to Sam.

Sam pushed. "How could you know that would help?" He kept the rest to himself. Dylan was as emotionally available as a junkyard dog, so how could he have possibly known better than Sam how to help a hurting omega?

Dylan turned back, face somber but not as angry as it often was. "Do you remember after my stepdad got taken away?"

Sam nodded, recalling the mess after the beta who took care of Dylan had gotten dragged away in cuffs for drugs, assault and a lot of other things that would keep him locked up a long while. He remembered the state of the house when Sam and his mother showed up to collect Dylan, to give him a place to stay. It had been torn to shreds. "Yeah. Everything was broken, tables turned over. I figured your stepdad gave a hell of a struggle."

Dylan shook his head. "Nah. He was passed out when they showed up, so they took him in without a fight."

A frown tugged at Sam's features. So what had happened to the house? It hit him so fast, he wondered how he could have missed it before. "You did that damage. Why?"

Dylan shoved his hands into the pockets of his jeans, looking like the kid he'd been when they'd picked him up from that dump of a house he'd lived at, when he'd hardly made eye contact, when he'd acted like none of it mattered. That was when Betsy had fully taken Dylan in, giving him a place to live. "Life isn't fair for a lot of people. Sometimes you get tired of it, tired of being something to kick when life gets bored, and sometimes?" He shrugged. "Sometimes the only way to deal with it is to ruin the reminders that were there, to trash some of the life that sucked. It isn't something easy to understand, and maybe it isn't healthy, but you know what? It's life, and it works." Dylan said nothing else as he left.

Sam wanted to argue the point, to tell him he was wrong, but what did Sam know about it? He'd grown up with what a lot of people would say was a perfect life. A loving mom, two alpha fathers who couldn't have been prouder, the only child of doting, middle-class parents. Maybe Dylan and Tracy spoke a language he didn't, had suffered a similar 'life isn't fair' history that made them understand something Sam never would.

Why argue it? Tracy had walked out of that room with her head held high, and that wasn't something he'd seen much of. If Dylan could bring that out in her, if he could make her feel like that, well hell.

Maybe Mason wasn't so wrong about them.

* * * *

Hours later and Dylan hadn't figured out a damned thing about the key.

Well, that wasn't fair. He figured it went to a padlock, though that didn't help much. Research told him the type the padlock, given the company and size. His best bet was that the padlock went to a storage unit, but with how many were around and how easy it was to sign up with a fake name, he wasn't sure how to narrow it down.

It's not enough, not nearly fucking enough.

Mason, Sam, Tracy and Karen had all gone outside to hang some sort of peanut-butter-covered pine cone. Karen had run in, showing it to Dylan with a smile on her face. A bird feeder, she'd explained, and Mason and Sam were going to put it up.

Dylan had offered the expected surprise and pride at the craft before she'd hurried off. He could have offered to help, but they didn't need his help, and no one had asked. Plus, he had other things to do, things far more important than joining in on some silly craft.

"Thank you." Tracy stood in the doorway to Dylan's room, her baggy clothing back in place.

He missed seeing more of her. Whether she saw it or not, whether she admitted it or not, she had a body he'd spent more than a bit of time fantasizing about. "For?"

"The music box."

"It was nothing. A little destruction is good for the soul."

"You understood. No one else did, but you did."

He sighed and closed his laptop when it was clear she wouldn't leave. "Yeah, I'm pretty used to breaking things. It's fine. You're welcome. We done?"

She came into the room, as though his attempts to scare her off only worked at bringing her closer. "No, I'm not done. Why are you so determined to push me away? What have I done to you that is so terrible?"

Dylan got to his feet, a glower painted on his face. He'd seen her pale at the slightest sign of anger, so anything from him should send her running, which was exactly what they both needed. The more he thought about her, the more he wanted her, and the more sure he was maybe even taking a taste wasn't a good idea. "Because, believe it or not, not every alpha can be led around by his balls just because some pretty omega bats her long lashes at him."

"I'm not trying to get anywhere near your balls." She took another two steps forward, then poked a finger to his chest. "I'm just trying to get along."

Dylan lifted a lip at her words and at the way she jabbed that finger into his chest. "Please, Red, I've dealt with enough omegas to know exactly what they're like. You might play innocent, but you aren't. You'll do what omegas always do, and you'll get your claws into an alpha and bleed them dry. If Mason and Sam want to be stupid enough to let you do it to them, that's their problem."

Her cheeks flushed a pretty pink that was far more interesting than it should have been. Made him wonder if she flushed like that when she came. Did her skin light up, all that red blotching over it in a display that couldn't be faked?

"What is this really about? Because it's not me you're this angry about."

"It's all omegas. I've had my share of them, thanks."

"So you met one who cheated on you and that means we're all bad? It means we all have to pay the price?"

Words snarled from Dylan's throat about a minute before his brain could tell him to shut the hell up. "You're all the same! Ready to use up alphas however you can, then throw them away. Nora did it when she fucked up our friendship, when she slept with Sam then moved on to greener pastures. My mom did it when she decided she was sick of dealing with my stepdad and left me there to take the brunt of his anger! She packed her shit in the middle of the night and took off. Didn't give a fuck about me, about what she was leaving behind, because all she cared about was what she wanted."

And there is was. Pity, dancing its ugly little steps across her face. "I'm so—"

"Don't you dare say it," he snapped to shut her up. "I don't need a fucking sorry from you. It's just a fact of life, huh? My mom was just like all omegas. Got herself knocked up by some alpha, no idea who he was, then sank her claws into a beta to take care of her. The beta, my stepdad, was an asshole, no two ways about that. I don't blame her for running, but fuck, she sacrificed me so she could get what she wanted. That's what I've seen, over and over again, that omegas are willing to take what they want and leave husks behind."

"We're not all—"

"The fuck you aren't. You're just waiting to get your claws into whatever alpha gives you the time of day. You want Sam to fix your problems, you want Mason to take care of you, and what? You want me to fuck you?" He should so shut up, but he wanted her pissed. Pissed was miles better than pity.

"I don't want to get my claws into anyone, and I sure as hell don't want them in you!" *Bingo.*

"Right," he sneered. "Like you don't get wet around us? Come on, let's be honest here, because I can smell you. You get one look at an alpha, one whiff, and you soak your panties, don't you? And you think that just because you smell the way you do, we'll do anything for you."

He should have shut up. Hell, he shouldn't have ever started. He knew it wasn't fair to unload on her, not with her past, especially about something she couldn't help. Biology and all that meant alphas and omegas reacted. Wasn't fair to berate her over it. Still, it was better she realized whatever fascination she had with him was a bad idea now instead of letting her linger in it.

She narrowed her eyes, that stubborn edge making his cock harden. Why did he like that, damn it? When she cowered, he wanted to protect her, but when she stood up to him? He wanted to fuck her senseless.

"Even if I was interested, it's not in you."

The fire in Tracy's eyes made Dylan yearn to kiss it clear. He wanted to wipe all that annoyance away and replace it with white-hot lust.

Which was crazy for so many reasons. One, she wouldn't allow it. Two, he didn't want her. Even scratching an itch with her would be a terrible idea. The more time he spent with an omega, the closer they got, the more likely he was to lose his mind and bond with her.

Which was something neither one of them needed and something he refused to consider might already be happening.

"So why are you in here, huh? If you're so opposed to me, why do you keep pushing this? Because I think the truth is that you *do* want me, Red. Fuck knows why. Maybe it's that whole bad-boy kick you females have, or maybe you like that I don't pussy-foot around you like the others do, but whatever it is?" He leaned in until his nose was inches from hers. "You. Want. Me."

Would she slap him for it? Maybe someone else would, but not her. What she did shocked him just as much, though. She wrapped her fingers in the front of his shirt and slammed her lips against his in a kiss so rough he might have gotten a cut on his lip from her tooth.

Fuck it, he'd take rough any day. He loved nails in his back, teeth in his throat, rough sex that left a person sore the next day.

Dylan replaced her violence with his own, backing her up until she hit the wall, where he shoved his thigh between her legs and right up against her hot cunt.

Even with her baggy clothes in the way, he knew where he was aiming.

The heat of her pussy seared him, and being so close, he could smell the mouthwatering scent of her drenched body. He lifted his leg, grinding hard against her, and she only clutched him closer, her fingers tight in his shirt as though she feared he'd get away.

The kiss was harsh and driven by something deep inside both of them. Dylan took her hot mouth, leaving nothing, no room for doubt, no room for fear. He kissed her like he wanted to fuck her—completely and without mercy.

Tracy didn't melt against him, didn't wilt. She met every movement of his with her own. No matter what he did, she returned it. She answered the press of his tongue to her closed lips by opening and offering a swipe of her own. When he pressed his thigh against her, she rolled her hips to rub her cunt against the hardness of his quad, a desperate seeking of her own pleasure.

He'd known there was something beneath that frightened omega he'd seen, something more than just fear and a bad past. In this moment, in this woman, he saw what else was there.

Passion. Desire. Need. They all poured from her as she took from him without reserve. She scratched her nails against his chest as if she could hold him still for her.

Not one to be passive or easy, Dylan upped the ante. He crowded her, kept her unsettled and off-balance so she had no time to evaluate or decide this was a bad idea. He could have her pants off in a heartbeat and inside her with a quick adjustment or two. Hell, he could fuck her against the wall and put them all both out of their misery.

And right then, he felt miserable. His skin had tightened, his balls aching, the knot at the base of his dick desperate to swell and fill her with his cum. Had he ever wanted anyone or anything more?

It made a mockery of how he'd wanted the other omega, of what he'd thought they'd had, what they could have had. That omega had enjoyed sex, sure, but she hadn't had this bone-deep need that Tracy radiated, as if she couldn't breathe without another kiss, without another stroke of her hard little clit against Dylan's leg. Nora had approached sex as a game she could take or leave, never above making sure Dylan knew she didn't need him, that he was only one of many choices for her. Tracy touched him like as though was nowhere else she'd rather be.

The slam of a door woke them up, and she darted her lust-drunk eyes around the room. Steps came down the hallway, fast but light.

Karen.

When Tracy shoved him, he moved backward to give her space. She had no clothing to rearrange, but Dylan sported a pretty obvious erection, and the last thing he needed was some kid bypassing all the normal don't-ask rules of society to point and question, 'what's that?'

Dylan grabbed his laptop, ignoring how stupid he looked, and held it in front of his crotch just in time for Karen to come charging in, calling, "Mom!"

Tracy answered, breathless still, her cheeks red, sweat matting her hair against her forehead. Yeah, he'd bet she'd flush hard when she came. "Hey, sweetheart, what's up?"

The girl beamed, grabbing her mother's hand. "Come on, Mom. We hung them up." She had Tracy halfway out of the door before she'd finished her pleading.

Before they got far, Karen twisted to cast a smile Dylan's way. "You, too. Come look!"

Dylan hesitated, used to the outskirts, to not being fully part of a group. Still, the idea of letting Tracy anywhere out of his sight didn't seem too likely. He chalked it up to some mating instinct, since he hadn't knotted the omega yet. Once he did, this feeling would go away, right?

And the other part, the part he didn't like to admit to, really liked the idea of being wanted.

It had been a long time since he'd been wanted.

Chapter Ten

Mason tried to ignore the mouthwatering scent of the omega, he really did. He'd pretended to not notice an hour before when he'd been in the kitchen. He'd taken himself outside for some fresh air. When, an hour after the first whiff, he could still catch the teasing scent of her aroused cunt, however, he realized he couldn't ignore it anymore.

Some things were more than just want. They were written in the primal areas of his DNA, the ones that had been passed down for generations. Those parts of him demanded he satisfy the needy omega who must be stoking the fire for such a scent to linger so long.

The needs of someone's body were biological requirements. He told himself that over and over while trying to give her privacy. Dylan had crashed a few hours before, and after taking his medication, Sam had followed suit. It left Mason up alone, as usual, and she hadn't appeared outside for their normal talks.

It seemed she had other plans for the evening, but given that the scent hadn't dissipated, he'd guess she wasn't managing shit on her own. Or was she edging herself? Was she taking herself to the precipice of release, then backing off? Was she keeping herself in that sweet torture? He could picture sweat on her brow, her hands shaking from the strain of unfound pleasure.

Whatever it was, it was asking too much from a houseful of alphas to ignore, and Mason knocked on the door gently. No need to embarrass her, but maybe she needed a reminder she wasn't alone. Maybe she needed someone to reiterate just how good alpha noses were.

No answer came, until a frustrated moan passed through the door.

Mason gave up on knocking, since clearly, she was too distracted to notice. Instead, he slid into the room, shutting the door behind him.

The sight nearly knocked his knees from beneath him. Tracy lay on the bed, covers kicked away, her legs splayed. She had a large shirt on, rucked up around her waist, but no panties. Still, her hand obscured his view as she plunged two fingers into her pussy, her body writhing with tension it couldn't seem to break.

The feral growl he let out was so deep it vibrated from his throat, like a mating call to a female he couldn't help.

Tracy reacted as he'd expected, her legs snapping shut and her body bolting upright. She tugged a sheet over her lap, stealing the sight he swore was tattooed into his gray matter.

"Need a hand?" He'd meant the corny come-on to break the ice, to show Tracy there was no reason for fear or upset.

The effect of it on him was something else, as he imagined replacing her small hand with his own, of filling her with his thick fingers. How wet would she be? How tightly would her body grip him?

There went pretending it was nothing, what with the next growl he let out.

"Get out," she whispered.

"I've been smelling you for over an hour, kitten. Having some trouble getting yourself there?"

"That is none of your business."

Mason crossed his arms so he didn't reach out, no matter how badly he wanted to. "Come on, I'm just here to help. Part of my job is keeping an eye on you, right?"

"I don't think Sam meant this."

"I'd bet he'd be here himself if he wasn't conked out on pain pills, so what sort of friend would I be if I didn't take care of his obligations?"

Her face didn't shift, telling Mason his humor didn't land. Then again, she looked rather put out right at that moment, so maybe it had more to do with her timing than his humor.

"Kitten," he tried again, softening his voice. "I don't have to help, but you really are distracting with that scent. You can't do this in a house full of alphas and expect no one will notice. It won't get any better until you take care of yourself."

Her eyebrows furrowed, an adorable discomfort on her face. "I'm trying."

"Yeah, I can see that. Not working?"

Her hair fell into her eyes she when shook her head. Her voice came out softly when she spoke. "I feel like there's this energy inside me. I didn't feel like this with Richard, but I can't get rid of it. I thought..."

When she didn't continue, Mason offered up some help. "You thought a little personal time would help? You ain't wrong. It's pretty damned natural that living in a house with three alphas would set you off, would get all those omega hormones riled up. It's the way we're made, kitten — it ain't a sign of weakness."

"It didn't work." And wasn't that a shit-ton of unhappy on her face as she admitted it? Sexual frustration wasn't something anyone wore well, and maybe it made Mason an asshole, but he sort of liked to see her pouting over being horny.

Adorable.

"Bet it's been a while since you tried. How long's it been since you gave yourself a hand?"

She didn't respond, but the movement of her eyes said she was thinking rather than avoiding the question.

"If it takes long division to figure it out, it's been too long. And when was the last time you got off, not counting a heat?"

Again, no answer, but this time her gaze dropped, shame coloring the motion. Poor girl blamed herself for it. "Richard wasn't very appreciative of the fact I stopped enjoying his touch," she whispered into the darkness of the room.

"Yeah, well, who could blame you for not wanting that asshole anywhere near you, and certainly not wanting to let your guard down? Look, I'm as big a fan of orgasms as anyone, but you're pretty fucking vulnerable as your body goes haywire, right? Everything sort of implodes, leaves you at your partner's mercy. Ain't the sort of thing you want to happen around someone you don't trust."

Jayce Carter

She traced a pattern in the comforter with her pointer finger, avoiding his gaze. "Yeah, that's what it was like. I stopped wanting anything with him, but he isn't here anymore."

"But you've been resisting a while, been used to not wanting it for a long time. You having trouble getting there? Sometimes fingers ain't enough."

That did get her to lift her gaze, and wasn't the suspicion there cute? "If that's your way of telling me you should help, don't think I'll fall for it. You wouldn't be the first to tell me your magical parts are the answer to all my problems."

Parts? The shy phrasing charmed him, but not as much as that little spark of attitude she gave him.

He grinned and gave her a wink. "Hey, my offer stands, but no. Look in the left side drawer of your nightstand. I know Sam pretty damned well, I bet."

She leaned over, and the action flashed her ass at him. The things that ass made him think were downright sinful. He'd bet it would give beneath his grip so well, his large hands cupping it perfectly. Hell, he wanted to grip it while he slid balls-deep into her tight, wet cunt.

A soft, scandalized gasp said she'd found Sam's fun drawer.

Sam might seem sweet, but he enjoyed toys, and he'd never have had her there without keeping a few in the nightstand in case she needed them. *Always taking care of people, ain't he?*

She moved back to sitting, with nothing to hide herself, probably too distracted by the pink vibrator she now clutched in her hands.

"Ever used one?"

"I'm not an idiot."

"Never said you were. Knowing what one is and using one are different, though. I heard you settled down with that prick pretty young. He doesn't strike me as the kind who would let you go playing around with toys. Seems more like a 'my dick is magic and oughta be enough' sort of bastard."

She pressed the button at the end, the thing buzzing quietly to life. "Yeah, he was." Another pause. "And, no, I haven't."

Fuck, I want to see her use it. I want to see her come unglued from it. Hell, I want to hold that toy against her clit until she's crying out.

"Go on," he demanded, voice husky, needing to see her come.

Tracy didn't move right away, and when she did, it was so slow, like the sweetest torture. She leaned back against the pillows, her thighs spreading wide. The sheet she'd pulled up covered her cunt, but he ignored the disappointment as she lowered the vibrator down her small body.

He didn't need to see her pussy to know when she'd touched it to her clit the first time. A sharp, startled gasp and the jerking of her entire body said she'd done it and probably too hard.

"Easy," Mason said. "It's stronger than you're used to. You don't need to use it as hard as you would your fingers. Glide it around your clit, kitten, to the side, above, hell don't even touch your clit at first. Thing is strong enough to get you off in just the general proximity."

Tracy's eyes slipped closed, and the next pass brought a breathy moan. She must have listened to his advice, and the idea of her getting herself off to the sound of his voice made him shift, his dick hard against his sweats. He'd love to jerk off to the incredible sight. Damn, it would feel great to stroke himself while she got off, to watch her little body writhe as she sought her own pleasure, to come just as she did. The moment his cock made an appearance, though, he was pretty sure the moment would be gone.

Pity.

Her hips rolled, and the sheet shifted. Another wanton movement, mindless and seeking, and that covering slipped farther. It wasn't long before Mason could see everything, before the wet pinkness of her slit came into view. She wasn't fucking herself on her fingers, wasn't using them to fill herself in some vain attempt to mimic a cock, but instead worked the vibrator against her body as he'd told her to.

She pressed it to the left of her clit, then the right, never fully touching the hardened bundle of nerves, never moving the hood for direct contact.

Good girl. Show me everything.

A tremble started in her thighs and her lips parted to release louder moans, ones that bordered on desperate whimpers. Her scent bloomed more, saturating the room, reaching inside him to demand that his alpha side satisfy her.

The need was bone-deep, an instinct so primal he struggled to resist it. He was an alpha and there was a spread, drenched, panting, needy omega in front of him. He could yank his pants out of the way and fill her in one brutal thrust. She'd bury her nails in his back and demand he knot her, demand more, and he'd give her everything. He'd fuck her until she forgot Richard, until she had no room for fear or doubt because he'd fill every last inch of her.

But if she was too lost to argue, then she hadn't agreed. It would erode any trust they'd built, so he'd stay put no matter what.

"That's it, kitten," he said in a voice he'd hoped was a purr but knew damned well was a growl. Even so, she showed no signs of fear, and her hips kept up that sexy, writhing, lifting thing so he didn't stop the dirty talk. Let her hear every filthy thing he was thinking. "You look delicious, like the best fucking snack. God, what I would do for just a taste of your cunt. Your skin flushes something pretty, and I'm drowning in your scent."

She thrust her hips up, the muscles in her firm thighs twitching. She was so close, he could see the strain on her face, the sweat on her brow, the panting of her chest through her baggy shirt, hell even her cunt twitched, like it was squeezing down, wanting to be filled. Even so, she couldn't get there, couldn't get over that last hurdle.

The struggle turned him on in a way that wasn't fair. It wasn't that he liked that she couldn't get there—though he guessed he did, in a way, because the sight was a pretty one—but he wanted to help her. He wanted to see her lost to the pleasure, wanted to get her there himself.

"Let me help," he all but begged in a broken voice, willing to drop to his knees and plead if that was what it took.

Her eyes opened, and all the lust there made him wonder if she'd heard him at all. "You won't…"

He'd agree to anything right then. Power of attorney? His first born? His left nut? Anything to get closer. "Anything you want. I'll do anything, kitten."

"Don't touch me," she whispered.

He frowned but nodded. *Fine, I'll make it work.*

She reached out to give him the vibrator, and slickness near the end said her pussy was beautifully drenched.

He couldn't touch her, but that didn't mean he had to resist everything. As a hedonist, Mason had never been any good at resisting anything and denying himself anything. He swirled his tongue around the head of the toy, tasting her slick that coated it.

Delicious. It woke up even more of his instinct, made his knot fucking pulse with need, as though it could annoy him into giving in. *Not happening, asshole,* he reminded it before crawling onto the bed between her spread thighs.

The first touch of the vibrator to her body was tentative, exploratory. Each female was different, and he had to figure out what she liked. Fuck, he wanted to spend all night figuring out what she wanted, teasing her luscious body for hours until he could play her like an expert. He glided it along her slit, testing by pressing in just a hair. It wasn't a great toy for penetration, too small and not shaped right for fucking her. Still, those vibrations would tease along her whole entrance, and he needed something inside her, to claim her somehow.

He pulled it back and moved it up, toying around her clit, avoiding the sensitive nub that peeked from beneath its hood.

How can I feel this out of control already? She'd used the toy on herself, and while it had gotten her close, she hadn't quite fallen over that edge.

The moment Mason had picked it up, when he'd brushed it against her, she'd known she'd been lost, any attempt to resist pointless. The vibrations ran through her body like a sensual caress, and the memory of him licking her juices off it made her pussy throb in desperate want. He'd done it with his gaze locked to hers, a promise in those whiskey-colored eyes.

He brought the toy to her clit, positioned to the side but firmly against the base. The vibrations sank deep into her, teasing her and overtaking her.

"That's right, kitten," he said above her moaning, above the filthy, wet sounds of him pleasuring her soaked body. "You're going to come for me, ain't you? It'll break you apart, because you need it, because it's been so long, but damn, it'll feel good. Let it happen, stop fighting it." His words might have made her laugh any other time.

Fight it? There was no way to fight the overwhelming pleasure he pushed into her nervous body, to fight the way he knew exactly where to stroke her with that toy, how to use it to torment her needy clit, to drive her body to a high she was afraid she'd never come down from. It was a madness spreading through her, a lust she'd never experienced before. Sex had been okay with Richard at the start, but it had never been *this*.

Mason ground the vibrator against her body, against the side of her clit, and she broke apart just as he'd said she would.

Her orgasm grew, prolonged by how he lightened the touch but brushed the toy against her swollen clit directly. She lifted her hips in broken, feral thrusts, her cunt pulsing and squeezing around nothing. She crushed the blankets in her fists as she tried to hang on to something, to keep some shred of control while her body shorted out beneath Mason's skillful touch.

Nothing worked, though, and the movement of the toy said Mason wasn't planning on giving her any way to resist him.

The orgasm went on so long that she pulled in a deep gasping breath when her muscles finally loosened, when her back lost its arch and she fell down limp on the bed.

He removed the vibrator immediately, giving her tired and overworked body a much-needed break. Again, he lifted it to his mouth and licked it clean, a wolfish grin on his full lips that matched his wild appearance.

The sight made her cunt tighten, and even exhausted as she was, she wanted more. She wanted to feel him push into her, to spread her pussy around his thick cock.

And, no, she wasn't ready for that to really happen, yet she still wanted it desperately.

"You look good when you come," he said in his deep, rough voice.

She dropped her gaze to find his erection tenting his sweats like a gift.

A gift? I always thought about that as more of an obligation. And yet, she wanted to see him. She wanted to peel the fabric away, to have nothing obscuring her view. She wanted to drag her tongue along his length, to have the same obvious pleasure he'd had when he'd swallowed down the taste of her he'd gotten.

"Don't worry about that," he assured her. "Can't help getting hard, but I'm not about to jump on you just because I helped you get off."

"You could take care of it," she said before she could think better of it.

"Here?" His eyebrow lifted. "You have a thing for watching? Will I get my own page in your sketchbook if I do?"

She pushed herself to sitting, not wanting to talk while she was lying flat, in a position of powerlessness. "Please?"

He sniffed deeply, the action primitive. Heat flashed brighter in his eyes as his smile widened. "You're not quite done yet, are you?"

"No. But, I'm not ready to—"

"I won't fuck you. You think I could touch you this time, though?"

She hesitated, and he waited. He didn't push her or try to coax a yes as she thought about it, as she decided if she wanted that. Then again, he'd had every chance to hurt her, to ignore her wishes, but he'd kept his word to her. He hadn't touched her when he'd helped her, even though his erection screamed that he'd wanted to.

Agreeing took more bravery than she'd thought she had, yet a moment later, Tracy nodded. "Just on the outside," she said quickly, needing some rules, some control.

"Sure, kitten, that'll be more than enough." He grasped her hips and pulled, causing her to fall backward and slide down the bed.

He might have frightened her, but his playful grin made it hard to be startled or angry. It left her lying flat on her back with Mason poised between her legs, a hulking presence that would have panicked her before. The way he'd moved her had shown just how strong the man was, as if his massive body hadn't already clued her in.

Now? Still basking in the glow of her first orgasm in too many years, she could appreciate his looks for what they were.

Because he *was* good-looking. His body was large, with little room for finesse. He was pure brute strength, with a broad chest layered in muscle and wide shoulders that went down to biceps easily larger than her thighs. His hair, wild and long and a lovely reddish-blonde, hung down as he rested over her. She leaned up on an elbow to get a look down his body, as well.

Mason pushed his sweats down his thick thighs to let her see everything else.

His waist didn't narrow much, all of him big. His thighs showed the separation in the muscles, his quads standing out, rigid as though holding still were difficult. He had hair on his thighs, the same that dusted his arms and his chest — light brown, almost blond. Her gaze traveled up his thighs to the thatch of reddish hair at his groin, and to the intimidating length of his long, thick cock. It seemed he was large all over, and the way his shaft stood erect, pressed against his lower stomach and so hard it had to ache made her moan.

Still, nothing but desire swam inside her. No hint of uncertainty, no worry. That surprised her. Did lust shove that all away so nothing else had room? Or did she trust him more than she realized?

Whatever the reason, when Mason stroked his fingers up her sex and wrapped his other large palm around his cock, she didn't fear. She surrendered to the touch, to the gentle way he ran his fingers across her core, like she mattered. He didn't push in, didn't try to take more than she'd been willing to give. His fingers were strong and sure as they explored her folds, never trying to gain entrance or take what hadn't been offered but instead teasing every wet, wanton inch of her sex.

His other hand stroked his thick cock, though even with his large hand, his fingers didn't quite meet when gripping it. That alone gave her pause, but the head of his dick disappearing into his palm then reappearing drove away her moment of concern.

She slid her tongue along her bottom lip, and he answered with a deep, masculine growl.

"This is a sight I won't ever forget, kitten. You make one pretty picture, all spread out for me, and I've never felt anything as good as your pussy. You're so fucking wet for me, ain't you?" He danced his fingers up to her clit, but even so, the touch remained indirect and teasing. "And your taste? Oh, kitten, I can't wait to eat you out, to swallow down mouthfuls of your sweetness."

His words sparked the thought, and she whined at how he'd look between her legs, staring up her body. His eyes, intense and wild, while those full lips of his, usually pulled into a smirk, would do something more interesting.

His hand sped on his impressive cock, and he stopped touching her to set that hand on the mattress, crowding over her. "This okay?" he asked, voice broken and rough.

Right then, everything was okay, so she nodded. The ease drained when the blunt head of his cock touched her pussy, when years of having Richard respect none of her boundaries crashed over her.

He stilled above her, so close they were nearly in missionary position. "Open your eyes," he whispered.

When had she closed them? She did as he said, looking up into his familiar whiskey-colored ones.

"Trust me, Tracy. I'm not going to fuck you. I won't take anything you ain't giving." He leaned down and trailed a kiss across her lips. "Trust me?"

When he didn't do anything, when he waited, Tracy shuddered out a tension-filled breath and nodded.

"Good girl," he praised. "You're so fucking brave. Now relax, hmm? I think you'll like this."

She still tensed, waiting for him to break that promise, to shove himself into her, to do what came natural despite her limits or his promises.

Instead, the first press of his cock to her clit sent her clutching hands to his chest. It wasn't a protest, and she didn't shove him away.

Mason waited, as though giving her time to decide if she liked it.

She did. It didn't take more than a split second for her to be sure she enjoyed the feeling of his hard cock grinding against her clit, a caress even more intimate than the vibrator, than his fingers had been.

"So you want me to keep going?"

She nodded.

"I want you to ask me to."

Her lips parted, but words wouldn't come. Asking for things was difficult. It was participating, and it was admitting her desires, and if she admitted them, they could be used against her. No one could tell her no if she never asked.

He brought the hand braced on the bed to her cheek, using his elbow to hold himself up instead. "Not used to asking for shit, are you?" His voice held no censure, no annoyance. If anything, it got kinder. "You gotta learn to ask—that way we both know you want it. I'll make it easy on you here—just ask me to keep doing that. Nothing hard about those words, is there?"

Tracy drew in a breath as she considered it. She'd have given up any other time, retreated to her own safe, lonely rut, but the simmering desire inside her, the sensation of his cock brushing her clit said she would play along if it meant more of this. "Please keep doing that?"

"Oh, I like the please. Wasn't so hard, was it?" He stroked his length again and took the opportunity to grind the wet head against her nub.

Pleasure sparked inside her, like currents of electricity that streaked through her body, travelling along her nerves. His cock leaked pre-cum, and she would swear it soaked into her like a balm she'd desperately needed.

She shifted her hands so that instead of pressing them against his chest, she slid them back to grasp his shoulders, testing the hard muscles there, amazed by the differences between their bodies. He was hard, large and confident. She was soft, small and unsure.

His facial hair tickled her as he stole a kiss, coaxing her with his lips as he used his cock to bring her nearer to that edge again.

And she wanted it. She *needed* to lose herself to another release after going so long without. She wanted to be so tired, so mindless and sated that she could do nothing but sleep happily.

The grinding of his cock against her clit pushed her toward that marvelous release. "I'm close," he said against her lips, the words a kiss all their own. "You want me to back off?"

The thought of him pulling back, of him moving even an inch away made her dig her nails in to keep him close. "Don't go," she pleaded.

"See, you can ask for what you want, kitten. Sure, I'll stay." A deep groan left his lips, her hips rising in response to the masculine sound of pleasure. "Your cunt will look good painted with my cum."

His words had an immediate reaction for them both. For her, an especially hard drag of his cock against her clit had her gasping, her muscles tensing right on the precipice of release. Mason's hand moved faster, almost frantic, and caused his solid dick to grind harder.

He came first with a growl, his hot cum spilling onto her waiting pussy. That sent her over, the sensation of his warm seed soaking into her, the way his lips stopped any movement, as though all his attention was taken up by his orgasm.

Tracy cried out as she came a second time, this one harsher, stealing her breath and thoughts as her back arched up against Mason's solid form.

He didn't stop the gentle nudges of his softening cock against her, the action rubbing his hot, thick cum into her skin. His weight settled on her, his body pressing against hers fully for the first time.

It again reminded her of just how large he was, of how much smaller she was.

She could have started to second guess it, but after the orgasms he'd gifted her with, the ones he'd wrung from her nervous body, she lacked energy to do so.

Instead, she licked his bottom lip, a sweet thank you, and settled in.

He cleaned her off once he'd caught his breath, the stroke of the rag against her over-sensitive pussy too much. The loss of his heat made her whine unhappily, missing his solid body. Only him slinging his heavy arm over her made her smile, when he'd returned to the bed and crawled in beside her.

I could get used to this.

Chapter Eleven

Sam couldn't get enough of Tracy. She looked better, again. During her time at the group home, stress had carved lines into her face. She gave so much of herself and took nothing for herself.

She might not like it, but she did better with an alpha around.

Or three of us.

The color on her cheeks and some of the fire back in her eyes suited her well. Her wild red hair was pulled into a low ponytail, and some part of Sam that had never really grown up wanted to yank it softly until she paid attention to him.

Still, something sat on her. It had been there all morning, and Sam didn't need her to say a thing for him to recognize what it was.

She carried Mason's scent.

The two must have gotten close the night before, because, despite a strong clinging of soap, he could smell the other alpha beneath it.

That explains why she won't look me in the eye, doesn't it?

Mason and Dylan had gotten the job of watching Karen on her new bike, the one which had arrived that morning, though Sam wasn't sure which of the alphas had ordered it. Karen managed to wrap them around her finger as easily as Tracy did.

It left Sam and Tracy alone, and the omega didn't seem comfortable with that, not given the way she'd avoided meeting his eyes all morning.

"It's okay," Sam said.

Her gaze darted to him. "What?"

"You slept with Mason, right?"

Shame washed over her pretty features first, trailing fear and guilt after it. At least the fear didn't last that long. "How can you..." She chewed at her bottom lip and sighed. "You can smell him, can't you?"

Sam nodded.

Her lip trembled. "I'm sorry, Sam, I shouldn't have. You've done so much for me, are letting me live at your home, and I betrayed you—" Her spiral into tears happened so fast it surprised even him.

"Woah, honey, hold on a minute." He caught her hand to try to get her to take a breath and a break from her little meltdown. "I'm not mad."

"Only because you're too nice to be mad."

That had him smiling. "No, that's not why. Mason's like a brother to me, and it's hard to blame you for getting pulled in. I've seen enough alphas and omegas who stay together falling into this sort of thing." He squeezed her hand, then sat back to not crowd her. He might understand, but he still needed a few answers from her. "I want to figure out what you're thinking, though."

"What do you mean?"

Sam fidgeted in the seat, both to relieve tightness in his back and to help with how much he didn't want to ask what he was about to ask. He'd been down that road before, had seen it go badly. Was he really thinking about trying it again? But, if he didn't, would he lose her? Finally, he came right out and asked. "No matter what your answer is, you've got a place here, you and Karen. I need you to know that, first, to understand that nothing you decide changes that. Okay?"

She nodded.

"Now, I want to know if you're feeling Mason and want me to back off. Maybe you fit with him better, maybe you and I were just a stress reaction, or hell, maybe it was guilt or just gratitude." He needed to stop talking. The more he said, the more he let the doubts creep in and the more he regretted this whole conversation.

He needed to have it though. It wasn't fair to Tracy to keep her in limbo, or to keep pushing if she'd settled on someone else.

And Sam wouldn't have faulted her. Mason was a good man, and he had no doubts the other alpha would take care of her. Even thinking that made his chest hurt.

Tracy said nothing for a long while, her gaze not dropping either, both locked in a staring contest, as if they could figure things out in the other's eyes. Her shoulders dropped. "I like you, Sam. It's not guilt or gratitude."

A relieved breath filled his lungs. That was a good first step, right? "Good. I mean, I'm glad that you like me." He gave her a smile, thinking about how she'd looked at him in the shower, how she'd touched him. That was more than just mild like, wasn't it?

Her cheeks flushed, and he knew she got exactly what he was hinting at. "I don't know how it happened with Mason. We didn't have sex, but we…" She couldn't seem to get out the rest before moving on. "I don't know what I'm doing. I was never like this before."

"Did you ever stay with three unmated alphas before? Because that makes a difference. You can't beat yourself up over a normal reaction."

"How is being interested in two alphas normal?"

Just two? Where does that leave Dylan?

"My mom had two mates." Sam thought about his fathers, about the two who had helped shape him into the alpha he'd become, who had guided him and could have given him no better role models in how to behave. "You know Claire has three mates, and so does Tiffany. It's not nearly as uncommon as people like to think."

Tracy pursed her lips before dragging her tongue over the full bottom one, wetting the rosy pink there. *What is she thinking about?* Given the way her scent had increased, he'd guess it wasn't anything innocent. As quickly as the scent bloomed, it dissipated and she shook her head. "It's not right."

"Don't say that to my mother or she'll give you an earful." He kept the playful tone in his voice, thinking of how much his mother would love Tracy. Plus, the woman had been clamoring for grandkids, and she'd dote on Karen like no other.

"I just mean, that's fine for other omegas, maybe, regular ones, but not me. I'm not the sort of woman who could do that. I can hardly manage being around one man." She sighed, setting her forearms on the table. "Besides, how can it be love if you're wanting a bunch of people? That's not love, then."

"And you want love?"

The question was met with a tense silence, but a soft exhalation later, she nodded. "Yeah, I do."

Sam drummed his fingers on the table, trying to decide how to address the issue. He thought back to his mother sitting him down and having a similar talk with him when someone from school had gone off about his mother being a whore because she had two mates. The kid had walked away with a broken nose and Sam had gotten suspended for a week. "You love Karen, right? If you had another kid, would you love the other less? Would you love Karen less?"

She shook her head, and the wheels behind her eyes moved.

"Then why do you think you can only love one mate?"

"It's different."

"Why? Because people say it's different?"

She huffed a frustrated sound, the sound of a woman trying to make a point but being outmaneuvered. "So you're fine with other alphas having me?"

And there it was. Preconceived notions were hard to fight, and Tracy had a hell of lot of them over this. Richard hadn't valued her, so it seemed she carried that same fear forward, that if someone didn't try to own something, they must not care about it. "You think that just because I don't mind sharing you with Mason, I don't value you? That the only way to treasure something is to hoard it? Trust me, honey, you matter a hell of a lot to me. Enough, in fact, that if you want Mason, I want you happy. I wouldn't say that about just any alpha. I can't say I'd react well to finding you in bed with just anyone, but Mason?" He had to admit, his friend's scent clinging to Tracy turned him on. "I don't mind that at all."

"And I don't get a say in any of this?"

"You get all the say. If you want me, I'm here. If you want him, he seems willing. If you want us both, that sounds good, too. The real question is what do you want?"

She turned her head toward a laugh so loud it echoed in through the open window. Mason had set up a small dirt jump for Karen in the garden, where Dylan was checking the straps of her helmet. The look on the girl's face said Dylan had done so many times already, the worrier never happy with safety. Still, her laughter, the contentment held there made Sam's chest tight. He'd always wanted family in that house, and for the first time, he had it.

The look on Tracy's face said she wasn't sold, and even though Sam had acted as though she was good with whatever she picked, if she didn't pick him, if she didn't pick *them*, she'd break his heart.

Everything rode on the decisions of one flighty omega.

* * * *

Dylan didn't normally have trouble sleeping, but a certain omega and her frustratingly tempting scent had made it impossible.

All day he'd smelled her in every damned room of the house. There was no place safe from it, and thus from her. Even his bedroom seemed infected with the scent, and he was ready to douse himself in a cold shower to rid himself of the erection that had plagued him every step of the way.

He wouldn't jerk off. That felt like ceding too much ground, like losing a battle. Instead, he ignored it.

As much good as that had done.

He rose from his bed, giving up. A glass of water, then an ice-cold shower. That was the plan.

The house appeared silent. Two a.m. was the time even the night-owl Mason normally slept, though. Dylan took it as a win, figuring he wasn't good company with the mood he was in.

The more he tried to ignore Tracy, the more she wormed her way into his mind. It wasn't just her scent, either. He liked her laugh, rare as it was. He liked the way she looked at her daughter, and the backbone she showed when it came to her. He liked…her, damn it. But he shouldn't.

He knew where that bullshit headed, and he wasn't looking to have his heart smashed apart again. Once was more than enough.

A rattle caught his attention when he reached the kitchen. The sound came from the den, and he frowned at the small cabinet tucked away beneath a bench seat. It ran the length of a row of large windows.

Dylan moved forward, steps light. He still doubted anyone would have broken in, and even if they'd managed to get past the security system, what sort of intruder would hide in a cabinet that small? More likely, some animal had gotten in.

Stay cats found their way anywhere, and Sam was soft-hearted enough to have probably been feeding them.

Dylan crouched on the balls of his feet before pulling open the door.

Inside wasn't a cat, but instead the tightly curled body of a trembling Karen.

All that ice Dylan liked to use so he didn't care, so people couldn't fuck with him, cracked at the sight.

Jayce Carter

She lifted her head, gaze startled. When it landed on him, some of the fear eased from her eyes. Well, the startled fear eased, but not the bone-deep one that had driven her to try to hide in a cabinet.

"Can't be too comfy in there, kid." Dylan schooled his voice carefully. Snapping at Tracy wasn't great, but even he wasn't dick enough to snap at a kid.

Karen shifted on the blanket she'd set up in there. "It's not so bad."

Dylan could yank her out, but he had a feeling that wasn't going to work too well. Instead, he tried for coaxing, despite that not being one of his skills. "Well, I'm going to get some ice cream, and I'd sneak you some, but Sam has this rule about not eating ice cream in the cabinets."

Karen's lips pressed together, and he got the sense she knew he was playing her. Still, ice cream proved too great a temptation, and she crawled out.

Within fifteen minutes, they sat outside, a bowl of ice cream in Karen's lap and an obligatory bowl set on the side table by Dylan, untouched.

The girl ate half the bowl before she spoke, and that was fine by Dylan. Helping people, doing the whole emotional thing, that wasn't his trick. If someone fucked with Karen, he'd step in. He'd happily skin anyone he needed to, break bones, bloody noses. If someone endangered her, that was where he excelled. Not this.

Even so, before long, Karen decided Dylan was the right one for the job. "I couldn't sleep."

"And cabinets are comfier? Because, while sleeping isn't much of a problem for me, I've never tried crawling into the shelves."

Karen slid her spoon across the melted ice cream at the bottom of her bowl, drawing designs in the mess. "I used to have a big dresser in my room, and sometimes I hid in the bottom of it."

'Sometimes' being when her father had been on a rage was the obvious part of the story she didn't need to say. The thought of that girl, even smaller, even younger, crawling into some dresser to hide had Dylan's already shitty control of his temper slipping.

"Well, you're safe as could be here. Sam has this place wired to hell, and between your mama and the three of us? Nothing to worry about."

"I don't want to be afraid anymore," she whispered. "I don't like being afraid."

That's when he saw it. It wasn't just the fear. Fear came and went, it happened, but helplessness? That clung. The girl had been helpless her entire life, helpless to the temper of her father, helpless to protect her mother or herself. Sure, there was a security system and alphas around, but she wanted to feel safe, and at the end of the day, that feeling of safety only happened when a person could defend themselves.

Dylan recalled nights as a kid, never sure when his own father-figure would go off. He'd lie awake just waiting, waiting for his stepdad to find some reason to get mad, to take it out on Dylan. Yeah, he knew what that sort of stress did to a kid.

And, while his plan wasn't something Sam or Mason would have done, they never really understood this. They couldn't.

"I'll be right back," he said, taking his bowl in and dumping it in the sink before grabbing something out of his room. Once back outside, Karen staring at him with more than a little suspicion, Dylan held his hand out with the small piece of metal.

She didn't reach, as though expecting a trap.

Dylan rolled the metal over, then used his other hand to pull out the blade from the pocketknife so it rested flat on his palm.

She recoiled, as though the blade might reach out and strike at her.

Still, Dylan didn't stop. He pointed out the parts of the pocketknife, showed how to open it and close it again. The handle was small, and the blade was three and a half inches long, setting snuggly into the handle when closed.

Despite the blade being small, he'd always taken good care of it, and it was sharp enough to make a formidable weapon.

Dylan held his hand out and waited.

"My mom wouldn't like it," Karen whispered even though her gaze never wavered.

"She doesn't need to know. This is about you, kid. You're the one who has to sleep at night, right? And at the end of the day, you're the one who has to look after yourself. Us, we're here to help, but you gotta know you can handle shit all on your own, too."

She wrapped her fingers around the handle and pulled it back toward her, eyes wide.

Good girl. Dylan pointed at the edge of the handle. "There's a hook there that'll let you tuck it into pants pockets. You want me to show you how to use it?"

Karen bit her bottom lip in a motion identical to her mother. After another breath, she nodded, fingers tightening around the handle and pure determination in those young eyes.

Dylan had to shove away the sensation of looking at himself, at remembering how it had felt to be little and vulnerable and knowing the only one he could really count on was himself. The lesson might have been a shitty one, but at the end of the day, it was true. It didn't matter the friends someone gathered, the family, people had to know they could take care of themselves.

So he stood up, Karen following, and smiled at the girl.

She'd be a hellion when he was done teaching her. He'd make sure of it.

Tracy forced herself to remain still when she finally found Karen. The panic she'd had when she'd found the girl's empty bed still forced her heart to race and sweat to rise above her eyebrow.

All the terrible thoughts swirled in her head. What if Karen had run away? What if one of those associates of Richard's had found her? What if she'd been kidnapped?

She'd located her daughter on the back deck, Dylan there, too. It let her take a deep breath, at least until she watched them.

Dylan wrapped a hand around Karen's mouth and pulled her against his front.

A rage that frightened even Tracy rose inside her, until she heard his voice.

"There's not much to hit right now, right? Except you're little, so use that to your advantage. Bring the knife down for a good swing and go for fatty areas. Thighs, stomach, anywhere the blade can sink in pretty far without hitting bone."

Karen's movements weren't frantic. She brought her hand down, something tucked in her fist, and hit it against Dylan's thigh in a controlled arc.

Dylan let out a laugh and released her, looking more relaxed than she'd seen before. In fact, a laugh from him seemed completely at odds with the alpha she'd come to know.

"Good job, kid. If you'd had the blade out, that would have been a good hit. Feel free to twist the blade, too, because that'll tear the wound up even more."

That was what was in Karen's hand. A closed pocketknife. *Did Dylan give my child a knife?*

Tracy lost her battle to remain still and stepped fully onto the deck. "Karen, it's time for you to go to bed." She knew her voice was laced with anger, but she didn't bother to hide it.

Karen didn't shrink, didn't cower. She curled her fingers around the metal like it was a lifejacket before offering a whispered *thank you* to Dylan and retreating.

She'd learned long before not to get involved in the arguments of adults.

Dylan turned, all the excitement and happiness melting off his face as though it had never been there at all. "If you're here to bitch, it's too fucking late to listen to that."

Tracy slid the slider shut once she heard the click of Karen's door. The girl's room was on the other side of the house, meaning she wouldn't be privy to the conversation that was about to occur. "Don't you speak to me in that tone of voice when you're the one out here manhandling my daughter."

"Manhandling?" He huffed a mocking laugh. "You know damned well I was giving her a self-defense lesson, something she should have learned a long fucking time ago."

"She doesn't need self-defense, because protecting her is my job!"

"You try to tell her she doesn't need it when you find her hiding in a goddamned cabinet at two in the morning!" Dylan's voice raised to meet Tracy's, neither fully yelling, but rather tossing vicious and angry whispers at one another.

The jab landed, and Tracy didn't bother to hide the flinch. She still didn't give in. "I may not have done the best job keeping her safe before, but that doesn't mean it should be on her shoulders. She shouldn't have to learn that, because by learning it, you're telling her she isn't safe."

"She already doesn't feel safe. You can't put this back in the case, Red. That girl has already seen the hell this world can be. She's lived it and trying to act like she's some innocent kid now isn't going to do a damned thing. She doesn't need everyone acting like she's fragile — she needs people telling her the world fucking sucks, and it's dangerous, and she can handle every single bit of it that comes snarling her way."

Tracy opened her mouth, ready to argue the point, but she found no argument. She wanted Karen to have a normal childhood. She wanted her to be ignorant of the dangers of the world, but that wasn't the life they'd lived. Trying to give her now what she'd never gotten before maybe wasn't the right way.

Even still, she couldn't let Dylan win. That fear she'd had shifted to frustration with the alpha before her.

Maybe it wasn't with him, but he seemed a safe place to put it. Sam was injured and had done too much for her. Mason was too damned easy going to lash out at.

Dylan though? He liked to push her buttons, and no matter how mad he made her, she didn't feel a speck of fear when putting all that frustration at his feet.

She pointed a finger at him, even poking it against his chest as she had the last time they'd argued. "I don't need your help raising my daughter."

Dylan dropped his gaze to the finger, then glared. "I think this isn't about her at all. I think you just want this to end like last time."

No. I won't think about last time, about his thigh against me, or his strong hands, or his rough kiss.

She ignored the heat in her cheeks at the reminder. She also chose to ignore the tightening of her nipples and the rush of wetness in her cunt. His brash behavior should at least turn her off, right? The others were so careful with her, each in their own way, but Dylan wasn't careful. He didn't treat her like she was damaged.

"You think too much of yourself."

He leaned down until his face was a breath from hers. "You shouldn't try to lie to me. I can smell exactly how wet you are right now. What, is this some sort of foreplay to you? Come out here, yell at me some and hope I'll get pissed enough to go for a repeat?"

Tracy said nothing back. What was there to say? The more he spoke to her, the more she felt the wetness of her panties, the more she thought he might be right.

And wasn't that a depressing thought?

But there was something about the way he stared at her, those dark, lidded eyes devouring her. In the dimness of the porch, his expression was even hungrier, even more dangerous.

She waited for him to scold her for it, for him to laugh and go inside, to tell her yet again he had no interest in her.

"You think I'll just give in and fuck you?" Dylan took another deep drag of her scent, savoring it, before his lips curled into something that wasn't friendly enough to be a smile. "No argument? Good, because that's exactly what I'm going to do, Red."

Chapter Twelve

A soft yelp escaped Tracy as Dylan tossed her over his shoulder then dropped her on a patio chair near the outside of the deck, away from the main light source. It gave them a sense of privacy, but also made her realize she was alone in the dark with a very intimidating alpha.

Dylan wrapped his fingers in the waist of her pants and tugged them off with no semblance of gentleness. "Don't get scared now, Red. You just yelled at me for the second time. If I was gonna hurt you, don't you think I'd have done it by now?"

His smart-ass comment scoured away her nerves. Tracy rewarded him with a soft kick to his shoulder, and he only cast her a half-hearted glare before yanking free her panties.

She doubted he could see much with the darkness, but the way he zeroed in on her pussy said he saw enough to tantalize.

He didn't touch her though, not at first. Instead, he swiped his thumb across his bottom lip. "Top off, too."

"I'm not getting naked outside."

"Like everyone hasn't seen it already."

She remained silent.

He tilted his head. "Really? Not like I haven't smelled Sam and Mason on you, figured they'd have stripped you down already. Useless alphas too eager? Fine, just pull that ugly sweater up, hmm? I want a good look at you."

Hesitation tugged at her. Even in the darkness, she lacked confidence. It was one thing to think about something sexual, about twisting bodies and mindless lust. She didn't want to see his disappointment when she showed him anything, though, when he got a look at how lacking she was. He'd been with enough other females to know how far short she'd fall.

He tsked, a soft sound, before his hands went to the bottom hem of her sweater. He caught her tank top, as well, tugging both up more gently than he'd done with the pants. A soft groan echoed inside him with each inch he revealed. "You worry too much, Red. Wouldn't want to see if I didn't already know I'd like it."

"Richard always said I was too skinny."

His growl took on a dangerous edge, and he didn't bother to hide it. "He was a fucking idiot. I don't even like you and I can say every glimpse I've gotten of you has made me hard."

He spoke with such bluntness, as if it didn't embarrass him at all that he'd been turned on by her, that despite his not-so-nice comments and attitude, he'd been attracted. She probably could have smelled it if she hadn't been so busy trying to ignore it.

176

He moved the fabric above her breasts, and the cool breeze tightened her nipples into hard peaks. *Who am I kidding? It's him that's doing it, not the breeze.*

"Fuck, Red," he almost purred, the sound so sinful she whined a moment before he lowered his mouth to her waiting breasts.

He didn't offer gentle kisses. Instead, he left a love-bite on her left breast, near the lower curve. A trail of stings remained as he moved his lips and teeth until he reached her nipple, causing her to cry out. Forget careful or cautious—Dylan sent her body into chaos with his rough touches.

He didn't move away from her, so close she could feel his lips curl into a smirk. "I like that sound better than you bitching at me. Hell, maybe we can actually get along if we do it like this. Never talk, never get in each other's way. Nope, I'll just fuck you whenever you annoy me too much, and you'll love every second of it, won't you?"

She didn't have time to respond—couldn't have thought of anything to say back anyway—before he switched to her other breast. Between the nipping of his teeth and the slide of his demanding tongue, he kept talking. "It's a fucking shame those other idiots didn't pay any attention to these. Look at those perky little nipples of yours, just begging for my touch. I bet you anything your clit is the same, isn't it?"

It was. They both knew it, even though he hadn't touched her there, yet. Her clit was hard and aching, peeking out from its hood and pulsing with each of his touches to her breast, as though they were connected.

He settled his hands on her thighs and pushed them obscenely wide. Even with her spread like that, he took up every inch of space as he lowered himself to his knees before her.

His expression was ravenous, as though he'd spotted a meal he intended to finish off. *I want him to finish me off.* The thought hit her so fast she didn't have time to counter it, to doubt herself.

His large, strong hands moved up her thighs until his thumbs bracketed her cunt, then moved to the top of her pussy to brush the sides of her clit.

The touch was so sure. He had the confidence she didn't. His lack of doubt grounded her, and when he used those thumbs to pull back the hood of her clit, to expose her fully to the cold night air and his hungry gaze, she surrendered.

She let go of her past, of every single fear Richard had created in her. They wouldn't be gone forever, but for the moment was enough. It was more than she'd thought she'd get.

She stopped worrying about her body, about a future, about what she should or shouldn't be, and narrowed her focus to the man kneeling between her legs as he lowered his mouth to her waiting pussy.

The first swipe of his agile tongue was slow and languid, and a guttural groan spilled from him. "You are delicious." His growled words blew warm air over her drenched sex, but as soon as he'd rasped them out, his seeking tongue was back. The laziness of that first touch gave way to hard licks, harsh and wild. He laved her clit, her folds, pressed his stiffened tongue as deep into her tight cunt as he could manage. He took her over entirely, like an animal poised between her thighs at the most sensitive part of her.

Tracy trembled with the overwhelming sensations, with the way he drove her body hard and how she wanted — no, *needed* — more.

Without thinking about it, she set a hand on the back of his head, a demand she'd never made before. She was passive in bed, someone who gave what her partner wanted but never more. His hair was soft against her palm, and she threaded her fingers through the short brown strands.

A mocking chuckle came from Dylan's lips even as he never stopped pleasuring her. Tracy used the grip to pull him impossibly closer, the edge of her release so close her thighs trembled. The way her skin tingled, the blurring of everything just on the sides of her perception told her how close she was to coming, and how badly she wanted to break apart beneath Dylan's tongue.

Except, as soon as she started to topple, when she wanted nothing more than to dive off that precipice, everything stopped.

Dylan moved back, his tongue swiping over his lips to clean them. He must have thought it funny, because without her saying a word, he let out a soft laugh. "You look good like this, all needy and denied."

A wanton whine was Tracy's response, her brain in chaos as her body struggled with the stolen orgasm and searing need. "Why did you stop?" The words were broken and panted out.

Dylan dragged his thumb against the side of her clit, the touch so light it only teased her, only kept that fire sizzling inside her but didn't let her come. "Because you've been pissing me off for days, Red. You really think I'm going to let you get off so easily? Plus, fuck, I just like to see you like this, all undone and at my mercy." A stream of cool air blew over her hard and tormented clit.

Tracy pulled at the back of his head, but he didn't budge. The orgasm drifted out of reach, but the moment it did, as soon as she pulled in a more controlled breath, Dylan dove back in.

This time, his finger toyed with the flooded entrance to her sex. He didn't push in, but the constant pressure drove up her desire up another level, another pleasure denied to her. His lips latched around her needy clit, sucking hard on the bud.

Tracy arched her back and rolled her hips, but Dylan never changed a thing. He didn't give her more or less, just stayed locked on her clit. The release he snatched away roared back to life, to the forefront of her mind and body. It rushed toward her, almost frighteningly powerful, enough to drag her under.

Just like the first time, as it started to crest over her, when goosebumps sprang up over her skin and the first tightening of her cunt hit her, Dylan pulled away, her grip sliding away from his head as a sob of need escaped her.

He offered a kiss to her inner thigh, then turned the one into a trail, going from knee to the juncture of her body. He spoke between them. "God damnit, Red, those sounds you make? I'd knot you right here if I thought I could get away with it. I can see your cunt pulsing, just begging for my cock. You want me to fill you?"

She nodded. *Yes. Something. Anything.* Any fear was gone, any questions. As long as he kept touching her, anything was good. He'd driven her mad with the pleasure and the denials, and the fire he'd grown to a blazing need inside her wouldn't be denied.

He pressed a kiss directly to her cunt but avoided her clit, the bastard. "With a welcome like that, how can I resist?"

She expected him to stand up, to strip out of his pants and shove deep inside her.

Instead, a deep growl left his lips and two thick fingers plunged into her sopping wet heat as his mouth returned to her pulsing clit. He didn't pull away this time, didn't deny her anything. He fucked her with those demanding fingers, stroking against every sensitive spot of her, even curling to torment the area behind her pelvic bone where a knot would stretch her, would lock inside her. Between his relentless tongue and his harsh fingers, she almost cried out as her body finally snapped.

Her orgasm had grown, each denial increasing it. Every muscle inside her tightened—her womb, her cunt, her thighs, even her hands clutching the back of his head. The release stole her breath and turned her thoughts to sludge. She could do nothing but endure the rushing pleasure so intense it bordered on pain. It slid through her until she fell backward in the chair, sinking into it without an ability to even think about moving.

Dylan withdrew his fingers, even that sensation too much on her tired body. When she whimpered, he offered an unrepentant smirk and an unnecessary twist of his fingers to pull a gasp from her.

He righted her clothing before lifting her to his chest. Against her better judgment, she allowed it. The heat of his skin, the sensation of his strong arms wrapped around her were nicer than she'd have thought.

He settled her into her bed, stripping off the sweater with a disgusted grunt and another comment about hating it. His annoyance made her want to buy more of them, made her want to watch him tear them off her.

Tracy caught his wrist before he could pull back, questions in her mind that she didn't dare ask. What did it mean? Where could this go? Was he going to stay?

Whatever openness or almost kindness Dylan had found during their moment of insanity must have drifted away, because back was that annoyance, that wall. He always did that, turning into someone else afterward. "Don't get things twisted, Red. We aren't whatever you're thinking."

"Why did that just happen, then?"

He gave a chilling look, the sort that made her flinch back. "Because you needed it? Because I wanted to? Sex doesn't have to mean shit. We aren't kids who believe in fairytales."

Tracy released his wrist. What was there to say back to that? Besides, it wasn't as if Dylan was the sort of man she'd want anything to do with, anyway.

Or the sort who would want anything to do with me.

He sighed, some of that armor he'd strapped back on slipping. "Red—"

"Goodnight." She tried to fill the seemingly nice word with as much 'get the hell out' as she could. Even with her cunt still sticky and her body thrumming from her orgasm, she tried to tell herself to get over it.

He didn't respond with another sigh, but instead a vicious growl. It didn't land. He'd had the chance to hurt her enough times—she wasn't afraid of a little growl he tried to use to get out of fights.

"Fine," he snapped when the growl didn't work, then all but stormed out like the kid he pretended she was being.

Fine. It's not like I have to deal with him. I have other choices.

And yet, as she closed her eyes, as she couldn't help but think about her life and future, she'd started being unable to picture that future without Dylan as well.

And she was pretty sure that fact would break her heart.

Chapter Thirteen

Mason had to admit, he liked Joshua. The other alpha had a similar sense of humor. In fact, he rather liked the entire other grouping.

With the stress of all the unanswered questions, with the risks to Tracy and Karen, with everyone on edge, it had seemed a good time to try to get their minds off it.

That had landed them at the home of Sam and Tracy's friend, Claire, and the three alphas she'd claimed.

The four lived in a cute house that seemed a good mixture of all of them. The happiness was obvious from the moment he'd stepped into the home, from the way the alphas watched her to the way she instinctually leaned against which ever one was closest at the time.

Envy sparked in Mason as he considered the future he wanted. He'd always thought a similar situation would be good, especially after spending so many of his days as a kid with Sam and his family. Still, this was one of the few he'd seen as an adult, that he'd been able to really observe.

Claire was tough but suspicious. She'd yet to warm to Dylan, but who could blame her? A few good smiles from Mason had won him a reluctant smile back. Karen loved the omega, and the longing on Claire's face made him wonder if they'd already started to try for children.

The funniest part was despite the presence of six alphas—each who could have sent anyone running with a good growl—they all bent over backward for the young girl. No matter the issue, they were there, ready to play along with whatever game she came up with.

And Karen ate the attention up. When Bryce offered a warning snarl in Dylan's direction over some tiny slight, as happened when alphas spent time together, Karen had grabbed Dylan's hand and told Bryce to be nice. And hadn't that been an amusing look of confusion on Dylan's face over the defense?

Seemed while he'd say fuck off to anyone else, the little girl could render him speechless.

"I don't know," Joshua admitted as he rolled the key over in his palm. "I've looked into anything I could find, had Kieran do the same, and I've got no clues where this might go. Most of those storage places can be paid off in cash under a fake name. Could be anywhere."

Karen came in holding two plates with brownies stacked on them. "Mom told me to bring these."

Mason took the plates, offering a thank you.

Karen didn't move, though, her gaze on the key, her eyebrows furrowed. "That's Dad's key."

Joshua lifted the key. "You know what this goes to?"

Karen nodded and took it from him. "To the place with all the boxes."

Mason set the plates on the side table. "You've been there? How do you know?"

Karen turned to face Mason, expression unsure. It meant Mason needed to ease off a bit. "Dad took me there when we went to the doctor. He said it was a secret."

Mason tried to plaster a smile on his lips, tried to look reassuring. "Do you know where it is? Can you take us there?"

She nodded.

Well, finally a break.

Claire and Karen sat on the back porch, chalk in hand, while Tracy and all the alphas remained inside. It seemed Claire wasn't quite done playing aunt.

Tracy tried, and probably failed miserably, to look comfortable. It was too much, too many, too overwhelming. The scents of them all made her awareness tingle. She felt like a cat stuck in a room with six dogs, and all she wanted to do was arch her back and hiss.

But that wasn't okay to do in polite company, so she tried her best to play nice.

They'd found the location of the storage unit Richard had taken Karen too, with her explaining the directions. It gave them a plan, options, hope. She hadn't had hope in a long while.

"Why don't you have Karen stay with us a few days?" Bryce asked, tension lacing his words.

Bryce always made her the most nervous, an intensity in his stare never failing to drive Tracy back a step or two. He rarely spoke, never smiled.

She trusted Claire, and she even trusted the three alphas her friend had chosen, but that didn't mean she was comfortable around them. "Why?"

"You have a lot going on," he said, but something rested beneath the words, a truth he was side-stepping. "She'll be fine here, and Claire will love having her again for a few nights."

"I don't want to just send her somewhere." Tracy didn't bother to hide her offense at the offer. Why were they trying to get her daughter away from her?

"Easy," Mason said, setting his large hand on hers. "You're growling, kitten."

"Kitten?" Joshua laughed at the endearment. "With the way she was flashing her teeth, I don't think I'd go with kitten."

"No one is trying to take your kid," Bryce again tried. "But you need to consider everything."

"Consider what? Just come out with whatever you're trying to say."

It was Kaidan who answered, his voice soft and his gaze down. "They may not smell it because they're with you all the time, but you're going into heat."

Heat. The word drained the color from her face. She couldn't be going into heat, right?

Then she thought about how she hadn't slept much, hadn't wanted to eat. She had chalked those things up to stress and changes. She hadn't wanted to nest, but then again, that usually happened hours prior to the start. Even then, she hadn't made a nest in years. The idea of making one for Richard, of that closeness had felt like a mockery of something sacred. "You're wrong," she whispered.

Kaidan shook his head, voice kind. "No, we're not. It's why we're suggesting Karen stay here, to give you privacy."

Tracy lifted her gaze to Sam's, unable to hide the fear in her eyes, not even having the ability to try to hide it.

Who cared if the others saw it when she felt like the world was crumbling around her?

A heat?

With these three alphas in the same house? She hadn't even been willing to sleep with any of them, and soon she'd have no choice. She'd be driven to do so, no matter her personal feelings, her reservations.

No matter theirs, either. Biology trumped everything.

Sam didn't respond with words, a blessing. Nothing he could say right then would reassure her, and the last thing she wanted was to have that conversation in front of others.

Not just others, but alphas she didn't know well or trust.

A hand on her leg made her jump, but when a side-glance revealed it to be Mason, she scolded herself for overreacting. An upcoming heat didn't change anything that they'd built thus far. The alphas didn't change just because she would be going into heat.

Even as she told herself that, she couldn't quite believe it. Instead, she struggled to see anything but alpha, but aggression and lust and her being defenseless.

Mason squeezed her leg, and the reassurance had her able to pull in a breath, unsteady as it was.

They said their goodbyes quickly, with Tracy meeting no one's gaze. Karen agreed to stay, no push needed. The girl had jumped at the chance, already halfway to the guest room without more than a quick hug goodbye.

It left Tracy in the back seat of the large crew cab truck, Sam beside her, Mason in the passenger seat and Dylan behind the wheel.

Sam pressed a hand to the back of Tracy's neck, pushing until she bent forward and her head fell between her knees. It was only then she realized just how lightheaded she felt.

"It's okay," Sam told her. "It'll be fine."

"How is this fine?" Her position muffled her voice, and the loud truck engine helped drown it out.

Even so, he answered, his strong hand kneading gently at her tense nape. "You've had heats before, honey. You know they aren't that scary."

Easy for him to say.

"What are you afraid of, kitten?" Mason twisted to look back at them. "Afraid one of us will force you?"

She shook her head. Even if she was terrified, it wasn't of them, not exactly. They hadn't hurt her, and they'd had plenty of chances to do so.

"So what is it?" Sam pressed.

Tracy sat up, her elbows resting on her knees. "I haven't done this in a long time," she admitted. "I'm not ready."

"Biology is biology. It doesn't wait till we're ready. But we can get sedatives if you want. Just because you're going to have a heat doesn't mean we have to service you. Any of us." Mason spoke with the same ease he always did, the sort that made her feel like whatever was wrong wasn't that big a deal. "None of us would force you, Tracy. It's your choice."

She wet her lips with her tongue as she thought about taking a sedative. Could she willingly drug herself just to avoid the heat? Could she be even more vulnerable? To agree to be at the full mercy of the alphas, to accept unconsciousness instead of suffering the natural effects. It would be easier, wouldn't it? No need to think about her future, about what she wanted. She could sleep it away.

"What do you want?" Sam asked. "I'll call the doctor right now to get sedatives for you. You won't have to do this if it isn't what you want."

Tracy worked her bottom lip between her teeth until it hurt, slowly sliding her gaze among the alphas. Sam sat there, form silhouetted by the passing streetlamps, his eyes soft as they always were, his hand a reassuring presence on her back.

Mason twisted from the front seat, his amber eyes intense. She thought about the way he'd used the vibrator on her, the way he'd taken only what she'd been willing to give. His wide shoulders, a source of fear normally, sent desire scorching through her veins.

And Dylan, who sat at the wheel of the car, his gaze on the street? His strong jaw and shrewd gaze said he was listening, even if he pretended not to be. Even he, with all his sharp edges and rough demeanor, hadn't pushed her for anything she wasn't ready for.

What would that be like with them? With any of them? With all of them?

Tracy knew the answer without doubt. She might be terrified, but she may never have this chance again. She wouldn't lose it. "I don't want the sedative. I want you."

Chapter Fourteen

Mason tried to ignore his idiot friend as he closed the door to Tracy's room, with Dylan hiding out in his own.

He should have been there. Worse, it wasn't that Dylan didn't want her. It wasn't that she didn't want him. It wasn't even that he didn't *know* he should be right there with Sam and Mason. No, instead it was Dylan's own stupid stubbornness that kept him on the wrong side of that door.

His loss.

Nerves shone bright in Tracy's eyes, but they didn't dull her beauty. She stood near the window, having stripped off the large, baggy clothing she liked to wear and replaced it with a long shirt that reached nearly to her knees. Sam's? Mason's cock perked up at the possession of her dressed in their clothing.

She is ours. The thought was so deep he couldn't even question it. No matter what happened, she was his. Maybe it had taken a while to find her, but fuck it, she'd always been theirs.

"We don't have to do this," Sam said, always too sweet for his own good, even if he was right.

They didn't have to do anything. Even though she'd rejected the drugs, she wasn't in heat just yet. More of the scent covered her, telling him it would happen in the next day or two, but not yet.

However, Mason had suggested a heat might not make for the best first time, especially with her as uneasy as she was. Heats were hard and fast, just bodies and need and hormones. Make no mistake, they were fucking wonderful. They released a primal side of people normally locked away by civility. They broke people down to their base instincts, to their real truth.

He'd rather take her slower that first time, to create something worth remembering, though. He wanted to spread her out, to take his time and tease her until they were both desperate. They all needed to ease her into it, to show her she didn't need to be afraid. She'd agreed, though hadn't seemed entirely convinced.

And Dylan? He'd scoffed at the entire idea and stormed off to his own room.

Tracy rubbed her left arm with the other hand, over the goosebumps that covered her flesh. "No. You're right, this is better."

"Doesn't have to be both of us." Mason forced himself to say it even though he knew that was what he wanted, what she wanted. Hell it was what Sam wanted. Losing either of them would make it incomplete — well, more incomplete since the idiot one of their trio was pouting in his room. Still, she deserved options. After everything she'd dealt with, she should be able to make the choice. "If it's too much, if we're too much, we don't have to do this together."

"I wouldn't be able to choose," she admitted in a whisper. After a moment, she pressed on, as though that didn't explain it well enough. "I don't want to choose."

Sam went forward, cane in his hand, his other arm still in the cast. That meant there wouldn't be wild sex anyway, given his condition. Though, knowing the other alpha, he'd more than make do. He dropped the cane when he reached her, wrapped a hand behind her neck and pulled her in to a kiss that was far too sweet for the things Mason was thinking.

Even so, Tracy melted into it. She leaned against him, returning the kiss, teasing her lips over his.

Mason reached down and cupped his groin, giving his already aching dick a good squeeze before removing his shirt. He took a place behind Tracy, then stroked his hands up her thin back, over the baggy shirt.

She shivered, a tiny tremor that ran out through her shoulders in waves.

"You smell good enough to eat, kitten," Mason purred into her ear and lowered his lips to her shoulder. He kissed along the soft, warm skin bared by the too-large neck of the shirt, using his teeth to scrape softly. Not hard enough to mark her or even sting, but hard enough she couldn't forget he was there.

And wasn't that a thing of beauty when she moaned into Sam's kiss? When her scent strengthened like some beacon for them?

He slid a hand around her, down her front, to the hem of the shirt. Her feet inched out — a welcome if he'd ever seen one — but he wanted more. She *needed* more. "Tell me what you want."

"This."

He let out a chiding click of his tongue. "I want to know exactly what you want."

Sam broke the kiss entirely, his good hand grasping her breast through her shirt. He teased his thumb against the pebbled nipple that already showed through the thin fabric.

Tracy's head came back to rest against Mason's chest, her eyes closed and her cheeks flushed. "Please, Mason."

Her needy plea almost got to him. He almost broke and gave her everything she wanted, wanting to spoil her until she understood just how precious she was.

But he wanted more. He didn't just want to service her during her heat. He didn't just want to help her out of this problem, then be gone. That meant she had to accept her own wants, that she needed to be present instead of a passive body content with allowing others to take.

She needed to take.

He nipped her shoulder harder. "You need to tell me what you want, Tracy. This all happens the way you want it to, and only because you want it."

"It's easier if you just do what you're going to do."

Sam closed his fingers around her nipple, not quite a pinch but a steady caress that had her back arching. "Easy isn't what we're going for here, honey. It's okay to want us, to want this, and the only way you're going to realize that is if you ask for exactly what you want."

A disgruntled sound left her throat, and again, Mason thought about giving in. A look exchanged with Sam got his strength back.

No. No matter how hard it was, how much he hated to see her struggle, she had to do this. She had to want them, want this, and the only way she could accept that was if she took control of it.

Tracy took far too long to speak, indecision rushing across her lust-colored cheeks, until in a soft voice, she spoke. "I need you to touch me."

"I am touching you, kitten. You'll need to be a little more specific."

She took his hand, the one still toying with the hem of her shirt, and slipped it beneath the fabric until she pressed his fingers to her cunt.

To her bare, soaking cunt. *Guess her not wearing any panties helps say she wanted this, doesn't it?*

He let out a sound more desperate than any he'd made before when he felt the heat and wetness of her aroused pussy directly, when the proof of her desire coated his fingers and he stroked her in a one long rub along her entire slit.

Maybe it wasn't in words, but he'd take that. His control wasn't about to stop, not when the first touch of his finger to her clit caused her to cry out, her hands flying to clutch Sam's shoulders.

The other alpha's eyes were predatory, skirting from her face, down her body to where he still toyed with her nipple, then to where Mason played with her tight pussy.

Right. Better places for this.

Mason let go of her and backed off. "Let's get more comfortable, hmm?" With a quick flick of his fingers, he undid the button of his pants and took them off. "Shirt off, kitten. I want to see what we're working with."

It took another long moment, making it clear the entire night was going to take a while, but Tracy grasped the bottom of her shirt and slipped it over her head.

Mason got one look at her perfect body, the lithe frame, the freckles, the flawless skin, and the jerk of his cock said he was in trouble.

This omega might just kill me.

Sam wasn't as smooth as the others in removing his clothing, but he figured getting it all off without help was the best he could hope for. Besides, it was hard to feel too put out when he caught sight of Tracy naked for the first time, every inch of her revealed with nothing hidden or obscured.

She was small, even smaller than he'd realized, with a petite frame that reminded him of a pixie. Her red hair hung loose around her shoulders, highlighting the freckles on her chest and her collarbone. Her waist was narrow, and she didn't have the curves of some women, yet each new detail he found only made him want her more. Her small, pert breasts, her erect nipples, the brownish-red hair between her legs.

Mason naked wasn't something that bothered or enticed Sam, and with how normal this felt, he wondered why they'd never done it before. Why had they never considered taking an omega at the same time? All their dating, all the times they'd had women, why hadn't it even occurred to him that this was something he'd want?

A nod from Mason toward the bed had Sam pulling in a relieved sigh. He took the hint, settling himself on Tracy's bed, enjoying the way her scent clung to the blankets, to the pillows. He set his back against the headboard, the position allowing him to take some of the strain off his still healing body.

Not that his injuries would have stopped him. He was pretty sure he could have lost limbs and he'd still have crawled himself into that bed to have Tracy. Biology was a funny thing, the lengths an alpha would go for an omega he wanted. Nothing as trivial as broken bones would keep him from his goal.

Mason pulled Tracy against him, making quite the sight as he kissed her. Her size was only further highlighted by the difference, by the way Mason dwarfed her, and Mason's hard cock, pressed against her stomach, made Sam groan with the realization they'd finally have her.

The woman who had haunted him for so long was finally naked, finally there and nothing would stop him from having her.

Mason broke the kiss quickly, then offered a quick swat to her ass as he pushed her toward the bed.

Tracy cast a soft glare, the sort she was far too sweet to pull off, before crawling onto the bed. She moved up until she knelt between Sam's spread thighs, her gaze locked on his cock, desire warring with unease.

Sam wrapped his own fingers around his thick shaft, giving himself a long, slow stroke. She'd already touched him, already knew exactly how his cock felt in her small, soft hand.

"You know," Mason said as the bed dipped beneath his weight. "Tracy here is quite the artist."

Her cheeks heated further, and she went to turn, to look back at Mason, but the alpha's large hand settled on the back of her neck to keep her facing forward.

"Ask her to show you the picture she drew of you." Humor colored Mason's voice. "Let's just say she did a pretty detailed job on some pretty private specifics of your anatomy."

The meaning only took a moment to sink in, and Sam gave his cock a harder squeeze at the thought of Tracy drawing something so risqué. Did that mean she thought about him like that? She must, if she was there with him. Had she touched herself to the image? Used it like some version of a dirty magazine?

Mason leaned closer and dragged his tongue up the dip at the center of her spine. "Go on, kitten, why don't you touch him?"

"What about you?"

"Oh, I can keep myself entertained." As Mason spoke, he dropped his calloused hands to her breasts, cupping them both, his palms rubbing against her nipples.

Tracy's gasp went straight to Sam's dick, but only a heartbeat later, she leaned forward. She set one hand on his thigh and wrapped the other around his shaft. She had less hesitation than before, less nerves.

Good. It meant she'd started to trust him, or maybe the lust was stronger than her unease. Whatever it was, he moved his hand from his dick, giving her the space to do what she wanted, and replaced Mason's hand on her tempting breast with his own.

Mason shrugged and moved the hand between her thighs, seeming content to play with her anywhere he could. His growl was low when he sank a deep finger into her waiting cunt, and the sound of how wet she was had Sam struggling to keep things slow.

Not that Tracy wanted slow. Her hips rolled in a seductive plea, and she stroked Sam quicker. How she managed to get him on the edge only minutes into this, he had no idea. He would have sworn he had better control, but already he gritted his teeth to keep from coming in her eager palm.

She whined, hips thrusting against Mason's hand. "I need more," she finally admitted.

"So take it," Sam answered.

The hesitation lasted seconds before she moved forward. Mason helped position her, turning her so she faced out instead of Sam. Her knees sank into the mattress on either side of his thighs, and she rose.

His hard cock ached at the need to be buried inside her. He wanted to plunge so deep, to feed her every inch of his hard dick until nothing sat between them. He needed to knot her, to fill her with his seed, to watch her come undone because of him.

However, she didn't grasp him, didn't lower herself. She froze.

For him to take care of things? Again, she'd tried to resign herself to a watcher, to a passive bystander in the action.

Mason chuckled, resting on his knees in front of her. "You can handle it, kitten."

Sam couldn't see her face, but from Mason's wide grin, he could imagine the glare she gave him. Her need to be filled by Sam's thick shaft must have been greater than her embarrassment, because she leaned forward and reached between her thighs to grasp his cock. She nestled the blunt head against her snug cunt, against the searing wetness he needed to bury himself in.

Still, he waited. It took torturous moments before she let out a whimper and sank down onto his length. Her cunt was so tight and hot, gripping his shaft as she took each solid inch of him. Her pulsing body was divine, snug around him and stretching beautifully, as though made just for him.

They both let out shuddering breaths, as if connected, when he bottomed out, when he'd fed her every inch of his cock, when he had her impaled on his length without any space between them.

Mason released a growl of his own, his large hands sliding over Tracy's front, teasing her breasts and tugging her hard nipples before falling to her thighs to spread them more. "Damn, that is a sight." He dragged his fingers around her pussy, around where the lips pulled snug against how his girth stretched her small body. "How do you feel, kitten?"

Tracy clutched Mason's shoulders and lifted her body a hair before grinding back down. "Good."

"Full? Like he's fucked you open? Because, he has." Mason didn't stop stroking her, touching from her stretched entrance to her clit, even as she began to ride Sam.

Tracy's cry was full of pleasure, her body never rising far, as though she hated losing even an inch of Sam. "Yes," she panted. "He feels so good." Her words weren't filthy, but Tracy wasn't the sort for filthy talk. If she'd tried to talk dirty, it wouldn't have sounded like the omega he'd fallen for. Instead, her honest, shy words made his dick jerk and harden.

Sam wasn't much of a talker, so contented himself with his hand on her breast and the tightness of her pussy. She rode him hard, but he didn't care. Even if he was sore later, even if his still healing injuries protested, he wanted more. He wanted her to take everything from him, to have all of him, for him to know he'd taken care of her.

Mason moved back to lie flat between her spread thighs. A hard jerk of her back had Sam looking past her.

Mason flicked his long, pink tongue against her swollen clit, the move easier since she didn't move far on Sam's cock. The other alpha tilted his head and tormented her sensitive bud, his hands on her hips. Mason didn't lick her carefully, gently, controlled. Instead, he lavished attention to her clit, to everywhere he could reach. He drenched the entire area — as if it wasn't already — like some claim to her. The reaction of her body — the writhing and the tightening of her perfect cunt — drove Sam mad.

He wouldn't last, and who could blame him?

Mason grasped her waist tightly and latched his demanding lips around her clit. The reaction was immediate, Tracy's head sailing back, her spine arching, her cunt tightening into an almost painful grip around Sam's dick.

He let himself go, the ache of his balls undeniable. His knot swelled, and the small thrusting of her hips shoved him all the way in, let him lock deep inside her.

Mason never let up, and between his grip and Sam's knot, Tracy had nowhere to go. Her hands went to Mason's hair, but she couldn't dislodge him as he forced whimper after whimper from her overwhelmed body, as each draw of his lips made her pulse around Sam's thick, swollen knot again, made her twitch and tremble and fall apart.

Filling a female had never felt so good, so right. Sam's body thrummed as he emptied spurt after spurt of cum into this omega — *my omega.*

Our omega.

Dylan stroked his cock with hard, punishing motions, his other hand bracing himself against the hallway wall as Tracy's cries of pleasure spilled from her room.

He should have been in there, should have drawn some of those sounds out himself. Instead, he stood in the hallway like a pervert, unable to leave, unable to join, stuck on the periphery. He'd tried to go to his room, but something had drawn him back, something he couldn't deny.

Each sound she'd made through the door had him picturing how she'd looked outside the other night, when he'd stared up her tight little body from between her spread thighs. Would her cheeks be flushed? Would sweat drip down her body?

Dylan sped his hand in time with the slapping of bodies, with the filthy sounds of the three inside that room. The scents were even better, Tracy's aroused body throwing off such deliciousness that Dylan had to struggle not to open the door and get a taste himself.

Instead, he contented himself with his hand, with the fantasy, while remaining safely at a distance. He couldn't have more. It never went well. The more he gave, the more it would hurt when it all went to shit, and it *would* go to shit. That was the basic truth of life. It always went to shit.

Even with the depressing thoughts, his cock leaked pre-cum, not caring about facts, not caring about anything but the omega behind that door.

When Tracy cried out again, louder and drawn out and familiar, Dylan knew she'd come, probably stretched out on someone's knot, and his own release washed over him.

It was a joke, a pathetic stand-in for what he wanted, what his body needed, but it was all he could give it.

He panted in the hallway, cock not even softening after his release, the scent of Tracy's body too powerful to allow it. Nope, it stood there still hard, mocking him, ready to service the omega he couldn't have.

Even so, he grumbled, pulling off his shirt to clean the mess. He chastised himself for the stupidity, for the sentimental longing, and took himself to his room before he did anything worse, like opening that door.

The soft sounds that heralded a second round followed him, but he tried to block them out.

What was behind that door would ruin everything, and he couldn't go through that again.

Tracy shifted, locked tight on Sam's thick knot. It made her feel full and taken over in a way nothing else did. It didn't hurt, but each twitch of his cock, each time that knot pulsed, she whimpered again as it set off another aftershock in her chaotic body.

Sam's good hand ran over her side, a soothing touch meant to calm her, no doubt.

Mason was less soothing, having removed his lips from her clit, but not far. He still lavished attention on her inner thighs, her mound, even her cunt. He licked up every drop of wetness he could find.

The fact he must have brushed Sam's cock with his tongue, that there was no way he didn't touch the other alpha should have made her uncomfortable, right?

She'd grown up with sex being a private thing, and she could only shudder at how Richard would have reacted to such activities. Still, Mason didn't seem to mind, and Sam didn't care and so why should she?

Each pass of Mason's tongue kept that heat sizzling in her womb, kept her pussy drenched and wanting and not nearly finished. He forced her to ride that edge of desire, not letting the fire go out beneath his attention.

"It feels good to have you knotted, honey," Sam whispered into her ear as she rested against his broad chest. His arm curved around her front, solid and warm and enough to make her feel safe no matter what.

And it felt good to her, too. No, not good. That wasn't enough. It felt right, like it was how it should be. It felt like she realized she'd had it all wrong before. With Richard, she'd feared this. With Sam and Mason, she couldn't get enough.

Mason took that moment to flick directly against her clit, and she jerked at the rough touch. It pulled at Sam's still swollen knot, and both she and Sam groaned in unison.

"Damn it, Mason," Sam growled down at the other alpha. "Can't you wait a minute?"

Mason offered a smirk before repeating the action as though Sam's growl didn't mean a thing to him. "Like you don't love that feeling."

"It's a bit—" Sam snarled dangerously when another lick from Mason had Tracy's body cranking down around Sam again. "Sensitive," he finished between gritted teeth.

Mason sat up, grinning before dragging his tongue along his lips slowly, mocking them. It reminded Tracy of Dylan, of how he'd done the same thing to her.

An ache in her chest threatened to steal the moment, but she pushed that away. Dylan hadn't wanted her, and she wouldn't let his rejection take this from her. He didn't deserve that.

Mason leaned in and traced her bottom lip with his tongue. She twined her tongue with his, licking her own juices from him, setting her hands on his wide, solid chest to steady herself.

His firm muscles flexed beneath her touch, and she allowed herself to enjoy the feeling of his strength. It wasn't dangerous, not scary. Right then it was just another part of him she liked. He took her lips, turning her tasting into a full-blown kiss.

He so distracted her with that kiss, with the stroking of his tongue to hers and the gentle caress of his lips, that before she realized it, he pulled, and Sam's knot slid free.

The loss was immediate and substantial. She missed the way his body felt inside her, the way he took up all the space she had. She missed how it shrank the world to something safe and warm and manageable. How could she miss him already? How could she miss that almost painful stretch so fast?

Mason's grip was unshakable, however, and he tugged her from Sam's lap.

A few quick motions and she was turned around, her body on all fours, facing Sam. Mason wasted no time sliding his long fingers through her folds, drenched with her own desire and Sam's thick, hot cum. He pressed the blunt head of his cock against her, then waited.

"Ask me," he demanded.

Tracy pushed backward, but Mason shifted his hands to her hips to keep her still in his iron grip. He was too strong. She'd get nothing until he allowed it.

"Ask me for what you need, kitten."

Pride abandoned Tracy. What did pride matter? Her nerves and reasons to keep silent drifted away as the pressure of Mason's dick teased her tightly strung body.

"Please, Mason."

"Please what?" He rocked his hips forward, the pressure so strong he nearly entered her. Leave it to him to walk that line without tripping over.

"Please, take me," she whined. She wished she could have done better with the dirty talk, but she'd never been that girl. Even that burned on her tongue, made her feel like some vixen she'd never been.

Mason's purr was soft and pleased, mild as her pleading might have been. "What a good kitten." He plunged into her, taking her in one hard thrust that filled her waiting pussy to the brim.

The stretch was so fast Tracy gasped and leaned forward against the intrusion. Mason's cock was so thick, that even soaked as she was, even though she'd already been fucked by Sam, her body struggled to adjust. He tested her limits, forcing her body to adapt to the rigid fullness of his dick.

Sam set his hand on her cheek, thumb tracing her bottom lip. "You can take him, honey." He leaned in, distracting her with a kiss that was too sweet given that Mason fucked her with such ferocity.

Mason didn't let her set the speed as Sam had, didn't go slow or easy. He took her with long, quick thrusts that had her gasping and struggling to focus.

Sam's kiss worked to further unsettle her, to give her nothing to hold on to. Mason's cock was thick and solid and it throbbed inside her. He plunged every last inch into her before pulling back until only the tip remained. Again and again he did so, their bodies meeting in frantic, noisy motions built on what they'd both wanted since they'd met in that hallway in the hospital.

Until he paused deep inside her, a massive presence in her small body, impossible to ignore.

Tracy released a growl, frustration battling pleasure. It sounded so much like the animalistic ones the alphas used, she struggled to believe she'd even made it.

Mason ground against her, but it only teased her further. "Ask me again, kitten."

She gave what he wanted before he'd finished the request, too needy to care about waiting. "Please, Mason, more."

He pulled back then filled her again.

The words fell from her lips like a prayer. "More. Please. Yes, Mason, more. Again." She begged him to keep going, but those words grew from weak pleas to growled demands, into her ordering him to give her what she wanted.

And Mason did that and more. Each demand she gave, he followed. He slid into her wet pussy with powerful thrusts that knocked her forward, that forced her to lean against Sam, to rely on him to keep her from falling on her face.

Mason's groan turned into a full growl, so deep in his chest it sparked a desire have all she could get from him. She wanted to push him past thinking, until he was ruled by need alone, just like her. He would take her with a ferocity that matched his wild looks, to be the animal he so often resembled. His fingers on her hips cranked down as his hips pistoned into her. He pushed her, taking her hard enough that if she wasn't so lost to the passion, to the sensation, she might have found it painful.

As it was, it was intense, and overwhelming, and exactly what she needed. It swept away everything else, her drive to feel his knot locking into place stronger than anything else.

Mason's growl turned into a hard snarl as he delved as deep as possible, as he buried every hard inch of himself into her, his knot swelling to stretch her.

His hot cum seared inside her as he came, as he ground into her like he could brand her deeper, the knot tugging when it grew enough to lock there.

That delicious fullness, the heat of his cum filling her, the growl of the alpha behind her and the lips from the alpha in front of her that still offered gentle affection all set her off. She squeezed down helplessly around Mason's cock and his swollen knot.

The world disappeared as she came, shrinking until only the three of them existed inside it. Sam's lips, Mason's cock, their warmth and strength and stability.

Suddenly, the thought of going into heat, of being at the mercy of these alphas didn't terrify her so much.

She could do worse.

Chapter Fifteen

"You're an idiot." Mason tossed the insult Dylan's way as they stood by the car, waiting for Sam and Tracy to deal with the storage unit office manager.

Dylan had thought the same thing himself since he'd first woken. He'd thought it when he'd seen the three walk out of Tracy's room, and when he'd gotten a whiff of her scent and the way it held that of both the alphas', and pretty much every second since he'd made the dumb decision to not join in.

I am a fucking idiot.

It didn't mean he was wrong, though.

"If you and Sam want to line up for part two of the omega disaster, go for it. I personally got my share the first time on that ride."

Mason leaned against the car, tossing a pebble into the air and catching it. "Just because it went to hell before doesn't mean it will this time."

"Don't they say that the reason we learn history is so we don't repeat it? Well, buddy, I learned."

"Are you really going to say you don't want her? Because don't think I missed that little show you two put on on the deck the other night."

Dylan offered a shrug, as casual as he could make it, trying to give nothing away. "She was there. She wanted it. No reason to turn down a pretty omega who offers. Didn't mean a damned thing."

Mason's huff was all sarcasm. "Right. All those looks you've been giving her, they mean nothing, too. Just normal, everyday eye-fucking."

Dylan gave a soft growl like a warning, not that Mason had ever taken those to mean shit. "How do you really see this going? You and Sam are gonna live all happily ever after like his parents did? That shit doesn't happen."

"It can."

"Not for people like me. Why are you bitching at me, anyway? You three are all shacked-up, all fucking picture-perfect family. I've got nothing to do with that." The words sat bitter on his tongue.

Even if he thought for a moment sharing an omega actually could work, it never would for him. Dylan had struggled for every damned thing he had, and even though Sam and Mason had taken him in as family, even though Sam's parents had given him a home after his own had been torn apart, it didn't change that he wasn't like them. Good things didn't happen for him, and if he tried, if he stepped up and tried to be part of that, the only thing that would happen was she'd see how different he was. She'd realize he was the one let in out of pity, and that would be the end of it, probably for them all.

Maybe if it had just been Tracy, he might have looked past the whole omega thing. Maybe he could have put aside his past and taken the leap, but with Sam and Mason?

Dylan had never lived up to them, and he didn't need Tracy, or anyone else, seeing that.

Mason's gaze was steady on him, that rock flying up then slapping down into Mason's large palm. The other alpha could be intimidating as hell, between his large frame, his beard and his overall 'I don't give a fuck' attitude.

Before he could respond, the bell above the door chimed, and Tracy and Sam came walking out.

The look on Tracy's face said they'd had some luck, and why did that slight grin have such an immediate reaction in him? *I want her to smile at me like that.*

"Go well?" Mason asked, finally pulling his gaze from Dylan to Sam.

"Unit 456, near the back. Tracy played the part of the overwhelmed, bereaved mate perfectly."

Dylan spotted the slight wince from the girl, as though she felt bad for not being that.

Then again, Richard didn't deserve her fucking tears. He'd gotten too many of them when he'd been alive. Fucker didn't deserve shit, now.

Mason snatched the key from Sam's hand. "Come on, Sam, let's check out the area first. Tracy, you stay here with Dylan until we're sure it's safe." At the confused stares of Sam and Tracy, Mason only took a step in that direction. "Could be someone waiting, who knows? Just give us a minute."

Dylan glared, the asshole not nearly as sneaky as he thought, but Sam either caught on or didn't care. The two alphas walked off.

Tracy fidgeted, but each movement caused her scent to spill out. The other alphas' smell clinging to her should have disgusted him. It should have had all his possessive instincts envious and prowling. Instead, it only made his shaft fill, made him want to add his own mark to her. He didn't want to cover their scents — he wanted to add to them.

Tracy inhaled, then turned a look full of shock on him. Right, sometimes he forgot how good an omega's sense of smell was.

"Like you don't already know you turn me on," he muttered, moving his gaze to the far mountain range. Safer than staring at her when he might do something stupid like kiss her, or fuck her, or tell her the truth about how badly he wanted her.

"So why do you keep pulling away?"

"You mean why wasn't I fucking you along with the other two last night?"

Ah, the wince he caught out of the corner of his eyes made him lift his hand and rub the back of his neck. Couldn't rub away the guilt, though.

When she didn't answer, he sighed. "Sorry. Just on edge today."

"Being with two alphas wasn't my plan," she said softly. "I didn't wake up and go 'oh, I think I'll seduce a couple of alphas.' I didn't want even one after Richard."

"And what changed?"

"I met Sam. I tried to ignore it, to tell myself I couldn't get involved again, but he's hard to forget. Then I thought, okay, maybe there's something there. Then I met Mason, and I couldn't believe I could feel something for him, too." She shifted and slid her hands into her pockets as though she wasn't sure what to do with them. "Then I met you."

He let out a harsh laugh. "Yeah, then you met me, and we really clicked, huh?"

"Maybe not in the same way. You…" She paused, dragging her tongue along her full pink bottom lip. "You don't see me as broken. You don't see me as weak. You don't let me wallow. I didn't plan any of this, Dylan, but I don't know what to do now that we're here."

He wanted to pull her into a kiss. He wanted to whisper to her that he'd make things up to her the moment they were back at the house. Hell, he wanted to make them up to her right then, to open the door to the car, bend her over the back seat and fuck her right there.

Except, all that doubt ricocheted around his skull, blasting the sides when he tried to think about a future. If she liked them all, it was probably just hormones, and hormones lessened with time.

So instead of what he wanted to do or say, Dylan stuck with what he did best and scoffed. "That's nice and all, Red, but pretty words don't change a thing. You enjoy whatever the fuck it is you got with Sam and Mason, but us? You and me? Or me as a part of that mess?" He shook his head, his gaze down. "There isn't a chance I'm stepping foot in that disaster waiting to happen."

He risked a side-eye when she didn't speak and found her staring at him.

It wasn't hurt in those eyes, though. Instead, she studied him, just like Mason had. Having someone stare at him so intently didn't sit well, especially when, no matter how much he scolded himself for it, he cared what the person thought.

"I'm not Nora, and I'm not your mother, either."

Ouch. Dylan struggled not to show how deep those words cut, how she'd hit the exact right mark.

"Never said you were." He tried for flippant, but fuck if he managed it.

"You've had some bad experiences with omegas. If anyone gets that, I do. Someone once told me that just because things have always been one way, it didn't mean they always had to be. You just have to be brave enough to try."

Dylan didn't let the words touch him. He couldn't. It was too risky to let him believe that bullshit, even for a second. If he believed it, if he really let himself think he could have more, he'd just end up hurt again. He'd end up at the ass end of another joke from the universe, fucked over by yet another omega in the endless line willing to screw him.

He opened his mouth to snap out a response, but for the smallest second, the thought found a way through his armor. A flash of a future came to him, threatening him. Tracy. Karen. Mason. Sam. Him. All of them together and…happy.

He shoved that shit into the smallest, darkest crevice of his brain he had before it could get a foothold, before it could do any more damage. *Nope. Fuck that. Not going to happen.*

Sam and Mason turned the corner, Mason's lips pulled down in an unhappy line when he spotted the clear distance between Tracy and Dylan.

Fuck you, Mason.

Tracy walked off without a word, and Dylan stood alone.

It was what he wanted, right?

Sam couldn't help load the boxes, so he stood with Tracy near the open tailgate. Annoyance nipped at him over his injuries. He hated being unable to do things, unable to help even load boxes. Hell, even the sex the night before, as amazing as it had been, had required specific positions for him to participate.

It wouldn't last forever but that didn't make it any less frustrating as he watched Mason and Dylan take all the work on their shoulders.

"That's a lot of files," Tracy said.

There were six large boxes, and another two full of different electronics and drives. It would take time to sort through all the items, and out in the open wasn't the place. They'd drag it all back to the house where they could properly survey it.

He couldn't turn it over to anyone until he had an idea of what there was. Clearly some police were being paid, which meant those files might let him know who was safe to give them to and who wasn't. Plus, he didn't need the embarrassment of dropping it all off only to find out nothing useful was inside.

Tracy leaned against him, her arm to his, the touch soft and yet moving. She rarely reached for him, rarely came out of her shell to touch any of them on her own.

The touch shifted as she lifted a hand to trail her fingers over his arm, against the bare skin below the sleeve of his T-shirt.

An inhalation told him what was up. Her heat was even closer.

She twisted, pressing her nose to his neck.

"Okay, honey." He groaned at the closeness, at the way the smell of her heat drifted from between her thighs and intoxicated him, making harsh demands of his body. "We're almost done here."

He'd hoped they'd have until the next day before the heat struck, but it seemed time wasn't on their side. Biology wasn't something he could just ask nicely to wait until a more convenient moment.

Mason turned his head toward them, gaze taking in the position of Tracy who nuzzled Sam's throat.

"Let's get home," Sam said, voice rough as Tracy's hands tried to slip beneath his shirt.

Mason nodded, hefting the last box into the truck before slapping the tailgate closed. "Sounds like a plan. Dylan, you drive."

If Dylan complained, Sam didn't hear it. He pulled away from Tracy awkwardly as she tried to regain contact and got himself into the truck. Tracy sat in the large back seat, with him on one side and Mason on the other. It left Dylan driving and up front alone.

Sam didn't bother with feeling bad or worrying about the other alpha, not when Tracy shifted again as Mason tried to get on her seatbelt. She breathed Sam in as though she needed him more than oxygen, and her hands curled in, nails digging into his side. It aggravated the rib, but his own answering hormones, the ones that rose in him in response to her heat, quickly drove all the pain away.

"Seatbelts are a must," Mason muttered as he strapped her in. "No fucking in the car."

That seemed to wake her up, shaking loose the desire in her amber eyes.

That was how heats were, though. As they started, a moment of insanity, of desire so strong it couldn't be resisted before the omega regained her senses. Eventually, though, she'd fall headlong into it. Before long, nothing would break its spell except a knot and the hot, thick cum from an alpha.

She'd become mindless with need to sate the primitive part inside her that demanded she reproduce. She'd bury those nails inside her mate to keep him close and use his body to ease the demanding ache inside her.

And Sam was so in for that. He wanted her to use him to slake the want inside her. He wanted to fill her again and again, to let his cum give her what she needed.

Color warmed her cheeks as she pulled back. "Oh, god," she whispered. "I'm sorry."

Sam set his hand on her thigh and squeezed to stop her. "It's fine, honey. We'll be back home soon."

She took her bottom lip between her teeth in that damn, distracting biting thing she liked to do. He wanted to replace her teeth with his own, to nip at the fullness there, to have her so desperate that she had no room for fear.

He cast a look past her at Mason, whose predatory stare said he wanted the same.

And the scent filling the truck cab? That delicious mixture of feminine heat and desire and something uniquely Tracy?

Well, they couldn't get back to the house fast enough for him.

* * * *

Tracy buried her nose in the soft pile of blankets Sam and Mason had left in her room.

They smelled of her alphas, and they soothed her heat. She'd set them on the floor, pushing the pillows and the bedding around until it was perfect. It took a long time, tiny adjustments as she made enough room for everyone.

The instinct inside her made building the nest mindless. Each place she shifted, each area she moved was created by the understanding inside her she couldn't identify, one deeper than conscious thought.

It felt good. Natural. It filled her in a way her past heats hadn't, not in a long time.

She worked to perfect it all, to make a nest that would see her through the heat, that she'd invite an alpha into.

Well, two alphas, she supposed.

Even that couldn't make her panic, and her body only hummed at the thought of the two, at the memories of the night before when they'd spent so long pleasuring her, when they'd ensured each touch and stroke would drive her need higher only to satisfy her at the end.

Once she'd finished her work, when she'd gotten the blankets exactly where they needed to be, she snuggled into the warmth. She pressed her nose into them, trying to drown in the scents of the alphas, the only thing that helped at all. She even picked up Dylan, faint as it was. Had they included something of his?

Sweat had started to bead on her brow, and her pussy clenched with each growing wave of need. Still, she'd done this before—she knew that was just the beginning. These were the long hours she should rest, because once it really started, there wouldn't be any rest.

Sleep came easily, though her dreams were as filthy as could be. She pictured things she'd never ask for, things she'd never imagined before. She saw Mason using his strong arms to hold her up against a wall, fucking her with a strength that was staggering. The dream was so real, so powerful she could feel the way his hips would snap forward as he forced his hard dick inside her. The dream shifted, and with Sam, it was different. Then again, Sam was a different alpha, and even in a dream, he showed it. He'd have her above him, urging her to ride him, his lips paying homage to her breasts, to her tight nipples. And Dylan? He appeared, too, even though she knew he didn't want to be there. He'd push her thighs apart, no matter how sensitive or tired, and he'd lick her as though possessed until he'd made her come again and again. No matter how she begged for a break, he only drove her harder.

"Kitten." A rough voice she'd heard in her dream drew her from sleep, though the moment it happened, she only snarled at the ache through her body.

How long was I asleep? She tried to roll over, to ignore the person bothering her despite the fact she knew the voice, and some still asleep part of her knew he could help.

Again, the voice came from closer. "Kitten, wake up."

Finally, Tracy opened her eyes to find Mason crouched beside her.

He smelled…*delicious*. The moment she inhaled, it hit her hard, her stomach clenching and pain crawling out from that spot, spreading through her like an infection. She pressed a hand to her lower stomach as though to stem that hurt and curled around it.

"It's time," he told her, voice soft.

That was when it all came back, when even through her lust-filled mind she put all the pieces together. She was in heat, and currently curled up in the nest she'd made from items that smelled of her alphas.

And beside her, both alphas stood, waiting. They'd stripped down to nothing, just like she had, their bodies on display. Again, she was as fascinated by them as ever. The strong lines of Mason's large frame, his longer hair that went to his shoulders like the mane of a lion.

His eyes, bright with primal want. Sam's darker skin, his brown eyes that, while always sweet, had a sparking fire inside them as he devoured her with his gaze.

They were waiting for her to invite them in. Richard had never waited, never followed that simple, ingrained rule. It should be her choice, her right to invite in any alpha she chose to service her.

And so, despite their cocks being hard, despite the tension in their bodies and the obvious desire, still they waited. They gave her the chance to decide.

One more inhalation did it, made the decision easy for her. Tracy scooted back, the feeling of the bedding against her skin almost too much for her highly charged body. "Please," she said.

She needed the alphas to satisfy her.

Chapter Sixteen

No better sight existed, at least according to Sam. Tracy lay in the nest she'd made from the bedding they'd given her. It sparked possession in him, the desire to have her, to keep her. She'd already found comfort in his scent, the use of it like the first step of foreplay for her heat. He hadn't serviced an omega through a heat before. His time with Nora had been short, and she hadn't gone into heat during it. Even when casually dating, omegas rarely allowed alphas to service them, choosing instead to use drugs or allow a beta to watch over them.

It didn't make him nervous, however. When he breathed her in, he knew what to do, as if he'd always known somewhere. An instinct he didn't know he had controlled him, told him what to do. Nothing on him hurt besides the brutal aching of his heavy cock, beyond the demanding throb of his knot. His leg felt fine and his arm, while still in a cast, didn't bother him.

That was probably a reaction to her heat, a way for nature to assure an omega's heat couldn't be denied.

He crawled into the nest, the one she'd made large enough for all three.

Large enough for four. He tried to ignore the wayward thought, ignore the male who hid in his own room. Mason had added a blanket from Dylan to the pile despite Sam's glower at its inclusion. Sam could have gotten over his past with Dylan, but the fool had made his position clear.

Dylan didn't want Tracy, so he didn't deserve to be there, even in that form. A look from Mason had shut Sam up, however. It was about Tracy, not about them, and whether he liked it or not, the omega had a thing for Dylan as well.

Sam's hope that she'd get over it, or that Dylan would get his head out of his ass, had mostly gone away. If her scent when in heat didn't make Dylan put aside his nonsense, nothing would. There existed few things as powerful or ingrained as biological need. If Dylan could resist that, he was far more stubborn than even Sam had given him credit for.

A stroke of Tracy's fingers brought Sam back to the moment. She slid them over his chest, the touch lacking her usual hesitancy. In her eyes, lust swam, so thick and deep it hardly held a speck of her.

A deep desire drowned out the fear and shyness inside her. That was the thing, though, an omega's heat was scary and powerful and cleansing. It didn't care about the past, the future, about anything but satisfaction. It forced people to move forward, to dwell only in the things they wanted right then, only in the moment.

And Sam intended to do that. He grasped her hair and pulled her into a kiss. He let himself have her the way he wanted, knowing she wouldn't be frightened off by it, that if anything, she'd demand more. There would be no censoring themselves, no caution or doubt, and she'd need nothing less than everything Mason and he had to give.

Tracy kissed him back with all the fervor he gave her, then more. She pressed closer, sliding her leg over his lap as she tried to crawl inside his skin. She sought entry with her demanding tongue against the seam of his lips until he parted them, until he gave her everything.

She rocked her hips, grinding against his already solid dick, her pussy damp and hot and leaving wetness on his length. She caught his bottom lip with her teeth as she reached between them and wrapped her hand around his thick cock in a solid hold.

"Wait," he forced out. "You're not —"

She rose to her knees, pressed the head of his dick against her dripping entrance and slid down his long shaft in one quick motion that silenced him beyond a surprised gasp.

Mason's dark chuckle came from just beside them, with him having gotten into the nest unnoticed. "Oh, she's ready." He slid his hand between them, moving down her lush body to find her erect little clit.

Tracy rode Sam, her body lithe and beautiful. She didn't hide, didn't seem to care she was nude and on display. None of her worries could fit inside that space, filled as it was by the three of them and her heat. Her muscles shifted beneath her skin, her thighs tensing as she rose, her abs contracting as she rolled her hips in the most sensuous dance he'd ever seen. She used him for her own need, her thrusts and speed and focus on what felt best.

And he'd experienced nothing better. He let her take everything, sacrificed himself at the altar of her heat, content to watch as she fucked herself on his hard shaft.

Mason's body was so close, sliding his fingers against Tracy's clit even as she writhed, as she moved up and down over Sam. The drag of his fingers made her gasp and shudder, clutching Sam's shoulders for balance.

The bite of her nails made him harden further, made his need grow. Now wasn't the time for holding off, though. It wasn't the time to show how long he could last. She needed him to come, her heat only lessening with his release, with his cum soaking into her needy body. There would be many more rounds before the lust-driven omega would be sated.

It meant the next time her hips came down, when the sway of her pert breasts and hard, pink nipples became too much, he let himself go. His knot swelled so fast it hurt, locking into place behind Tracy's pelvic bone. Her body was tight around his, but Mason's fingers never stopped. He ground them against her clit until she threw her head back and squeezed down around Sam's knot like a vise.

His cum burnt as it left him, like every part of him had grown too hot, but Tracy's reaction was instantaneous. Her forehead came to rest against Sam's shoulder, her chest rising and falling in hard pants as she came, as his release filled her, trapped by his swollen knot.

He carded his fingers through her hair, the soft red strands as wild as ever in his grasp. He pressed a kiss to her temple as she leaned against his sweat-soaked body, a moment of quiet in the eye of the storm.

This was something he'd never thought he'd get.

Mason never let up on his tormenting touches to his omega's hard little clit. He wasn't a sadist, but he wouldn't deny enjoying a bit of 'too much' when it came to his partners. That lost look when lines sprang up between their eyebrows and they didn't think they could take more. Sure enough, Tracy whimpered, a slight squirm, but trapped as she was on Sam's knot, she wasn't going anywhere.

"Easy, kitten." He pressed a kiss to her ear, then offered a quick love bite to the lobe. A little sting was good, and the hormones raging in her body finally distracted her enough that he wouldn't frighten her off with it.

Even as they waited, even as the cum Sam had filled her with soaked into the needy walls of her pussy, even as she was stretched on Sam's knot, her scent said she was far from done. The clenching of her cunt, when Sam would growl and she would whine, showed her body had already started to wind back up.

That was how this went, though. Omegas took more than a couple of rounds to sate them, before their bodies finally collapsed at the end, exhausted. It helped ensure the best chance at reproduction, since they went into heat only once a year or so.

Mason had seen more than a few omegas through their heats in the years when trying to fill that void, the years before he'd realized the bond between he and his fellow alphas was the missing part. He'd driven himself to exhaustion trying to sate the desperate omegas, giving all he had to satisfy them. In the end, he'd been tired, and they'd been happy enough, but it had lacked any connection. It had been bodies and nothing more. At least he hadn't ended up impregnating any of them.

Taking Tracy together, caring for her as a group, that got to him on a deeper level, something no one-on-one relationship had ever come close to. It was the part that had been lacking before.

So when Sam's knot finally went down enough for him to slip from her, when her unhappy whine said she was empty and didn't like it, Mason wasted no time.

He put her on all fours and shoved her chest toward the floor, until her face was inches from Sam's wet and hard shaft.

Mason lined up and plunged into her waiting cunt, rewarded by an instant tightening and a cry from her perfect soft lips. She squeezed around him as she came, and he swore it wouldn't be the last time. He'd get her off until she was shaking and begging and pleading for a break. If she was going to milk them dry, he'd damn well do the same to her. He'd make it impossible to deny what they had.

She bracketed her hands on Sam's hips to give her leverage, forcing herself backward to take him deeper, harder. Gone was the timid omega, replaced by the seductive vixen who would drive him as hard as he did her, who would demand to be fucked and filled.

Deeper and harder he could do. Mason leaned forward and grasped her hair in a punishing grip, then moved her lips to Sam's length. "Go on, why don't you entertain yourself."

She didn't have to be told twice, stretching her pink lips around Sam's thick cock in a heartbeat, taking him deep into her waiting mouth.

Mason broke his thrusts off for a second as he watched. "You taste yourself, kitten? Because that's quite a treat. You are *mouthwatering*." His words came out rough, graveled, and he didn't wait for any response before he resumed fucking her with hard and quick motions.

He took her like he needed to—like she needed him to. He filled her entirely with each thrust, then pulled back until he'd almost left her before plunging back deep inside her hot pussy. It forced her body to stretch more, teasing and tantalizing every inch of her snug cunt with his straining cock. Every hard thrust that knocked her forward was met with a shove backward from her, as if begging him for more, to keep going, to give her everything he had.

Mason let her suck Sam's dick, that twisted part of him loving that Sam was likely too sensitive for it to be entirely pleasant. Still, Tracy needed all she could get, and the thought of her taking both alphas in some way, at the same time, nearly undid Mason. Besides, while swallowing the cum down wouldn't be as good as leaving it deep inside her, it would still help take the edge off.

Her pussy clung to him, tightening in erratic waves around his cock. He didn't stop or slow him, didn't change his speed at all. He gave her everything he had, knowing she'd be sore later, but also knowing she'd happily bear that.

We'll all be sore.

He grasped her hip in a crushing hold, the image of her pinned between Sam's and his dicks too much, too perfect. He swore right then that no matter what, he'd take care of her.

Always.

He pictured her years later, belly swollen with a child—their child—that glare she tried to give when wanting to look tough, the one she couldn't hold because of her sweetness. He thought about how it would feel to have this omega for good, to claim her fully, to have her be theirs.

It wasn't her snug, soaked pussy or the sight of Sam's dick filling her mouth that made him come. It was the future he finally saw.

The thought tossed him over the edge, his cock jerking before the base of it swelled, her pelvic bone locking him into place, her lips never fully relinquishing Sam's cock.

The first spurt of cum sent her moaning around Sam's length, the muffled sound so filthy and depraved Mason's dick gave another shot of cum, his balls aching as he filled her with every drop he had.

He leaned forward, resting his weight against her, against Sam, exhausted and sated and happy in a way he'd never felt before.

And his promise echoed in his head.

No matter what, I won't lose this.

Chapter Seventeen

Dylan had jerked off more times in the past six hours than he had in his entire depraved teenaged years.

Okay, so maybe that wasn't true, but it sure as hell felt like it. If he'd thought Tracy's scent and the sounds the day before had been bad, they were nothing compared to her being in full heat. And Mason and Sam? He had to give the alphas credit, because each time those waves started up again, when her voice turned needy and demanding, they seemed to step up.

Meanwhile, Dylan paced the house between his masturbation breaks.

The running of a shower surprised him as he walked back into the house, having stood on the back porch like that would help. Him in only sweats with an erection like a fucking tent-pole had driven him back to the safety of the house, because he didn't need Sam getting calls from his neighbors about some pervert flashing his hard-on around.

A few steps closer and Dylan caught a wafting of Tracy's scent through the closed bathroom door. The heat wasn't over — couldn't be — so what was she doing?

He opened the door, no sense of the other alphas inside. Cold air blasted him, and a soft whine came with it.

In the bottom of the tub, Tracy had curled into a fetal position, water raining down on her, her skin red from the freezing temperature of the shower.

He could turn around. He *should* turn around. He'd go get Sam or Mason to deal with it. This was their problem, their responsibility.

However, Tracy hurting and in heat hypothetically was a fuck-lot different from actually seeing that shit.

Dylan closed the door behind him, then reached in to turn off the water.

She opened her eyes, offering a weak glare. "Go away."

"What are you doing in here, Red? Because I'm pretty sure what you need is back in that room, not in a shower."

She shivered, yet even with that, new drops of sweat came up on her eyebrow. "I told them I needed a shower. They've done enough."

Enough? Not fucking close given the shaking she was doing, the way she was too worn out to even wince when another wave must have had her lower stomach cramping.

"They say that? Because I'd bet that's you over-thinking." He grasped her arm and pulled, getting her off the bottom of the tub. It gave him a look at her very naked body, but he tried his best to ignore it. Enough temptation without spotting those perfect breasts with an almost invisible spattering of freckles, all wet from the water. "Come on, let's get you back."

She shook off his hold, but the movement lacked strength. "Just leave me alone."

"I would have if you'd stayed where you were fucking supposed to."

"Fuck you," she shoved out, the curse odd from her, though the way she stumbled over it made him grin.

At least, it did until she cried out, leaning forward, knuckles turning white on the edge of the tub as another wave of that scent hit him.

"Come on, let's get you back. There's no reason for you to hurt." He tried for kindness. He could do kind, right?

"Just leave me alone!"

Fuck kind. Dylan leaned down and got right in her face, pulling his lips back into a snarl. "Look here, Red, you're fucking hurting and there is no way I'm leaving you in here like this. You either take your ass back to that room and let Sam and Mason deal with it, or I'm about to bend you over something right here and fuck you myself. We clear?"

He tossed the threat out there as if it would send her running, as though she'd realize how stupid she was being, that she'd rather have Mason and Sam and she'd stop being stubborn. She just needed that good push for her to get her head out of her ass.

Instead, her pupils blew wide, the black eating up the amber that had been there. Another inhalation told him the same thing. *She wanted him.*

Dylan tried to tell himself no, that he needed to take her back, that this was crazy. Except, the way she leaned toward him, the want in those eyes, the acceptance there? He'd never really been wanted before.

He couldn't let that go. Before he'd even fully realized what he was doing, he'd pulled her from the tub. Her legs were shaky, so leaning her forward against something was out of the question. They wouldn't hold her up.

Fine, he was nothing if not inventive, especially when he had a good fucking reason to be. Dylan grasped her thighs and set her ass on the sink counter, his lips finding hers, hungry and dominant. She challenged him, and he wanted to rise to that challenge. He wanted to prove to her that he could handle her, and that she could handle him.

Her legs spread around him in a welcome, and between them he found her drenched sex. Her slick, the other alpha's cum, all of it only served to make his dick harder. Even the water of the shower hadn't fully washed away the evidence of her heat. A jerk of his sweats to free his erection was all it took before he pressed himself against her soaked, tight slit.

He breathed her in once more, savoring the moment, the heat, the spark between them that he'd spent all that time trying to ignore.

She panted against his lips, breaking the kiss to dig her nails into his sides in a clawing grasp. "You said you'd fuck me if I didn't go back," she taunted him.

"Oh, I will, Red." Dylan slammed into her, silencing any other quips she thought to make.

Her pussy made him suck in a hard breath, the way it wrapped around him in a perfectly tight grasp, the softness and heat that seared deeper than skin. He felt branded, like he wasn't claiming her at all, but she was taking some part of him, instead.

All the reasons he'd had for why he hadn't wanted this, couldn't have it evaporated under the searing heat of her body into nothing. Her chilled skin, still damp from the shower, was the only thing he knew, the only thing he cared about. He grasped her ass to keep her still as he gave her punishing thrust after punishing thrust. He fucked her with the madness he felt, with the growing desire that had started that first day he'd seen her, when he'd told himself there was no way. Each thrust was a response to each time he'd scolded himself, every fucking time he'd pulled back when he hadn't wanted to. He offered them up like apologies, like penance for his stupidity.

Tracy clung to him, her nails deep in his sides, probably drawing blood, her thighs tight around his hips, her cunt squeezing down on him.

Why had he resisted so fucking hard? What was so terrible about this?

Dylan couldn't find a single answer, so he plummeted into that madness with her. Their lips met one another, hungry and angry and wild. The movements of their bodies mirrored that, untamed. For everything Dylan gave, Tracy took. No fear sat between them, all that frustration melting into something that burned impossibly hotter.

Dylan bit down on her bottom lip, mimicking the way she would do it to her own. "Fucking hell, you're perfect," he whispered, the words flying from his lips before he could censor them, before he could protect himself. He let her see how much he wanted this, how much he'd needed it, how damn afraid he was of losing it.

And that was stupid. He knew it, knew giving anyone that sort of ammunition to use against him was asking for trouble, but he couldn't help it. Buried inside her like that, when he'd tried to resist for so long, had worn down all his defenses.

So he let her see it all, consequences be damned.

He was tired of fighting it. He was so sick of telling himself not to want her, of having to remind himself that it would only end badly. Right then, he didn't care. Let her rip his heart out and stomp all over it, because he couldn't fucking resist her anymore.

A tightening in his balls drew a growl against her lips. He didn't want to come. He didn't want this to end. When it did, when he'd satisfied her, would she walk away? Would she return to the room, to the other alphas, and leave him alone? Would he end up on the wrong side of that fucking door again?

Despite trying to hold off, her body dragged him past the point of no return. He pulled in a ragged breath as his body gave her exactly what she needed, as their kiss slowed, grew softer. Even after all the times he'd taken care of himself over the past hours, it was like it knew he was finally where he belonged. Somehow, he wasn't dry, and the frantic, tiny jerks of his cock as he came inside her let him add his own scent to her, completing something between them all.

He could no longer pull out of her, but that didn't stop him from occasionally grinding against her, from setting her body off to tighten around him in another delectable tug. Her shivers had drifted away, replaced by hard breathing and occasional whines. She'd reached the point of her heat where she still came but lacked the energy to do much about it. She'd cry out softly, and her pussy would squeeze, but that was all her body could manage.

He eased her through the wait while he had her knotted, his lips trying to say something with the kisses that he knew he'd fuck up if he tried with words.

When his shaft pulled free, when a broken moan left her at the loss, he cupped her cheeks and gave her one more kiss.

With her energy sapped, he drew on his own, pulling her into his arms. Sam and Mason were both asleep in the room, snoring loudly despite their hard cocks, as though even in sleep they knew they were needed.

Dylan settled Tracy into the nest on the floor, the one that had likely looked more made when they had started. He caught sight of one of the blankets. *Mine.*

Once he'd set her there, she snuggled against the bedding, and Dylan's chest stung. He wanted to crawl in after her, to stay and be there for the rest of her heat.

Hell, he wanted to be there for a hell of a lot longer.

But that same doubt crept back in. *They don't want me here. I don't really belong.*

He took a step backward, ready to leave her be, but those soft amber eyes of hers opened. She held out a hand to him, then waved him forward, inviting him into her nest.

The action humbled him, stunned him. It was so much more than he'd expected and far more than he deserved.

Helpless against the request, against the desire in him to do just that, Dylan stripped off his sweats fully and moved into the nest behind her. He hauled her against him, fitting her so closely no space remained between them.

He danced his fingers over her bare side, giving himself the chance to touch, to explore, as he tried to rest.

He didn't know what was to come, but he knew he had more hope than he'd ever had before.

* * * *

Tracy woke as a hard, thick cock filled her, but the easy slide said her body was more than a few steps ahead of her mind.

Even so, she was tired. Exhaustion hung on her bones like a shroud, heavy and dragging her down.

Not that her body cared. A moan slipped past her lips before she'd fully woken, before she'd had a chance to take in any detail beyond the warmth of a body behind her, the scent of alphas surrounding her and the stretch of her pussy around a thick cock.

"You feel good, Red." Dylan's dark voice tickled her ear, warm and promising and with the same gruffness he always had.

She shuddered as she surrendered to the width of his hard dick, arching her back to let him deeper, to let him take her over.

Soft lips teased hers, and Tracy opened her eyes in confusion. Dylan was clearly behind her, given the slow, languid thrusts and his hard body against her back.

She found Sam's smiling face in front of her, and he traced her jawline with his fingers. "How're you feeling, honey?"

Tracy opened her mouth to answer, but an especially hard thrust from Dylan turned her words to a gasp.

Dylan chuckled as he wrapped his fingers around her hip to steady her.

"Is it over?" She asked the question in a rough voice, tired from the moaning, the cries, the lack of water.

She recalled Mason forcing her to drink a few times when all she'd wanted was more of the males, when she'd have been happy to dehydrate if it meant swallowing down the alphas, instead.

"Almost," Sam rasped before offering a flick of his tongue to her bottom lip. "You're almost done. Another hour, maybe, and it'll be over."

An hour? After what had been an all-night event, the idea of even another hour made Tracy want to curl into a ball. Even as she thought that, she rocked against Dylan's thrusts, seeking the delicious way he filled her, how he delved deep inside her.

"You were moaning in your sleep," Dylan said. He tightened his fingers at her waist and rolled his hips, the action causing his cock to stroke against her inner walls in a new, toe-curling way. "I haven't had as much work as they did, so I figured I'd take one for the team."

Take one for the team? What a smart-ass. Tracy elbowed him, but he responded with a nip to her earlobe and another delicious roll of his hips.

Sam chuckled at the display, as though charmed by their interaction. He gave her another kiss before working his way down her body, over her chest, down her sternum, over her stomach. When he reached the place where silver stripes sat on her stomach from carrying Karen, he didn't avoid them. Instead, he lavished affection over the stretch marks, his tongue paying homage to the imperfections. He traced her hip bones, where they stuck out due to her thin frame, and each area she had hidden, each flaw, he loved.

He didn't love them with words, but with action. With the brush of his soft lips and the stroke of his hot, wet tongue, he helped erase each unkind word Richard had hurled, replacing them with his own admiration.

He ended up kissing her mound, the glide of his lips to her sensitive skin better than any massage.

Dylan moved from her hip to taking her thigh in his hand and pulling the leg backward, resting it against his thigh.

Sam took the new position to drift impossibly lower still, so his lips played against her newly exposed pussy. He slid his tongue against her clit, a flash of pleasure racing through her.

His growl was low, as though he'd tasted nothing better, as if it woke up the vicious, primal side of him she so rarely saw.

Her heat remained, but it had seemed subdued, as though the alphas' efforts had quieted and tamed it. They'd turned it from a wild creature to a house pet who purred at the attention Sam lavished to her clit, to the way Dylan stretched her body.

It then occurred to her the missing part, as her pleasure-addled brain caught up.

She searched the room for Mason, for her wild-looking alpha whose easy smile and contagious joy never failed to make her grin.

She found him seated near the top of the bed, making her wonder exactly when she'd moved from the floor. She recalled complaining about her knees at one point, when Mason had lifted her with ease and deposited her on the mattress. She'd missed her nest, but the softness of the mattress, the fact she was already covered in their scent, meant she'd stayed put.

When her eyes met his, he offered her that easy smile as if she wasn't being fucked by Dylan, as if Sam wasn't feasting on her. He looked at her with heat, but also a sweetness that had no place in such a filthy moment.

"Hey there, kitten." He slid closer, taking the space Sam had vacated when he'd moved between her thighs. "Bet you're tired, huh? Probably sore, over-sensitive?" He pressed a thumb to her bottom lip, toying over the full flesh there. As soon as she nodded, he kept speaking. "You're almost done for, then you can sleep. You'll take Dylan's knot once more like a good girl, won't you?"

The idea of her body stretching again, of Dylan's thick knot locking inside her overly worked body made her whine a weak protest.

It was too much. Even as her cunt squeezed down, as the hormones inside her swore up and down that was the best plan ever, she whimpered against the exhaustion.

She needed it like she needed a cold shower during a fever, something that didn't always feel great but was necessary. She craved his knot, his cum a balm, the only way to chase away the deeper, molten ache inside her.

Mason pressed his forehead to hers while his large hand found her breast, fingers teasing her nipple in a gentle caress. He spoke, his lips brushing hers, his mustache tickling her. "You can do it, kitten. This is the last time, and after he knots you, by the time he can pull free, you'll be done. Tell me you can do it, hmm? Really, with Sam's tongue on you, I doubt you'll notice much of anything."

Sure enough, Sam took that moment to latch his lips around her clit, his fingers holding her hood out of the way and keeping her spread.

She cried out against Mason's lips, trying to arch but having nowhere to go, not with the three alphas pinning her between them. Mason swallowed down the sound, a soft rumble in return as though he could taste her distress and loved it.

Tracy gripped Mason's shoulders as the sensations overwhelmed her, as they crawled through her.

"Fuck, Red, your cunt is so tight. There's no better feeling than you milking my knot, and the way you struggle is even better. Are you going to come for us again?"

Us.

Up until then, it hadn't been *us*. It had been Sam and Mason, then Dylan on his own. He might have gone down on her, and he might have had sex with her, but it had always been on his own. He hadn't been part of anything with them, more than reluctant to join anything between them.

Hearing him say *us*, feeling him take her along with the others, moving as a unit, it went deeper than even his dick. Of anyone, Dylan had been clearest that there was no us. Not between he and her, and certainly not between he and any of the other alphas.

Mason closed his fingers in a pinch, and between the pull of Sam's lips, the tightness of Mason's fingers and Dylan's hard thrusts, Tracy came weakly, her body too tired for much fanfare.

The orgasm was harsh, washing through her, and she was too tired to stand against it, to do anything but feel her muscles contract, her sore abs tighten, her pussy clench in quick pulses.

Dylan's teeth closed on her shoulder, not hard enough to break the skin but tight enough for her to whine at the sting, to have something to focus on as every nerve in her body rebelled in chaos. The bite was as clear a claim as anything else, of him holding her still, of him wanting her and not letting her go.

Dylan's knot was thick as it locked inside her, his bite loosening to turn into a kiss.

Meanwhile, Sam brushed his lips against her mound, against the top of her slit in some sort of silent thank you.

Mason never stopped his lips to hers, praise falling from his deep voice, whispered along with Sam's kisses and Dylan's growl.

She relaxed against them, against their warmth and strength and the familiarity of their scents.

She rested, refusing to overthink the connection, the sense of security between their large frames, between their gentle touches. Tired as they were, they seemed content, shifting slightly to find comfort in the large bed.

Even with Dylan's knot still pulsing, with her cunt still tightening around him, darkness pulled her under.

And she gave in to it, refused to worry. She'd worried for a long time, had never thought she could have this, and even if it was just for that moment, even if she couldn't commit to it, she enjoyed it for then.

Chapter Eighteen

Tracy ached, a deep burn inside her that made moving painful. Even so, she couldn't stop the grin she'd had since waking.

After a heat, the alphas tended to need more sleep, exhausted from the effort. All three of hers still slept in her room.

Hers.

The claiming title felt right. Strange, perhaps, but fitting. After that night, they felt like hers.

They'd spent all night caring for her, taking turns satisfying her. First it had been Sam and Mason until, after the first six hours, she had seen the weariness weigh on them. She recalled Richard, who had enjoyed her heats at the start, but it had been all about his pleasure. He hadn't cared for her, for anything she suffered.

That doubt had driven her from the room, when she'd told them she needed to shower off, when she'd tried to let them rest.

Jayce Carter

The time with Dylan had surprised her. It had been hard and meaning so much more than she'd expected. It hadn't just been sex, even if had started with them snipping at each other.

Would they always be like that?

He'd spent the rest of the night behind her, never leaving, never trying to get space. She'd woken first, leaving the others to sleep as she'd crawled from the nest.

A shower had washed away all the dried cum that sat on her, the evidence from the night. What it meant kept lumbering through her mind.

What did it mean? What did they want?

What do I want?

That one she was stuck on. Could this really be a home? Could she settle Karen there and create something out of them all?

Would they even want that?

Sure, the males had taken to her daughter, but having a child stay for a few days was very different from living together full time. Did they want to be parents? After the heat, she could even be pregnant. Were they ready for that?

Could she really put Karen or herself through that when she had no solid answers?

"You look like you're thinking hard." A kiss to her head accompanied the words, tearing her free of her musing.

Tracy turned, and the action allowed Mason to stealing a kiss from her lips, as well.

"Morning, kitten." His charm was unfair, the way he managed to say anything and make her want to smile. Well, that and the fact he hadn't bothered to put on a stitch of clothing. Every inch of his flawless body was on display, and he walked as though he either didn't know or didn't care. "How're you feeling?"

"Why are you naked?"

"You noticed? I'm flattered."

Tracy didn't bother to try to one-up him. Especially with him naked as sin, with his wild hair and wilder gaze, she didn't have a chance. Instead, she only offered a mocking glare.

He huffed a laugh. "What were you thinking about?"

Tracy took a sip of her coffee, nodding toward the pot to show there was some left. "About what I want."

He grabbed a cup down and filled it with coffee. "Oh, hard things, then?" He took a seat at the dining room table across from her, still moving as though being nude was the most normal thing in the world to him. Ignoring it, pretending not to be affected by it. "Seems way too early for such hard topics, especially given your late night." He waggled his eyebrow. A full waggle that had her groaning with the absurdity of the motion.

"You just think you're so charming, don't you?"

"Yeah, pretty much." He flashed her a grin before taking another drink. "Finish up that coffee, kitten, because afterward we're going to breakfast."

"We slept through breakfast. It's almost six."

"Want to know a secret?" He cocked up an eyebrow, mischief across his features.

"Sure."

He leaned across the table and gave her a deep kiss, the sort that made her wonder how he could still have any energy or desire after her heat. Yet, it stirred all those feelings in her again. No matter how much they'd done the night before, or the fact her body ached at the idea of coming again, she warmed for him.

How did he make her want him again so fast?

He pulled back, then tapped her chin in a chiding move. "Diners serve breakfast all day. Go on, kitten, and get dressed. Your alphas need to feed you."

He took his cup and walked out, leaving Tracy speechless staring at the broad expanse of his bare back and his perfect ass, his words soaking into her.

My alphas.

She liked the sound of that.

* * * *

Mason popped another fry into his mouth, his gaze pinned to Tracy. She ate an omelet with ham, which wasn't what she'd wanted.

She'd wanted some salad, but a bit of coaxing had gotten her to order something with more protein. That surprised him, how she wasn't comfortable with anything any of the three of them did for her.

Holding doors open, a hand on her back as they walked, or when Sam had offered her some of his fruit cup when he'd seen her staring at the strawberries, it all brought on a look of confusion. She wasn't used to someone caring about her.

The way she hesitated when they did it made him want to keep at it. He wanted to offer those little bits of sweetness until she learned to accept them, until she realized she was worth it, that they weren't just a trick to get something from her.

"Now that we're here, kitten, and you're stuck in a booth between us, let's talk."

The words had her back straightening and, he was damn sure, if she hadn't been sitting right between Mason's and Dylan's large bodies, she'd have bolted.

Better yet, Sam was on the other side of Dylan, keep both their flight risks properly contained.

"I don't know what you're talking about." Tracy didn't meet Mason's gaze, poking at her omelet with her fork.

"This isn't the time to pretend. You're not the type who bullshits, so let's put it all on the up and up."

Still, Tracy didn't look up, didn't respond. She didn't want to make the first move, huh?

Fair enough.

"I want you to stay," Mason said, risking everything. "Not just until this Mario bullshit is handled, but for good."

"Easy for you to say. It's not your house."

Sam chuckled, seated on the other side. "It's his house, too, Tracy. Always has been. Even if he and Dylan left for a while, it was built for us all. Mason's talking for me, too."

Tracy's chest lifted as she took a deep breath, then braved a look up. "I can't put Karen through any more uncertainty. She's been through enough."

"No one's asking for some trial run here," Mason pressed. "You like me. You like Sam. You tolerate Dylan. So, why not? You can't say you haven't been happy with us, that Karen doesn't like it there."

"Sure, she likes it. And if you change your mind? If you decide that a ready-made family isn't the life you guys want after so many bachelor years, then what? Then my daughter is heartbroken yet again." She shook her head as if decided. "I can't do that to her again. She deserves something forever, to not worry that people are going to hurt her or leave her."

Mason thought about that little girl, about the things she'd seen that no child should. Tracy wasn't wrong—

she deserved a hell of a lot. How could he make Tracy understand that he wanted to help give that girl the life she should have? He wanted to make that family for her, that home? He thought about Karen's smile when she'd seen the bike, her laughing as they hung the bird feeders, about Tracy's half-hearted glare over the times Karen would manipulate the alphas into treats or gifts.

Yeah, he liked that all.

But Tracy's face made it clear she wouldn't believe it.

"Things can always change," Sam offered. "I want to tell you this is forever, that there's nothing that could break it up, but that isn't life, and I wouldn't lie to you. Five years from now? Who knows? Maybe you'll wake up and realize you're sick of us. Maybe you'll decide you don't want three alphas hanging around. What I can say is that for now, I know what I want, and it's you here with us, and I don't see that changing."

Mason wanted to add more. He wanted to tell her it would be forever, but as usual, Sam was honest to a fault. It wasn't fair to tell Tracy anything but the truth, and the truth was that no one could promise another person forever.

So he waited, the stillness at the table unnerving as they all thought.

Tracy lifted her gaze to Dylan, then. *Ah, Dylan, the asshole who never fails to be an issue.* Also, the asshole who Mason cared about like a brother. He might be a shitty person when it came to emotions and, well, dealing with people, but no person would do more or risk more for those he cared about. Hell, even when still rightfully angry about Nora, Dylan had come running at the first sign of a problem.

"And you?" She asked the question in a soft voice.

Dylan didn't answer right away. He sat there, his gaze drifting from person to person. Lines of tension bracketed his mouth and his lips blanched as he pressed them into a stern line. Finally, he set his arms on the table in a loud, unhappy drop. "Yes, I want you to stay, damn it."

"You're not allowed to talk to omegas anymore," Sam snapped. "You're terrible at it!"

"She knows I didn't want this, you all do. I didn't plan on this, and it went so well last time, that sure, let me fucking line back up for another trip on that ride." He huffed, his shoulders drawn up near his ears, his face full of annoyance.

It was almost enough for Mason to break into a deep laugh at how the other alpha resembled a pouting child.

Tracy chimed in instead, her hackles risen as seemed to be common between those two. "If you don't want this, I don't have to stay."

Dylan lifted his lip, a mock snarl without sound. "We both know I want you, Red. I even like having that kid around. This is what I want. I'm just not very happy about wanting it."

Tracy didn't stop looking at Dylan while he stared right back, like the two had some sort of stand-off by just staring, as though that way they could figure things out.

Instead, she shook her head. "Well, I'm not very happy about it either, if that makes you feel better."

"A little."

Silence fell at his snarky jab, at least until Tracy's laugh was the first to break it. Damn, he rarely heard that laugh. It was soft, unsure, like she still wasn't entirely comfortable doing it. When Mason joined in, then Sam, her laugh grew.

Even Dylan chuckled at the end, so all four of them were laughing enough that a few other patrons turned to send glares their way.

Mason shook off the censure. What did he care what they thought?

When the laughter petered off into gasping as they tried to catch their breaths, and Mason wiped a thumb beneath his eyes because they'd started to water, Sam was the first to recover.

"Does this mean you're staying?"

Tracy's humor faded away, but at least she didn't look like she'd try to go over the table to escape. "I don't for how long, I'm not sure what will happen, but for now?" She nodded. "For now, I'll stay."

And Mason swore he'd make it so she never wanted to leave.

* * * *

Tracy didn't know what to do with her hands. When had she become twelve again, so uncertain how to work her body? She recalled being a child, back before expectations and age and experience had taught her differently, when she'd lounge on furniture and laugh and not worry.

Now she sat in the back seat beside Mason and felt like an awkward teenager who'd never been beside a boy.

"How are you feeling?" Mason solved the issue by tossing an arm over her shoulders after a loud—and very fake—yawn. The absurd move managed to be charming, probably only because of just how cringy it was.

"Better," she admitted. The protein had helped settle her stomach, and while she was still tired, while she still wanted to sleep, she felt better than she had after any other heat. "Normally I'm exhausted, still achy after a heat."

Mason turned and pressed a mindless kiss to her cheek. "That's because you've only ever tried to go through a heat with one alpha. Works better when there's a few to share the load." He paused, then laughed hard as if his own innuendo pleased him.

Tracy elbowed him softly, the action so natural she didn't even consider that a few weeks before, she'd have never done such a thing. She'd have never trusted an alpha enough to play like that, for fear of their retaliation.

The moment she'd done it, that she'd made contact with his side and he let out a soft huff of air, which was probably playing up the strength of the hit, she froze.

Mason twisted and nipped her earlobe. "Hitting isn't nice, kitten."

"I did not—"

"You really should keep your elbows to yourself," chimed in Sam from the front seat, humor glinting in his eyes through the rear-view mirror.

Before she could offer up another denial, Mason twisted and took her lips in a deep kiss that chased away all her rebuttals.

Dylan spoke up from the driver's seat, his dry voice waking her up as Mason broke the kiss. "Great, now you've rewarded her for it, so she'll keep elbowing people."

Tracy turned to snap back at him, but Mason took that chance set a hand on her upper thigh, high enough for her breath to catch. His pinky finger drifted higher still, rubbing a feather-light touch against the crotch of her slacks.

The touch made her whine softly, her body still off from her heat, from the orgasms they'd wrung from her during it. Even the light caress sparked a deep lust.

"I can't," she said but didn't remove his hand. "I'm sore." Even saying it was hard, since she'd never refused sex before. There hadn't been reason to try before, because it wasn't as though Richard had ever listened.

Mason paused the touch and offered a squeeze to her leg. "Too sore to take any of our knots, sure. Last I checked, that wasn't the only way for a bit of fun, and I'm always up for some fun." Even as he spoke, he didn't bring his hand back to her pussy, didn't force the issue. Instead, he waited, pressing his thumb to her thigh with gentle, reassuring pressure. "You gotta tell me yes, kitten."

Tracy didn't even hesitate that time. That was something, right? Progress? Instead of letting herself get wrapped up in her own head, in her own worries, she turned and took a kiss of her own. She didn't ask, didn't wait, just took as though she were owed it. She pressed her lips to his, hard and needy, and Mason gave her everything.

He returned his hand to the juncture of her thighs, to the part of her already growing wet for him. His teasing touches made her want the trip home to go faster. *They make me want to ignore good sense and take my pants off right now.*

A soft growl from the front seat pulled her gaze to the rear-view mirror. Dylan watched with a ravenous stare, and he dragged his tongue along his bottom lip as though he could taste her already.

Tracy let her head fall back on the seat as Mason twisted his hand to caress her sex through her slacks that seemed far too thick all of a sudden. She wanted those deft fingers of his against her heated flesh, to be playing directly with her without the barrier.

Mason placed his lips to her throat, kissing over where her pulse hammered against her skin. His dark chuckle said he felt it, and as though she couldn't help it, as if she didn't control it at all, her hand moved over to his lap. She grasped his thick erection through his pants, and they both let out simultaneous groans.

The car pulled to a hard stop, waking Tracy from the lust that had consumed her. They were already home?

Mason undid her seatbelt, but Dylan was already at her side of the truck, pulling her out, his hungry lips seeking hers. It made her dizzy, the way she went from Dylan, to Mason, to Sam who pressed her against the truck for both their balance. She bathed in the attention, in the way they fed on one another's lust until nothing but that lust existed.

They got to the door, but as soon as they entered, they all froze.

Sam twisted away to the alarm and all three alphas went rigid.

A clash from down the hall made Tracy catch up.

The alarm was dark.

The power was off.

Someone was in the house.

Chapter Nineteen

Dylan moved first, because, for all his faults, he was best in a crisis. "Sam, stay here, call nine-one-one."

"Forget that, I'm calling the station directly." Sam took his phone out, hitting a few buttons for what must have been a saved number.

Dylan was thankful Sam hadn't fought that, because the truth was that if people were in the house, Sam would be most useful in his current state staying back and keeping Tracy safe. Mason and Dylan were in better shape to confront an intruder directly.

Dylan didn't carry his weapon with him most of the time, not when he wasn't on a case, and he wouldn't take Sam's. Instead, he moved the opposite way as the sound, to Sam's room, and used the code that never changed to Sam's gun safe. It was closer than his own weapon would have been.

When he returned to the living room, pistol in hand, Mason had grabbed a crowbar from the closet by the front door where Sam kept the tools. A lifted eyebrow was met with a shrug from the larger alpha.

Then again, Mason had always been more comfortable with something blunt. He wasn't really a man who used much subtlety, and given his size, a crowbar could be lethal.

Dylan moved down the hallway first, gaze searching for clues in the dim house, lit only by the moonlight from outside. The security panel had been dark, and the lights hadn't worked. It meant they'd turned off the power in addition to bypassing the alarm.

Another sound from down the hallway had him quickening his quiet steps as he neared it. Then the scent of smoke hit him, and he frowned.

Fuck. They're after the files.

The moment the thought occurred to him, when he realized what the target must have been, Dylan gave up the stealthy route. If whoever it was managed to destroy those files, Tracy would lose her only leverage.

He turned the corner to find more smoke and the crackling of fires on the boxes. The asshole must have put an accelerant on them, because he'd just smelled the smoke and yet they all were going up in flames like fucking gasoline.

Dylan locked eyes with the intruder, something he hadn't expected. It wasn't a male at all. Instead, a very slight female stood there, ski-mask obscuring all her face except her bright blue eyes, a lighter in her hand. She tucked it into the belt at her waist but didn't speak.

Dylan raised the gun toward her. "Come on, nice and slow."

The woman lifted her hands and walked forward.

"Mason, get water to put these out. We can't let them get destroyed." He reached for her wrist, to twist it behind her back.

The woman moved with a speed that surprised him. She spun, knocking the gun from his hand and landing an elbow against his lip. It happened so fast he didn't even have time to be ashamed for letting it happen. Not because she was female, but because he should have known better than to let anyone get the upper hand.

As fast as it happened, it stopped. Mason was too large and strong, and when he grabbed her by the arm and hauled her against him, the fight ended. He pinned her wrists easily, his crowbar dropped and forgotten, while Dylan shook off the pain in his lip and the way the strike had rattled his brain around in his skull.

"How about you put out the fire," Mason said, his voice that same amused tone that Dylan hated, full of more than a little mockery. "I'll handle the little hellcat."

Dylan did as requested, rushing into the hallway for the fire extinguisher that he knew Sam would have there, the ever-prepared alpha who had seen what fires could do.

Mason held the girl tight, an arm around her throat, her hands pinned behind her, while Dylan put out the flames.

Sam and Tracy came in, though all three alphas tensed at her presence. None of them liked her around anything potentially unsafe, and that included standing in a recently burning room and beside the strange woman who had done it.

Even so, no one was about to stop her, either. The smoke rose from the boxes, and all of them stood silent as they stared.

Everything had been destroyed. The files they needed to keep Tracy safe, to get Mario to back off, they were all gone.

No one spoke. What was there to say?

They were fucked.

* * * *

Tracy stared at the woman in cuffs, the woman who had so quickly shattered the plan she'd thought they had. The moment Tracy had felt like she had solid footing, when they'd had the files, when she'd given in to the alphas and made it through her heat even stronger, this woman had torn it apart.

Why?

The woman — an omega — sat on the porch, her hands cuffed behind her back, police nearby. Now the intruder's mask was off, Tracy got a good look at her face. She had short, brightly colored blue hair that matched her eyes. She wore a black outfit, tight but old, and she sat without a care.

"She won't say anything," Dylan said from the side, his gaze hard. The woman might have been small, but Dylan stared at her with all the aggression of an enemy.

The woman cast a smile full of mockery toward Dylan, as though she weren't in handcuffs, wasn't on her way in jail.

Tracy lifted her gaze to Dylan. "Can I have a minute with her?"

"No. In fact, fuck no."

The woman huffed out a soft laugh and shook her head.

Tracy tried again. "Please? She's cuffed and you all can watch from over there. I just want a minute."

Dylan's eyes narrowed, and his face screamed no.

"Sure," Sam said, interrupting from behind her. "I think we can give her just a little room."

It only took a few moments for Sam to shoo away the officers and Dylan, with Mason already inside. They didn't go far, and Tracy could feel their eyes on her even from that distance. Still, it made her feel safe, made her feel protected.

The woman's gaze followed where the men had gone, but she made no move to run. "I'll never understand omegas like you."

"Like me?"

The woman nodded toward Sam. "Omegas who give up everything for a man. Or, a couple of them, in your case." She paired the words with a mischief-filled grin. "Dicks are a dime a dozen, and even with three of them, they aren't worth the trouble."

Tracy folded her legs and twisted toward the woman. "They're not so bad."

The woman shifted as well, wiggling. After a few seconds of quick gymnastics, she'd gotten her hands below her butt and pulled them in front of her. She lifted them toward Dylan who had already crossed half the distance toward her, as though to show she'd moved her hands in front of her but didn't plan to do anything else.

Tracy waved the alpha off. If the woman wanted to hurt her, she would have already. The conversation was too important to let it end.

The woman continued to speak once Dylan pulled back. "Mario had some shit to say about you and that mate of yours. Didn't figure you'd jump all back into that hornets' nest so fast."

Tracy ignored her comment. *What does she know?* "If you know what Mario is like, why are you helping him?"

"Same reason anyone does anything. Money."

"You're ruining my life over money?"

The woman leaned back against the post of the porch. "Trust me, I did you a favor. The shit in those files? Do you have any idea what people would do to you to get it?" She whistled low. "Believe me, they aren't the kinds of people you want to fuck with."

"Coming from someone who works for Mario?"

She waved her bound hands dismissively. "First of all, I don't work for him. He's small time, and he's an idiot. What was in those files, though? It was more than enough to bury you and set a lot of fucking fires if it got out. That mate of yours collected information for well over a decade, and letting everyone know where some of those bodies are buried?" She shook her head. "Nope. Best no one sees what was in them. Well, no one but me."

A frown pulled at Tracy's features. "You said you did it for money, so what do you mean you don't work for Mario?"

"Mario's job was quick money but that doesn't mean I work *for* him. Once I saw what you had, though? Idiot had no idea what was there, and the last thing I'd do is turn those things over to that useless asshole."

"How did he even know I had them?"

The woman shrugged. "Probably had you tailed. That's what I would have done, at least. He told me he figured you had the files but he didn't know where you hid them, so wanted me to check the house."

Tracy's temper simmered. The woman talked about those files as though they were unimportant, as though they weren't discussing Tracy's safety and that of her daughter. "Well, because of what you did, I can't negotiate with him anymore. I have nothing to make him go away."

The woman cocked up an eyebrow. "He was never going to just go away. Problems never do, not until you make them."

Tracy let her shoulders drop, mirroring the woman's stance, leaning her back against the opposite post. Envied swamped her for that woman's life, for that easy confidence, for her 'I've got this' attitude. "Easy for you to say. I'm not you, though, and I have people to think about."

After a long silence, the woman let out a soft sigh, the first sign of anything but mockery, the first indication anything sat beneath the woman's attitude. "Seems to me you've got mates and a kid, so you aren't doing so badly." Her head struck the post as she let it drop back. "And the shit in those files? The people it outted? You should be really fucking happy it's gone."

"So what do I do now that you burned all my leverage?"

The woman offered her a smile full of the same humor she'd worn the whole time. "You woman up and deal with shit. It's all we ever do."

Sam sighed as he stared out at the leaving cop cars. The electrician had left just before, after getting their power and alarm system working again. *Not that the alarm did any good.*

Helplessness ate at him from the inside. It had been the injury before, but now? Now it had worsened. He wanted to take care of Tracy, to protect Karen, but he had no idea how to do that.

The files were gone. They'd been reduced to ash and a few useless scraps of words without context, the woman having used enough accelerant that they were lucky the fire hadn't destroyed the house. He'd made copies of the few pieces left, the originals going to the police station along with the mysterious woman. His boss had sworn the woman would be under constant guard, and they'd keep her arrest quiet, especially about the files. They couldn't have Mario finding out about their destruction. Better he just think she failed.

What would happen to her, he had no idea. So far, they hadn't figured out who she was beyond an omega, the fact supplied by Tracy's sense of smell. It would take more digging before they knew anything more, and Sam doubted it would help them much anyway.

At least Mario had no idea the files were gone. That was something, right?

So now what he was he supposed to do? No matter how many rocks he turned over, people from above him kept putting roadblocks through official channels. Without hard proof, he couldn't go to the police or FBI. He'd thought those files would open doors, would give him something solid to force someone's hand, but now?

Now he didn't know what the hell they were going to do.

"Well, this fucking blows." Dylan's harsh words hardly surprised Sam, though the fact that the other alpha had followed him outside did.

They'd yet to talk much, despite living in the same house together. It seemed they both excelled at ignoring one another.

"Pretty much." Sam rested his forearms against the railing of the front porch, trying to stretch out his tense, knotted muscles.

Dylan walked up beside him and leaned a hip against the wood. "So, we going to talk or what?"

Sam twisted, mirroring the other alpha's stance. "About?"

"Come on, don't be an asshole. This whole talking bullshit isn't exactly my favorite thing."

"So why are you doing it?"

Dylan's dark gaze darted toward the door, to where they both knew Tracy was.

Guess that answers it, huh? Whereas Sam's mom couldn't have forced them to make up, whereas he doubted a well-placed blade could get them to talk, it seemed the little omega in the house managed the miracle just fine.

"She wants this," Dylan offered as though that said it all.

It does, right?

Sam took a deep breath, then forced himself to have the conversation he'd avoided for years. "I'm sorry, okay? What happened with Nora should have never happened. I was stupid, and I should have known better."

Dylan said nothing for a long while, so long that he expected Dylan to just flip him off. Finally, though, Dylan let out a long breath, his shoulders falling as though a weight had finally fallen free. "Wasn't your fault. Looking back, I think she always planned it. She wasn't ever happy with just me."

"It doesn't matter if she planned it. I went behind your back, and I know that, and, well, damn, Dylan, I'm sorry, okay?"

Dylan dragged his fingers through his hair. "I know you are. I've had a lot of time to be pissed, and trust me, I was. In the end, being pissed is just going to bite me in the ass, and I'm sick of doing that. I'm tired of fucking up my future because of my past. We're good, okay?"

Guilt Sam hadn't realized had settled so deeply in him eased at those words. How had he been so burdened by the rift between Dylan and him and never noticed it?

Because he'd cared more about that female who hadn't wanted either of them than he had about the friend he'd had for all his life. He'd been too busy obsessing over an omega, and in doing so he'd helped to shatter the relationship that meant everything to him.

He swore right then to never let it happen again.

However, it still forced him to broach another topic, one he wasn't looking forward to. "How do you really seeing this going with Tracy? Because the last thing I want is her hurt because you and I can't get this thing put behind us. Can you see this working, between all of us?"

At least Dylan mulled the question over. He twisted so his ass pressed against the railing and he stared toward the house, his arms crossing. "I wouldn't have thought so before. If you'd asked me that first day if I thought we could make this work, if we could seriously share an omega between the three of us, I'd have told you to fuck off."

Sounded just like him, didn't it?

"And now?"

He sighed and shook his head, as though he couldn't believe it himself. "And now, I'm struggling to see a future any other way. How'd this happen? How did I end up in this place where, yeah, I can see this with all of us and for the first time, it feels right?" He shook his head. "The fuck have you all done to me?"

Sam reached out with his good hand and patted his friend on the back, a sense of contentment he'd missed swamping him. Being without Mason, without Dylan had made him feel as though he had no anchor. He'd missed that sense of home his friends had given him, that family, that solid foundation.

As he patted Dylan, the first good real moment between them in five years, he was forced to confront just how much he'd missed, just how unsettled he'd been.

And, maybe that was what hit him as he looked through the window of the house, as he spotted Tracy sipping coffee by the counter in the kitchen.

Sure, he loved that omega. The more time he spent with her, the more he fell hopelessly in love with her. He'd been lost that first night, when he'd stared at her in the ambulance, when she'd protected her child with that ferocity. It had only grown with time, as he'd seen her sweetness, her humor. But, maybe besides any of that, he realized he owed her more than he could ever repay.

His omega had given him back his family.

Tracy sipped her coffee, despite the hour, as Sam and Dylan stood outside after seeing the cops off.

They'd taken the woman, who hadn't given any sort of information about who she was, to the station. Tomorrow, they'd have to deal with her. They'd need to figure out who she'd worked for, though that seemed obvious. It had to be Mario, because Tracy refused to consider someone else could be after her as well.

The files had been destroyed save for a few scraps of burnt remains, ones that gave no useful information, just tidbits without meaning. She'd glanced at them, but they'd meant nothing to her.

Still, the warmth of the coffee helped chase away the coldness that had settled inside her.

Karen would spend another two days with Claire. Tracy had called while they'd waited for the cops to show, needing to hear her daughter's voice, to know she was okay. The girl was having a wonderful time, being spoiled rotten by Claire and her alphas, no doubt.

It helped ease the guilt of not being able to protect her own daughter.

Mason walked into the kitchen, his gaze careful. "Should probably get some sleep, kitten."

"Probably." She took another drink instead.

He sighed, then came closer. "We'll figure this out."

By *we'll* he meant he, Sam and Dylan, because other people took care of Tracy. Claire had Karen, and these three had to handle all Tracy's problems.

She'd never taken care of herself. Never dealt with her own issues. If anything, she just made more of them then waited around for someone more qualified to fix them.

She grunted out a sound that was less classy than she usually tried for before twisting slightly as Sam and Dylan came back inside.

The three alphas filled so much of the space of the house and so much of her thoughts, too.

Sam set a hand on her back, rubbing as if that could take away the issues of the night. It didn't, all the problems still hanging on her shoulders, yet it did ease the tightness in her chest. She leaned back, letting herself rest against his solid body behind her.

Dylan picked up her cup, gaze narrowing at the coffee. So, another one who didn't care for her drinking caffeine so late at night? Then again, Dylan liked his sleep, so she supposed she understood. He dumped the cup in the sink without anything more than a quiet huff.

Mason caught her chin, lifting her gaze to his. "Come on, kitten, let's go to bed."

"Why? Is that going to fix any of this?"

He pressed his large thumb to her bottom lip before slipping into the warmth of her mouth. "Nope. However, I promise that tomorrow ain't going to be any easier to deal with if you're sleep deprived and grouchy."

Tracy tried to glare, she really did. When he pulled his thumb back, then fed it past her lips again, her brain went an entirely different direction. She imagined his thumb being something far more interesting.

Suddenly the tension in her body melted, not going away but transforming into something new. Mason's lips curled up after a slow inhalation.

Sam pulled her hair back, then toyed with the sensitive skin over her neck. "Come on, let's get some sleep."

Dylan snorted as he checked the newly fixed alarm and locked the doors. "Yeah, with the way she's smelling, I doubt anyone is going to be sleeping."

Mason kicked up that eyebrow and flashed his lazy grin at Dylan. "Hey, you're welcome to go to bed and get your precious sleep if you'd rather."

A playful growl left Dylan before he grabbed Tracy, tossing her over his shoulder as he had the night he'd gone down on her. The action forced a startled yelp from her, his hard shoulder pressed against her stomach. "There's no fucking way you're having all the fun."

Tracy smacked her hand on his back. "Don't I get a say in this?"

Dylan grasped her ass in one hand and wrapped his fingers around to press against her cunt through her slacks. He teased her, grinding against her clit, the action enough to bring back all the lust Mason had started in her from the truck ride. A low moan left her lips, one full of all the things she wanted and all the ways they could distract her.

"There's your say, Red," Dylan said. "And it sounds like a yes to me."

Chapter Twenty

Dylan hated having no options. He wanted to tell Tracy they had it all figured out, that she had no reason to worry. He wanted Karen tucked safely into her own bedroom knowing nothing would get her, knowing that Dylan would handle it all.

He couldn't say that, though. Every hour that passed, each time he thought about an option, he realized they didn't have many of them. Every damn time he found something he thought might work, he came up with a million reasons it wouldn't.

In short? They were completely fucked.

They had no leverage. If they told Mario the truth, he might kill Tracy and them just to tie up loose ends. If they went to the cops, they couldn't do a damned thing without proof. Sam had been adamant about people putting up roadblocks everywhere he looked in the official channels, which left them with fuck-all without some very clear evidence. Evidence that had just been burned.

He rubbed the heel of his hands against his eyes, frustration wearing him down. He hadn't slept more than a few hours. Even exhausted as he had been from Tracy, nothing had managed to keep him in bed.

Which sucked, because he'd really needed rest.

Her warm body had helped and, hell, even lying beside the other alphas had let him relax more than he had in years. After the three of them had lost themselves in lust, when he'd driven orgasm after orgasm from her body until she was begging him to stop, after she'd given as much pleasure as she'd taken, they'd slept in the same large bed.

It wasn't enough, though, not when a crippling fear of losing it all plagued him.

A kiss to his shoulder had him turning to find Tracy standing beside him.

Either she was silent, or he was far too distracted for his own good.

Probably a bit of both.

"Morning," he rumbled, trying to keep the stress from his tone, not wanting to burden her.

"You've been up worrying, haven't you?"

A smile he couldn't help toyed at his lips at her correct guess. "A little."

She slid in the seat beside him, and again he was awestruck by just how pretty the woman was. Her hair was wild, still damp from a shower, and the more she came out of her shell, the more he realized how well it suited her. At first, when she'd been the frightened mouse he'd met, he'd thought her hair an absurd feature. It was meant for a feisty female, for one with more backbone and spunk than the girl who cowered at ever sound. With time, though, he'd seen more.

She was brave, and she had backbone. Tracy might not throw her strength around as some did, but she'd do anything to protect those she loved.

Am I one of those people, now?

He shoved away the question. Even thought he'd accepted his place, he still couldn't accept she cared for him, not like she did the others in their grouping. It just didn't seem possible.

"I talked to Sam, and you guys are going to go pick Karen up today."

"Is that a good idea?"

Tracy pushed her hair from her face. "I don't know, honestly. At this point, however, I also don't have any other ideas. I don't have a plan, and I'm not sure what will happen. However, Mario gave me a month to find them. He still doesn't know for sure we found them, and at best, even if he did think we had them, he'll think we moved them after that woman broke in. I can't leave Karen with Claire for another two weeks until the clock runs down. She'll come back, and when we're ready to do something, when I know what to do, we'll send her off with Claire or Tiffany."

We'll. Damn, that sounds good. I like we'll. I like her thinking of us as a unit.

Dylan nodded, trying to keep his face blank. "Okay. Got to say, I miss her."

"No more self-defense," Tracy chided.

"She could use a lot more of that, and you too. Self-defense isn't about expecting trouble, but it's about knowing that when trouble shows up, you can handle it."

She narrowed her eyes but didn't argue with him. Instead, she changed the subject. "So you'll help get her?"

"And leave you here alone? Fuck. That." The very thought of leaving her on her own made his skin crawl. Mario could still show up, or another of his lackeys, and she'd be alone?

Like fuck.

Tracy's lips pressed together in a tight line. "You're going to be getting Karen. She means more to me than anything else, and we both know she's in far more in danger than I am. Mario hasn't come after me directly because he knows I'm the only who can get him what he wants — either I have them or I can find them. Either way, Karen's at more risk. Please, Dylan, I trust you, and I need to know you'll be looking after her. It's a long drive, and, honestly?" She rested an arm on the counter, looking as tired as he felt. "I could use a little time alone."

"For what?"

"Thinking."

"If it makes you that unhappy, I don't fucking suggest it."

She offered up a weak smile, as though the joke wasn't good but she wanted to acknowledge that he'd tried.

"I just want to take a long, hot bath and enjoy the silence. I want to be able to think about everything and see if I can't sort it out."

"And if you think and realize you're better off without us?"

"Well, I mean, how could I do without your charm?"

Dylan gave her a soft growl before leaning in and stroking his lips against hers in a kiss so quick and soft, she couldn't react before he pulled away. "I don't like it. What did Sam say?"

"Pretty much what you did, but he gave in. So did Mason."

"They always give omegas too much leeway. I'm not as soft as they are."

"Why do you think I waited until last to talk to you?" She leaned toward him to recapture the kiss he'd cut short. She was pure sugar, sweet and giving and so much more than he'd ever deserved.

Even so, he took the kiss, took all she gave to him. He'd always been a selfish bastard. By the time they broke apart, he was hard again, aching and breathless. Fuck, was there ever gonna be a time around her he wasn't sporting a hard-on?

"You are manipulative," he whispered, his forehead pressed to hers.

"But you'll do it?"

He hated himself but nodded. At the end of the day, he'd give her anything she needed, and if that was a bit of time to herself, fine.

She was right. Karen was in more danger, and Dylan wouldn't even consider what would happen if the girl got hurt. Just the quick thought had his chest tightening and his temper shortening.

"Fine," he snapped. "But when we get back, you're making it up to us."

She traced his bottom lip with her tongue, a teasing touch full of promise. "Gladly."

* * * *

Mason grinned at Karen, who sat in the front seat of the truck. One good look at Dylan and she'd stolen the coveted spot from the alpha, a miracle since Dylan didn't give in to anyone.

Then again, Karen had the same ability to twist all three of the alphas her mother had.

"Aunt Claire said no more ice cream, but later, Bryce brought me a bowl."

Mason didn't bother to hide his bark of laughter at the thought of the sternest of the three alphas sneaking Karen desserts.

Seemed Karen could manipulate damn near any male she wanted. Then again, her mother had managed to get herself some free time, despite the grumbling of all three alphas.

No matter how many times people said alphas were in control, Mason knew it was a lie. A good set of batting eyelashes or a grin and a female could bring any alpha to his knees with a smile on his face.

"I'm surprised you didn't try to weasel out more time there," Sam said from the back seat.

"I missed Mom, and my room, and —" She closed her lips, going silent.

Mason turned a side-eye on her, the lights from the street spilling into the truck cab. "What did you miss, kid?"

She fiddled with the frayed spots on her jeans, and Mason made a note to make sure they got her some new ones. He tried to remember how many bags she'd brought to the house with her, and he only recalled one small bag over her shoulder. She needed more things, and he wanted to shower her with them. He wanted to spoil her rotten with whatever he could.

A soft sigh, then Karen spoke in a quiet voice. "I missed you guys."

And there went any resistance Mason might have had before. Fuck, those soft words melted him.

Nothing was going to ever happen to her. He swore it up and down, that that little girl wouldn't ever have to be afraid again, that he'd do whatever it took to give her the life she should have had all along.

He went to respond, to come up with some dumb-ass way of saying what was in his head that wouldn't make either of them feel more award, but before he could think of anything, something knocked the truck to the side.

Mason gripped the steering wheel as the car jerked to the right. Squealing tires and Karen's startled scream filled the cab.

The truck shuddered as it hit the rough pavement outside the guidelines of the lane, but Mason slammed the brakes and steered it back before it hit the concrete wall on the shoulder.

Mason's other hand reached over, keeping Karen in place. She grasped his arm like it was far more comforting than the seatbelt, which was probably doing a hell of a lot more, but suddenly Mason understood why Sam's mom had stuck her arm out any time she'd slammed the brakes no matter how old Mason got.

Seemed that shit was instinct.

The truck came to a hard stop, and the first words came from Sam. "Everyone okay? Karen? You good?"

Mason twisted when Karen didn't answer, and while her eyes were wide, she didn't appear harmed. "Hey, kid, it's okay. Nothing hurts, right?"

She swallowed hard, the pallid tone of her skin speaking volumes about how shaken up she was. "I'm okay."

"I'm good, too," Dylan chimed in. "In case anyone cared."

"And here I thought we'd finally rid ourselves of you." Mason sat up, squinting into the darkness of the deserted side street to look for the other car involved. He'd caught a glimpse of a dark SUV. Did they end up swerving off the road?

Now that he knew those in the truck were fine, he grasped the door handle, ready to check on the other vehicle. Before he could open the door, the truck jerked hard again. The same dark SUV hit the driver side of the truck. It shook the entire vehicle, a terrible grinding as it fucked up the side.

The metal-on-metal sound stopped, and a shove showed the other vehicle had pinned the truck between it and the concrete sidewall, trapping the door shut. *What the fuck?*

Mason leaned past Karen and shoved at her door, but nope. Nothing. It didn't give at all.

The shattering of glass forced Mason over Karen, covering her from the falling shards. A hissing sound brought his head up to find the small triangle glass near the front windshield broken, and a black hose poked in.

"The hell is that?" Mason growled out the words, gaze darting for options.

Sam answered after a quick sniff, voice hard. "It's the same gas they used at the hospital."

"You're sure?"

A huffed sound said Sam wasn't an idiot. He had his cell out, the beeping of the numbers as he dialed punctuating the hissing of the gas and the lightheaded sensation Mason struggled to ignore.

He knew the gas Sam was talking about, the type used for alphas when they needed to be sedated. It meant it wouldn't harm Karen. In fact, it wouldn't affect her at all. However, if they didn't get something figured out fast, it would put all three alphas down.

And that wasn't acceptable. He'd just sworn to himself to take care of Karen and here he was failing her already.

Sam's voice from the back seat said he was talking to the police station, giving out the information he could, but the alphas had started to cough.

Mason couldn't break the window beside Karen. She might get cut. Instead, he shifted up the center console and scooted that way. If he could get far enough over, he could drive his boot through the window. He might not be able to get out that way because of the SUV, but getting some of the gas out of the cab could keep him conscious enough to do something.

One problem at a time.

He slid toward Karen, bringing his long legs up, the space not nearly enough for his huge frame. He kicked out his feet once, but the angle wasn't good for much drive. His heels bounced off the glass. His lungs burned, and his thoughts crawled at a snail's pace through his head.

He coughed, as though that could clear his lungs and his head, then lifted his feet to kick again. The window cracked, lines spidering out, but nothing else.

He tried for one more kick, but the gas won. He couldn't find the energy to break the window, to even deliver another kick to finish what the last had started.

Mason curled his fingers around Karen's shirt, as though he could do something, but darkness took him.

Chapter Twenty-One

The bath hadn't help to shed any additional light on Tracy's life. She'd sat back, resting in the nearly scalding water, hoping some epiphany would overtake her. She'd look around in the steamed bathroom and suddenly everything would make sense.

She'd know that the alphas were the right choice for her. She'd know how to deal with Mario. She'd feel like she had control in her life for once.

Instead, she'd only been warm.

Warm and still completely confused.

How could she feel so lost when she'd also never felt happier? Shouldn't that make it easy? The fact that she had within her grasp what she'd always wanted should have made the choice obvious.

Instead, it only made it cloudier. For the first time, she had the chance of losing what she'd really wanted, and now she knew how it felt to have it. Could she stand to lose it now that she'd had a taste?

She'd left the bath when her fingers and toes had wrinkled, when the water had drifted toward chilly.

The house felt strange empty. No Karen, no Sam, no Mason, no Dylan. The silence wasn't threatening, just sad, like a dead Christmas tree in January, and it made her miss the sounds of them all in the walls of the only home she'd had for a long time.

She wanted Karen's shrieking laughter, Mason's conspiratorial whispers, Sam telling them all to be careful and Dylan who would complain and yet join in.

They'd left three hours before, and she expected them gone another hour or two. Claire and her alphas had taken Karen to a cabin their friend owned out of town. She knew they wouldn't speed with Karen in the car, and the girl would probably talk them into stopping every half an hour for something.

The idea of those large, intimidating alphas being completely manipulated by an eight-year-old who couldn't weigh more than sixty pounds made Tracy smile. The reaction surprised and delighted her, that she could find not just passion, but humor with them. Lust was easy, that was biological, but fun? Comfort? Security? She could laugh at them and it wasn't scary, wasn't dangerous. *Is this what it's supposed to feel like when you have a mate?*

Her phone went off in the other room, and Tracy didn't bother to smother the smile. It had to be her alphas, right? She jogged over to it, and sure enough, Dylan's name popped up.

Strange. He isn't the type to call.

"Hello?"

Nothing came through at first, and Tracy pulled the phone away to ensure the call had connected.

Finally, a voice that sent chills down her back answered. "Hello, Tracy." *Mario.*

Tracy leaned against the counter her phone had been on, trying to keep herself standing as every muscle in her suddenly went useless. Mario had Dylan's phone. What did that mean? Was Dylan even alive? What about Mason and Sam? What about Karen?

"What do you want?" Her words came out quiet, and she knew they vibrated with a tremble. She couldn't sound confident. She wasn't.

Mario, however, didn't have the slightest quiver to his voice. He spoke with absolute authority. "You already know that, omega. I want the files."

"I don't have them."

He offered a soft *tsk*, as though she were a dog behaving poorly. "Don't lie to me. I had a tracker on the truck you've been using. That's how I know you picked something up from the storage unit. I had someone go in afterward to find out your mate had a unit under a false name there. It was why I sent someone to your house looking for the files. When I didn't hear back from her, I had to assume she'd been caught, and that the files are elsewhere. A pity, as she'd come rather highly recommended. That track is also how I was able to so easily find and subdue the alphas and your child."

"They're alive?"

"For the moment, yes. None of the alphas can speak, but here."

A pause, then a voice that did cause Tracy to collapse to the hard, wooden floor came through the line. "Mom?"

"Hey, sweetheart, are you okay?"

There was the slightest of unease in her voice, but Karen had always been stronger than she should have been, than she should have needed to be. "I'm okay. Sam, Mason and Dylan won't wake up, though."

"I'm going to get you, Karen, okay? Don't worry, it'll be fine—"

A rustle said the phone had been snatched back, and Mario's voice held nothing but pleasure.

He thought he had won.

Hasn't he?

"Don't make promises you can't keep, omega. Things will be fine if you bring me what I've asked for. Don't think I'm stupid, here. You've had the files for days now and no word. Were you hoping to find something in them to turn over to the police? The people in those files would have never let that happen. You realize that, right? Your only way out of this is to hand over the files to me."

But she didn't have the files. They didn't exist anymore. If she told him that, he wouldn't believe her. Even if he did, he'd realize he had no reason to keep any of them alive anymore.

It meant she had to lie. She had to make him believe she'd get him what he wanted, at least for long enough that she could figure out a plan.

"Okay. I'll bring them, just don't hurt them."

A hard laugh came from him, and she knew right there that even if she had the files, even if she turned them over to him, he'd never let them go.

Why would he? Once he had what he wanted, they were just liabilities to him. There would be no reason to let any of them live. Even if he got the files, they were dead.

"You've got three hours, omega. If you aren't here by then, I'll kill one of the alphas. Don't test me, because I have no problem following through. Tell me you understand."

The words bubbled from her throat like a trained response. She'd learned beneath Richard's thumb to follow orders when given with that tone of voice, so she sold the lie with everything she had. *Play the part. Be the good little omega just one more time.* "I understand."

He gave her the address, a place out of town she didn't recognize, then hung up.

Tracy stood numb for what had to be ten minutes, waiting as if someone was going to tell her what to do. She'd always relied on others, never trusting herself to figure things out. She had no one, now. She could call Claire, could involve those alphas, but what would that do? Mario had abducted three alphas and a girl without a problem. He'd given her the address, which meant he knew someone could come after him. All of that meant the same thing. He was ready for trouble.

The last thing Tracy would do was endanger even more people. If anyone showed up, Mario would kill one of the people she loved, one of the people she couldn't lose.

She pulled herself off the floor with no idea what to do, no plan in mind. She went to the only place she could think of, the room that still smelt of smoke and ash, where the remnants of the files had been taken away, save for the copies of the scraps left behind.

Tracy sat on the floor and spread out the crisp white pages from the file. The copies meant nothing, most of them not even full words let alone complete ideas.

One scrap had a date on it, another the first three numbers of a street address, maybe. She went from page to page, desperate to find something, anything.

Hopelessness dragged at her as ten minutes turned to twenty, then thirty and she'd found nothing.

She picked up one of the pages, squinting to try to make more out of it. She tilted her head, peering at the letters that didn't make any sense.

in Kansas

What was in Kansas? Why couldn't Richard have done this one thing for her, have helped her this one time? After everything he'd stolen from her, after all the ways he'd torn away a good life, he left her in this lurch at the end?

Tracy rubbed her eyes, thinking about the man he'd been at the start, at the way things had seemed so effortless. She recalled how he'd smile at her, the way he introduced her to friends back when they'd been young and still starting out.

Kansas

Tracy froze.

Maybe that wasn't a place. She recalled meeting a client back at the start, in the first years of their mating, when she'd come home early and found them both in Richard's home office.

She took her phone and searched the last name.

It couldn't be a coincidence, could it?

The face of the man she recalled meeting briefly flashed across the screen of her phone.

The same perfectly styled almost-white hair, the same dark eyes. He was older, but it was him.

Torrin Kansas. *in Kansas*. She read what she could on the internet, though it included little. He was a successful businessman, and it was only once she'd gone back a few pages that she found dirt, as if it had all been swept past the first few pages of results.

Tracy went off that, piecing together the scraps of information she had. Most had come from the same box, the one near the bottom that hadn't fully burned. The copies showed the charred tidbits of information left over, and she tried to turn them into something useful.

Together, it gave her a lot of nothing, but she had no other choice.

No other option came to mind, nothing else she could do that might save the people she loved more than anything.

Tracy might have been beaten down by Richard, but now it was up to her to clean up his mess.

He might have been the predator in their relationship, in her life, and she'd never thought she'd be able to fight him.

Mario had turned into the same monster, into the beast that stalked her and threatened everything she had. Standing toe to toe wouldn't work. Maybe she wasn't bigger or faster or stronger, but she was smarter.

The best way to deal with a predator was an even larger predator, and she suspected Torrin Kansas was a much bigger fish in their little pond.

It could work, if she didn't get killed first.

* * * *

Sam woke, groggy and with his head throbbing.

What the hell had happened?

It took a moment to force his eyes open, gunk having developed in his lashes to glue them shut. It reminded him of waking up after his run-in with Mario's goons, when his body had rejected the entire idea of being awake.

"Sam?" Karen's whisper shook his laziness.

Why am I sleeping upright? Where am I?

"Hey, kid," he grumbled, voice rough as he finally woke enough to take in the details of the room.

He was bound to a chair. His fingers brushed the wall, telling him he was against one. To his left, Dylan and Mason slumped forward in their own bonds.

Karen was on his other side, and while bound, she wasn't nearly as securely tied. Her hands were in front of her rather than behind, and her ankles had a zip tie keeping them in place. Still, she wasn't connected to the actual chair.

"You were asleep a long time."

"Yeah, seems that way." He swallowed to clear the dryness of his mouth. "You okay? Not hurt, right?"

She shook her head, wide eyes showing the white around her irises. Even so, she hadn't fallen apart.

The girl was tough, like he'd always said.

"Some people put us in the back of a van. I couldn't wake you up. When we got here, they tied us up."

Sam wanted to ask who *they* were, but he already had a good damned guess. Who else but Mario and his thugs?

He shifted his hands, testing the binding. The arm in the cast was bent at a bad angle, and he had more slack between his wrists because they couldn't quite meet in the middle. His attempt ended up giving him rope burn, but nothing else. Seemed they at least knew how to properly tie someone up. Not that being killed by a competent bad guy really made him any happier.

"The fuck did I drink last night?" Dylan's voice was even rougher than usual, but no less mean.

"Do you have any slack in your rope?" Sam asked without waiting for Dylan to catch up. He was smart, he'd get there.

The moment he did, the moment the other alpha realized where they were and what must have happened, a vicious snarl left his lips. "Kid okay?"

"I'm fine," Karen answered for herself.

Sam looked toward the other alpha in time to see him let out a long breath, and he got that sort of relief. They'd had one job, which was to watch after Karen, and look where they'd ended up.

Mason was the last to wake, but then again, from Sam's fuzzy memory, he might have been the last to go under. Sam recalled him kicking at the window in a bid to break it. He'd probably soaked more of that gas in beforehand, and given his size, they might have even dosed him a second time. He came to with the same unhappy confusion as the others, looking like a dog waking up as he shook his head and his long hair moved from the action.

Having them both awake helped Sam. It was harder to fall to despair with them beside him. Between them, they'd figure something out, right?

The door opened, and in walked a face Sam wouldn't ever forget. He'd sworn to make the bastard pay, but that promise felt even more important considering this newest slight. Putting Sam in the hospital he could let go, but frightening Karen? That he planned to hold against him.

Mario smiled as though they were unimportant but amusing nonetheless. "Nice to have you here," he said. "And Detective Franklin, you look as though you're healing well."

"Fuck off," Dylan chimed in before Sam could say a thing.

Anger flashed in Mario's eyes, reminding Sam not to underestimate the man. He was a coward, sure. He was a frightened little thing who hid behind others to do his dirty work, but for now he had the power to do anything he wanted. Pushing him wouldn't end well.

Mario seemed to pull the anger in, the face of a man who didn't want to admit anyone could get to him, especially those he considered beneath him. "You alphas are all the same, thinking you're special, that you run things. I assure you, you don't run anything here."

When Dylan opened his mouth, Mason growled lowly as a warning, one Dylan took by turning his likely stupid words into a glare instead.

"What are you hoping this gets you?" Sam asked.

A scratching sound filled the space as Mario pulled a chair through the empty room. He said nothing and no one could speak over the high-pitched complaint of the move.

Posturing.

Finally, Mario had moved the chair to the center, in front of them, and sat in it with slowness that reeked of arrogance. He folded his hands and set them in his lap, his moves unhurried. *All a game.* "I'm not sure why everyone keeps asking me what I want. I've made my demands clear from the start. I want the files. It has never been that difficult."

"We were getting them for you," Mason said.

"No, you weren't. I'm not as stupid as you seem to take me for. You had no intention of turning them over to me."

"So, you think tying us up so we can't get them is a good way for us to go get them?" Dylan's grating voice threw a lot of 'you stupid fucker' into his words without having to say it.

"I think that with you here, the omega will be inclined to do as I say. I had thought an abstract threat would be enough, but she is harder-headed than I'd have expected."

"She'd do better with help," Mason pointed out.

"I doubt it. In fact, I bet if you'd never got involved, she'd have handed over what I wanted without a peep. I've seen her files from the police, from the hospital. After what Richard did to her, she'd have given me anything I wanted without a fight if you three hadn't been giving her ideas. With you out of the way, she'll cave and come crawling in here like the broken thing she is."

Sam drew his hands into fists to keep his temper in check. If Mario thought that, he hadn't the first idea about who Tracy really was. He'd never seen her when protecting the things she cared about.

Still, it didn't matter how fierce Tracy could be, it didn't change that she lacked options. They had to figure a way out themselves.

Sam kept the fact there were no files to himself. If Mario realized that, he'd kill them, no question.

He had no idea how long they could bluff, but it was their only chance.

Mario rose, as though the conversation had grown tedious. "I have things to attend to."

"What's going to happen to us?" Karen asked, voice steadier than it should have been.

Mario stopped and stared at her, his head tilting as though he couldn't quite believe she'd addressed him. "If your mother doesn't bring me the things I want, I'll kill the alphas one at a time. As the female child of an omega, you'll possibly be one as well. We'll test you and if you are one, I'll sell you off. Omegas fetch good prices, especially young ones. They're easier to train." Mario's shoulders lifted in a casual shrug, as if he hadn't been speaking of murder and slavery. "Then I'll track down your worthless mother and kill her too, for the trouble."

Karen swallowed but didn't respond, didn't break down. Not even a tremble of her lip.

Good girl.

Mario waited, as if he wanted the tears, but when nothing came, when the eight-year-old outlasted him, he turned his back and stormed from the room.

The loud click of a deadbolt said he'd secured them in.

Dylan spoke first. "Hey, kid, you still got the knife I gave you?"

"You gave her a knife?" Sam couldn't hide the anger in his voice at the idea Dylan had armed the child.

Karen's face lit up. "I do! I tucked it into my boot!"

"Good girl," Dylan praised. "You can lean down far enough to grab it, I think, and cut your hands free."

Karen lifted her bound feet up while reaching down, fingers feeling inside the ankle of her boot. Slowly, she withdrew a pocketknife, and Sam felt the need to cut another glare Dylan's way.

The other alpha only shrugged, as though he didn't give a fuck what Sam thought.

Then again, it *had* come in handy.

Karen opened the blade with a surprisingly practiced flick and started to work on her zip-tie at her wrist, twisting the blade to get it between her and the plastic. It was slow going without much leverage, but eventually, she broke the tie.

Again, she went to work on her ankles, and after what had to be twenty minutes, she'd broken free of all the ties with only a few minor slices to herself to show for it.

Karen came to Sam first and worked on the much thicker rope that bound him. It took longer than he'd have liked, but she got him free, as well.

Unfortunately, the moment he went to rise, his legs gave out and he ended up pitched forward and flat on his face. He wasn't coordinated enough to catch himself, and even if he had been, the cast made it tougher. The gas hadn't cleared his system, yet. Karen worked on Mason, then Dylan, but both had the same issue.

The gas used wouldn't wear off all at once. They'd be disoriented and weak for at least a few hours, just like after Sam's last stay in the hospital. How could they do anything if they couldn't even stand?

Mason, already ahead, nodded toward an upper window. "Karen, sweetheart, there's a window up there. It's small, but you can get through it."

"What about you?"

"Don't worry about us, kid." Dylan had pulled himself back into the chair, since he probably hated sitting on the floor. Still, sweat on his brow said he'd paid for the move. "We'll be fine."

Karen shook her head and tucked the blade into her pocket. "I'm not going to leave you."

"You've gotta," Mason said. "You get out, that's the most important thing. We'll be fine once we rest a little longer, then we'll come out after you."

She shook her head again, face taking on the same hard lines Tracy's did, looking so much like her mother that Sam had a moment of regret.

He couldn't think he wouldn't see his omega again, even if he couldn't quite figure a way it would happen.

They had nothing, their belongings gone, taken while unconscious. The room was sparse, and even in the bits of damaged furniture—a desk, a dresser, some stained and ratty boxes—he doubted Mario and his goons would have left anything useful.

"Okay, kid," Dylan said, the first to bounce back after her refusal. Then again, given Dylan being the one who'd given her the knife, that didn't shock Sam. Seemed Dylan had more faith in the kid than the rest of them. "Go check all those drawers for anything we can use."

Sam watched Karen nod and move off, then exchanged heavy looks with the other alphas.

He had no idea how they were going to get out of this, but they had to figure it out, and fast.

Chapter Twenty-Two

Tracy feared her heart might crack her ribs as she walked into the large office building with the Kansas name across the roofline. The lobby was spacious, modern and freezing.

Despite the chill from an excessive air conditioning system, sweat rolled down between her shoulder blades. The receptionist at the front desk had tried to shoo her away, content to run her off as though she were some mistress looking to score off the boss.

However, when Tracy had dropped Richard's name, when the receptionist had called up to Torrin with that, everything had changed.

Suddenly, two men in black suits with scowls as intimidating as their shaved heads and large frames had shown up in the lobby to escort her in the elevator.

They were both alphas, a fact that might have sent her running just a few weeks prior. She'd have bolted at that scent, at the danger they posed to her. Any alpha would have set her off, but two who glared and didn't speak more than to tell her to follow were the worst of it.

She wasn't the same old omega, though. She wasn't the woman Richard had beaten down, the one Mario thought he could control, and she had all the reason in the world to hold her shoulders back and her head high.

One of the alphas snorted, a soft sound that wasn't entirely unkind. More subtly amused, as if he didn't really care what the outcome was but managed to find some humor in it.

They took the elevator to the top floor, and Tracy held it together, even as they exited the doors and passed a large desk with a scowling woman behind it—the secretary, no doubt.

Through the last set of doors—large metal ones with frosted glass—sat a stern-looking man behind a large, dark-stained wooden desk. The office screamed power. Or arrogance. It was hard to tell the difference much of the time.

The man was younger than she'd have guessed, or perhaps he just looked young because it had seemed so long since she'd last seen him, since so much had changed. His blond hair was slicked back from his forehead, and light eyebrows perched above dark eyes. The contrast was strange, the dark-oak eyes paired with the lighter coloring. "Mrs. Pera. You are the last person I expected to see today."

Tracy turned a gaze on the two alphas still there. "Maybe we should have this talk in private."

Torrin waved off the suggestion. "These two men have my complete confidence. I trust them far more than I trust you, so I believe they'll stay." He said nothing else, sitting back as if he had all the time I the world.

She didn't.

Tracy took a deep breath, then a step forward to gather her courage, her chin held high. "I have a deal for you."

"Really? And what is it you think you can offer me?"

"You know about the death of my mate."

"Yes. If you're expecting me to shed a tear, you've wasted your trip."

His words surprised her. Then again, she supposed criminals could still hate other criminals. One jackal could loathe another, but it didn't make either good. Just two different kinds of bad.

"I don't need your tears. Your protection, on the other hand, is what I'm after."

"I'm not in the business of protecting random omegas." His words weren't mean-spirited. He didn't gloat, but rather spoke as if it were a simple matter of fact. It was if he was explaining he couldn't save every single stray, and that while it was sad, the reality was that some perished.

"Richard kept files on all of the questionable people he knew."

"Questionable?" Up went that blond eyebrow.

Tracy wouldn't let herself be intimidated, not anymore, and certainly not by alphas drunk on their own power. She pushed forward, selling the bluff with everything she had. This had to work. He had to believe her. "I have all Richard's files."

"So? The fact you're here says you must know how many of the police force are on the payroll of any of your mate's colleges. You couldn't take any of those files to the authorities or you would have done so already."

Tracy took another few steps forward until she stood just before the massive desk. "They may not get any of you thrown into prison, but we both know you don't want them getting out."

Torrin didn't move, not a single reaction. He gave nothing away as he stared back.

Keep going. You can do this.

"How would all the other names in those files feel about knowing everything? Sending it to the police wouldn't do anything but sending it to—" She pulled memories in, trying to recall names Richard had used. He might not have spoken to her, but he'd often move through life as though she were a ghost, on calls without worrying about her. She took advantage of that, used it to her benefit for once. "Navarro, Tinkman or Harris would cause you a few problems. Not to mention releasing them to new sources. You might have friends in high places, but you know what they say about rats and sinking ships. No one would benefit from those files going public."

A muscle twitched in Torrin's jaw, the only proof that he'd heard Tracy. They stared, neither moving, neither giving in.

Torrin leaned forward, setting his forearms on the desk. "You are playing a dangerous game."

"Trust me, I know. Right now, Mario Navarro has my daughter and my mates, is threatening to kill them, so I understand exactly how dangerous this game is for me. The question is, do you understand how dangerous it is for you?"

Torrin narrowed his gaze further, his expression hard, but Tracy gave nothing away. She didn't let fear show. She'd spent so much of her life afraid, submissive, willing to go along with whatever was safest. *Never again.*

"It's a simple deal. I want protection for my daughter, my mates and myself. As long as we're safe, those files never see the light of day. If anything happens to any of us, they get out."

"And if something happens to you that isn't me?"

"Well, I figure it's in your best interest to make sure that doesn't happen."

"And you expect me to first step in and deal with Mario, I suspect?"

"If you want all those files to stay secret, then yes. It's a small price to pay for your privacy."

He tapped his fingers against the wooden desk, loud in the quiet room. "And you think this is a good idea? You think you can maneuver me like this?"

She met his gaze and let him see how serious she was, let him see the bone-deep determination built by a life of being run over. This had to work, because if it didn't? She'd lose everything. "I don't think I have a choice, and right now? Neither do you."

* * * *

Dylan wanted Karen out of there. He wanted her miles away and running as fast as her little legs would carry her. Instead, she was still in the room, having absolutely no intention of running.

The damn kid was just like her mother. Stubborn. Difficult. Too loyal for her own good. Worse, with the alphas down for the count, it wasn't like any of them could muscle her out themselves. Hell, she could have knocked them over with a small shove.

So Dylan used the time to work out his muscles, to try to get them responding worth a damn. Not that it was going well. No matter how hard he tried, his body was about as cooperative as that of an unruly foal. His legs wouldn't hold his weight and his arms had about enough coordination to manage to punch himself in the face when he was trying to push his hair back.

It was looking more and more like there was no chance of a good escape. Not that Dylan had ever believed in miracles or shit like that. The more he looked around, the more they came up with exactly nothing and the more he had to acknowledge they were probably going to die there.

Which he wasn't looking forward to, he had to admit. Dylan hadn't been a man afraid of death, but then again, he'd never had much worth keeping, either. Hard to worry about something like dying when his life hadn't been anything to write home about.

If he'd had a home to write back to.

Now, though? He thought about not seeing Tracy's smiling face. He thought about the way she fought with him, the way she squared up those thin shoulders of hers and tried to stare him down. He thought about Karen laughing and the spark in her eyes when she realized she was capable of so much more than she'd known. Fuck, he was going to miss that. He was going to miss the dinners where they all sat around that big table Sam had gotten, where they laughed and settled into such an easy routine that it seemed criminal they'd not been together all along. Hell, Dylan had come to regret the years he'd spent pissed, the ones where he'd held on to anger instead of letting it go and getting the fuck over his pissy attitude.

Didn't it just figure that, at the end, when he finally found what he really wanted, he'd lose it? Somehow that seemed to fit with his general life and luck.

And, fuck, for the first time, it mattered.

Voices from outside had him twisting his head to listen. Thus far, he'd seen no one else, hadn't heard anyone. The door had been locked, since Karen had tried it, quietly, to avoid detection.

Sam reacted first to the noises and lowered his voice to a whisper. "Karen, they're coming, so you need to go, now."

Again the girl shook her head, her hair swinging around her shoulders. "No."

Sam managed enough dexterity to grab her hand, squeezing it tight. "You've got to, sweetheart. You can go get help, okay?"

Tears swam in the girl's eyes, but they didn't escape. No, she sniffed once, hard, and again shook her head. "I'm not leaving you." Her voice broke, a tiny fissure in the walls she tried to put up. "I'm not going to lose you guys."

And there it went. Dylan's heart—useless thing that it was—cracked at the pain in that voice. Even so, she needed to get. The truth was that they weren't getting free, and any idiot with a brain would know to off the alphas first. While that made him happy, that Karen would be safe, at least for a while, she also didn't need to see that shit.

Before they could have the conversation further, before they could try to push her to go, the door swung open.

The moment Mario and his two goons walked in, they lifted their weapons at the sight of the alphas free.

Free, but all still seated, which showed more than anything the lack of strength they had. Mario scanned his gaze across them, then let out a soft laugh. "I suppose I shouldn't have underestimated you. However, even unbound, you don't seem much of a threat." He walked forward, making Dylan's shoulders bunch at the nearness, not wanting the fucker anywhere close to Karen. "I am forever amused that society likes to hold alphas up as something special. Clearly, that is in error."

Dylan opened his mouth to say something he shouldn't but snapped it shut when he thought about Karen. She didn't need to pay the price for Dylan's big mouth.

Mario cocked up an eyebrow, but let it go. He glanced down at his watch. "Unfortunately, the omega is late. She should have been here five minutes ago."

"Traffic?" The snark slid from Dylan before he could help it, and his reward was one of Mario's goons backhanding him. Copper filled his mouth, even though it couldn't have been much blood. Just a few drops from a sting in his lip where his teeth caught him.

He spat the blood out onto the floor, ignoring the desire to tell the asshole he could barely hit. That would only make things worse, and for the first time, he had someone else to think about. While Dylan would happily suffer a few extra bruises for his difficult attitude, he didn't want Karen seeing it. She'd witnessed too much shit in her life already.

He turned a glance her way to find her shrinking back, behind Sam, fear painted across her features. He could almost see her back when her fucking father had been alive, her hiding from him with that same face.

He gave her a smile, and while his chin tickled from a drop of blood that made its way down his skin, the smile seemed to soothe the kid.

Mario watched the exchange, gaze careful. He huffed softly, then shook his head. "This is the problem. Alphas do whatever they want, and we allow it. Betas outnumber alphas and omegas four to one, and yet we like to pretend you are special. You are mistakes, evolutionary screw-ups driven by hormones instead of your brains. And yet, even though alphas haven't shown themselves to be all that vital, we keep setting you on pedestals."

Dylan had heard such tirades before. Sure, maybe as an alpha, he wasn't the one to have shit to say about how betas had it, but everyone thought they had it bad. Alphas got blamed for shit all the time, were watched carefully, always suspected first before a beta for any crime. The fact was that there were shitty parts to any designation, and if anything, betas had it damned good. They flew under the radar, didn't have to worry about shit.

Some just took it to heart, as though it was some personal slight to them. He'd seen it in his stepdad, the way he'd blamed everything on alphas, like they'd personally fucked him over. Mario was the same sort of asshole beta with a chip on his shoulder, always feeling the need to show off that he was just as good as any alpha.

Mario kept speaking. "I told her what would happen if she didn't show up. Of course, I can't do away with all my leverage. That would be foolish. I still need her to follow through on her part, but she seemed to need a reminder about who is in charge."

Dylan didn't even need Mario to keep going. He knew exactly what was going to happen, and hell, maybe his shitty attitude was good for something. Mario was going to off someone to prove to he was serious, and since Dylan had managed to piss him off already, he was probably the best bet.

Fuck, that was just fine, though. If one of them didn't walk away, he'd rather it be him. If he could buy the others the time, it was worth it.

"You don't have to do this," Sam said, always the one to try to fix shit.

"I really do." Mario waved his hand toward Sam, and one of the goons lifted his gun.

"So, you get others to do your dirty work?" The words left Dylan before he could help them, desperate to pull the attention back. "Can't even take care of your own problems?"

Mario's gaze locked in on Dylan. *Here we are, back in the game.* "You don't know anything."

"I know that you hire alphas to deal with your problems. Doesn't matter how much talking you do, you're just a typical beta who hides behind others because you can't cut it."

Mario's face pinched into tight lines before he reached out, snatching the weapon from the other man's hand. He walked over to Dylan, and when he raised the pistol, the awkward tremble in his arm said he'd never held one before. "One of you dying is as good as any other. While I wouldn't have minded the detective going first, I've got to admit, I like the idea of ending you myself."

Dylan pulled his shoulders back and lifted his chin, unwilling to even flinch and give the fucker any pleasure of seeing him squirm. Mario's arm quivered, but he stood there as if he was the biggest, baddest asshole ever, high on his own inflated sense of ego now that he had the gun.

Before he could pull the trigger, something flew at him. A heartbeat later, a call from Sam. "Karen!"

Sure enough, Karen's thin body plowed into Mario, but due to her tiny size, he didn't budge. It was enough for Mario to be knocked off course, however, and distracted. He struggled with her but couldn't pull her off.

The click of her pocketknife's blade locking into place, a flash of silver, then a howl from Mario.

She'd plunged the blade into his side, and even Dylan winced when she twisted the blade, forcing the wound open wider and causing red to pour like a faucet.

That was enough for Mario to really yank back, to throw her off and deliver a punishing backhand to her face, one hard enough to drive her small body to the floor.

A phone rang in the background, the hulking bodyguard to the right looking at the number, then answering in a hushed voice.

Mario grasped the wound, the gun having dropped to the floor during his struggle with Karen. Blood leaked from between his fingers, staining his immaculate fancy clothing. "You bitch," he said, voice all hysterical anger.

Karen's wild red hair hung in her eyes as she pushed to her hands, picking herself up. *Strong girl. Mario would have been down for the count after a hit like that.*

Mario bent forward, gasping in pain as he grabbed the gun. He pointed it toward Karen, and Dylan moved.

Despite the weakness, despite the drugs still in his system, he moved. Seemed the gas couldn't quite overpower basic biological urges, like the one that told him to fucking keep that kid — *my kid* — safe. Because, she was his kid. Blood didn't matter, because he'd claimed her mother and that meant he claimed her, too. The feeling was strange, the knowledge of this ready-made family, the sort of thing he never figured he'd get, but he was done fighting it. Even if he died there — and it was looking pretty likely — he was going to die knowing he had something worth a damn.

He didn't throw himself at Mario. He had no chance at doing shit to him, not in that condition, but at Karen. He threw himself over her, shielding her body with his.

"Wait." The gruff voice was new, and Dylan lifted his head, expecting to see someone else in the room. Instead, it was the henchman who had answered his phone. He fired his pistol, but the bullet tore through the chest of the other guard, not one of the alphas.

Mario yanked back, too startled to lift his weapon at the bodyguard. "What are you doing?"

The bodyguard appeared unconcerned with the room, as though nothing there mattered more than whoever spoke on the phone. "Yes, Mr. Kansas."

"Kansas? You're working for Torrin?" Mario's cheeks went red.

None of it meant much to Dylan, beyond a possible chance at making it out alive. Of course, whoever wanted Mario out of the way might not have any better plans for them than Mario did, but hell, hard to get worse than where they were right then.

The man focused on Mario for the first time. "These people are under Mr. Kansas's protection." He held the phone out, finger pressing a button. "You are on speaker, Mr. Kansas."

An authoritative voice came through the line, one that held actual power rather than the pretending Mario liked to do. "You are supposed to contact others before taking action like this on your own, Mario, especially when they might affect more than just yourself."

"This wasn't about you. It was about me. I couldn't just let this bitch have those papers on me! They could send me to jail."

"She has agreed that no file will come to light in exchange for the protection of herself, her child and those alphas. I agreed to this arrangement and already informed a few of our mutual acquaintances. We have all come to a consensus that this is the safest course of action."

"You can't do this," Mario whined, having gone from an overconfident asshole to a child whose toy was being taken away.

"I can. Are the hostages unharmed?"

The bodyguard answered. "One alpha has a split lip, and they are recovering from the gas used to sedate them, but otherwise unharmed."

"The child?"

"Mr. Navarro struck her."

Silence crackled. No one drew breath, as though the voice across the line could reach out through the distance.

"He struck her?" Had any words sounded so dangerous, rumbled out slowly?

"Yes, sir. Hard enough to knock her to the floor."

An unhappy sound, not quite a growl but close, before Torrin answered. "He behaves like a wild dog and should be put down like one."

"Understood." The bodyguard pulled the trigger twice, delivering two rapid shots to Mario's skull, the skill at which he fired them frightening, even to Dylan who was no stranger to guns.

Mario's body fell to the floor, and for all his posturing and threats, he'd been reduced to nothing with only a moment's thought.

Dylan kept Karen's face shielded from the body, didn't want her seeing that. She trembled beneath him, but he wasn't about to stop shielding her. This Mr. Kansas, this bodyguard, they might not want to kill them right then, but that didn't mean he trusted any of them.

The voice from the phone started up again. "My employee will escort you all to your home, and I will have your omega meet you there shortly. You are all under the same agreement as she is. As long as those files never get out, as long as none of you breathe a word of what is in them, I can assure you, you will remain perfectly safe. It was nice doing business with you."

The line went dead, and Dylan turned his head to view each of the others in the room.

What the fuck had just happened?

Chapter Twenty-Three

Sam traced his fingers over the developing bruise on Karen's cheek. It was swelling, would turn all sorts of colors during the healing process, and he hated them all.

She was already asleep, had been since they'd gotten her home and she'd passed out on the couch waiting for her mother. She'd woken long enough to hug Tracy before exhaustion dragged her back under.

Mason had carried her into her room and tucked her into the bed. She'd rolled to her side, her small arm thrown around the pillow, and gone straight back to sleep.

Tracy stood with them, as though all of them needed to take a deep breath and accept everyone was safe. Everyone had lived. They'd faced down Mario and his plans and come out the other side together. And Tracy? She'd stood her ground when others would have crumbled. She'd drawn on all that strength she'd doubted she had to do what no one else could have.

Sam left the room first, with the others filing out behind him. Once back in the kitchen, far enough away no one would wake the sleeping kid, Sam said what he couldn't help. "What do you want, Tracy? I get that you're scared, that you're nervous, but after tonight? After almost losing everything? I want to be clear — no, I need to be clear. I want this, now more than ever. I want you here, in this house. I want to put Karen to bed at night and have her know without a doubt she's got a home and a family here. I wanted this before, but now? Now I need it. I'm not pretending anymore, not trying to go slow, and I need you to decide if that's what you want."

Tracy didn't respond at first, the same hesitation on her face she always wore.

Mason chimed in, setting his large hand on Tracy's cheek, rewarded by her turning toward him to nuzzle his palm. "Kitten, come on. You faced down someone who, honestly, scares the shit out me, all on your own. You've got nothing to be afraid of with us. Pretty sure you know what you want. You just gotta take it. And, in case I ain't being clear here, what I want is you naked and against me every fucking night."

Dylan didn't bother with the pretty words. Instead, he stepped up to her and leaned down, taking her lips in a kiss that had Sam's cock growing interested. He pressed her until her back hit the counter, then ravished her mouth.

Not that Tracy appeared bothered by it, since she returned his fervor with her own, clutching at his shoulders for purchase.

Dylan broke the kiss, both of them panting hard. "Give us everything, Red, and we'll give you the same."

That seemed to do it. All that fear of the known, of fully trusting someone else, of trusting herself to know what she wanted, all burned away. It was scoured clean by their declarations, and only a stark need in her eyes remained.

She wanted them. All of them.

Dylan must have seen it too, because he wrapped her legs around his waist and headed for Sam's room, the one farthest from Karen's.

They were taking their omega to bed, and after such a hard night, after almost losing everything, he planned to worship every last inch of her body until none of them could move.

And Sam had never wanted anything more.

Dylan loved carrying his mate, the way she clung to him, the way she trusted him. Even calling her his mate didn't cause him to stumble.

She *was* his. Body, mind, soul, all that shit. Maybe he wasn't someone with fancy words and pretty declarations, but none of that mattered. She was his, he was hers. The girl owned every fucking bit of him.

He dropped her onto the bed, warmed by her gasp, then her sweet smile as she bounced twice. Of course, it was the lust that won out as he stripped his shirt off.

He was naked in no time, needing to feel her warm body against his. She didn't just own him, no. He hadn't been worth owning before. Too angry and bitter and stuck in the past to be worth having.

She'd done more than that. She'd changed him, showed him he could want more, that he deserved more, that she could give him more. She'd mended him in ways he didn't know were possible.

Instead of the useless, angry male he'd been, he cared. He cared about her, about the child who felt like a part of him and about the friends he'd lost for far too long. She'd pulled them back together, made a family out of them and, as he blanketed her body with his, he tried to tell her how much that meant to him.

Her kisses were desperate, and she scratched her nails along his skin. He grasped her shirt, yanking it up until it slipped over her head. She'd stopped wearing those baggy things, stopped hiding, and it meant he got to see each beautiful inch of her willing body.

Dylan broke away from her lips as he moved back, wanting another, more intimate taste of her, and when she let her thighs fall open for him? When he got to look up her body, to find those trusting eyes of hers locked on him?

For the first time ever, he felt like maybe he deserved this, and even if he didn't? He'd go through hell to keep it anyway.

Mason chuckled at the way their flighty omega bumped Dylan's shoulder with her knee when she tried to close her legs. She might trust them, a whole hell of a lot, now, but that didn't fix good old-fashioned nerves.

And, always the selfless helper, Mason stepped in. He slid behind Tracy, pulling her body to his, her back to his broad chest. She melted against him, the glue that had put his life back together.

He reached around her small body to grasp her knees, then spread her thighs wide.

Her breath caught, but she didn't do more than give an experimental tug at his grip.

Mason nuzzled her soft cheek. "Come on, kitten, why don't you just lie back?"

She shivered, as though his voice were a chill that stroked over her naked body. It made him want to keep her on this edge forever, because he doubted that he'd ever grow tired of how she warred between shyness and lust. Her past would sneak up, whispering to her that she couldn't trust him. It would try to work its claws into her, to drag her backward, and that battle would flicker in her wary eyes.

Then Tracy would take a deep breath and choose to move forward, to lean against him, to not just offer but take the kiss she wanted, and Mason would lose himself again. Lost to her quiet strength, to her willingness and ability to build a life out of nothing.

She'd wasted the talent trying to give that prick she'd been mated to a life, but she'd done the same for Mason. She'd mended the family he'd lost, creating something out of the mess they'd made it, so he had more than just an omega. He had a foundation, a future and a real home.

He pressed a kiss to her shoulder, a smirk spreading across his lips at the first hard jerk of her body when Dylan found her clit with his tongue. Even with her moving, Mason held tight to keep her still and spread open for Dylan's attention.

Mason teased her ear with his lips, toying with the lobe, using his teeth as his gaze remained locked on Dylan's work. Her cunt glistened in the light that spilled in from the open bathroom, damp from Dylan's work and the resulting wetness of her own response.

It made the sort of image he'd never forget. Hell, he'd be happy to tattoo that shit on his brain.

Mason stroked Tracy's inner thighs, drowning in her scent and those sexy little gasps she made while trying to stay quiet even as Dylan ate her out.

Let her try. It'll be even more fun to drag those sounds out of her.

He left a trail of kisses along her shoulder, her collarbone, everything he could reach as he enjoyed her, the moment, the thing he'd wanted but never knew how to get.

This was the life he'd needed, the one he'd wanted forever, and it was the sexy, brave and sweet omega writhing against him who had given it all to him.

Tracy couldn't smother the loud cry when Dylan latched his demanding lips around her swollen clit. He drove her hard with the greedy sucks he offered up, and Mason was no better, his grip solid.

A hand at her cheek turned her face, and lips pressed to hers. It only took a moment before she knew who kissed her, even without opening her eyes, without counting hands or trying to think through it. Each male was so different.

Sam was sweet, cautious, like some guard who was forever by her side. He kissed her with that same devotion, the sense of security, the steadiness she'd always craved. Tracy had spent so much of her life unsure, in the lurch and never knowing where her feet might land. Sam offered security she had needed. She lost herself in that same safety as she leaned toward him, into his kiss, into that masculine taste that was just him, and the fact she'd been smitten and lost to him even when she'd tried everything to resist it.

Mason's strong hands on her thighs kept her pinned open, and she'd never confuse a kiss from him for either of the others. Mason was all ease, all fun, all comfort. He slid into any situation and made her feel like she fit, like no matter what happened, they had it handled, like she belonged. She'd spent so much time on the outskirts, afraid to be noticed, and Mason made her realize she didn't need to hide. She didn't have to be anyone else or worry what anyone else thought of her. She could just be herself, and she was never alone.

And Dylan? The alpha poised between her spread thighs who licked her as if starving for her taste? He was the most unexpected, the most frustrating. He'd nearly sent her running the first few times they'd met, and yet somehow, she'd fallen for him. He reminded her of a junkyard dog. He snarled to scare people off, but once she'd gotten past his defenses? She had no bigger supporter, no one who believed in her more, who would fight harder for her. And that was how he fit so well, because even though he could protect her from everything, he honestly believed he didn't need to. He pushed her to do what he knew she could, even if she doubted it. He gave her a safe place to fight, for her to rage against, and to know that if she could stand against him, she could stand against anyone.

Tracy had run from everything, hidden from the world. She'd ducked her head, done what she could to keep her daughter safe and just tried to survive. She'd stopped believing that she could have anything else, that life was ever anything better. Then these three alphas had come into her life and turned it upside down. They'd dragged her from her self-imposed solitude, from her fear, from the place she'd buried herself, content to let life pass her by.

Pinned between their bodies, their heat and strength and touches surrounding her, she gave herself over to what they offered. She kissed Sam, pressed back against Mason's solid body and lost herself in the stroke of Dylan's tongue — all the things she couldn't imagine losing.

She closed her eyes and basked in the affection, in her new life, the one she'd gotten when she'd been saved by her alphas.

Want to see more from this author?
Here's a taster for you to enjoy!

The Omega's Alphas:
Protected by her Alphas
Jayce Carter

Excerpt

Maybe pouting wasn't the most mature choice, but Emily could think of no better reaction when faced with her three new—and far too hot to be fair—alpha bodyguards.

Her father had discovered she'd been skipping out on her last protection detail. Not that it had been the first time she'd taken her security less than seriously. Men were easy to manipulate and convince to do whatever she wanted. It hadn't taken more than a week or two of work for her before a new bodyguard would start turning a blind eye to whatever she wanted. Not to mention, getting her way had never been hard, not with her classical good looks. Long blonde hair, bright blue eyes and a figure she spent plenty of hours of cardio keeping slim meant it didn't take much to tempt men.

Besides, her father hovered over her as though she were still a child. As an alpha, he couldn't help it, but that didn't mean she'd just put up with it. He'd been overprotective all her life, ever since her mother had been murdered when Emily had hardly been old enough to walk. Why should Emily suffer just because her mother had ended up the target of some deranged alpha?

Life as an omega had enough problems without factoring in a father who wouldn't let her go to the store alone.

"Miss Pitch," Levi, the head bodyguard, said with that professional, distant politeness she loathed as he gestured toward the waiting limo. He was dressed in one of the all-black suits that seemed obligatory in his line of work. Not that she'd complain with how he filled out that suit. Levi had that no-nonsense attitude, paired with dark green eyes and dark hair. His stern expression was the sort of thing that could melt panties, at least if he hadn't been such a buzz kill. Still, it made her want to see how far she could press him before she got a reaction.

Emily scowled, lifted her chin and walked ahead with the haughty "I'm better than you" attitude she'd learned at an early age. Arguing any more now wouldn't do a thing.

She'd argued for hours with her father when he'd told her about the additional security and it hadn't changed anything. It hadn't been the first time they'd had this fight, and it wouldn't be the last. Because she was his only child, her father liked to keep her wrapped up and away from any potential danger, and Emily? She liked pushing her luck.

Maddox moved in front of her to open the door, which put her beside the very large alpha. He'd unnerved her more than the other two from the moment she'd first seen him, when he'd stood, his height having to be six-four at least. Add to that a shaved head, serious eyes and the broadest chest she'd ever seen, and it was no wonder she'd taken an automatic step backward.

The third alpha, Grant, lacked the outwardly vicious edges of the others. Instead, he smiled like a lure, like the prettiest, most tempting trap in the world. Eyes so dark a brown they were nearly black had peered at her, coaxing her to fall into them, and all of it wrapped up in flawless dark skin.

Were all alphas so tempting, or was it just those three? Or, maybe her lack of exposure meant any alpha at all would draw her in.

As an unclaimed omega, Emily had plenty of eyes on her. No shortage of alphas would have loved a shot at her, since the possibility of mating into the Pitch family would tempt even saints. Money, power, prestige—her bloodline could offer them all to the lucky alpha who landed her as a mate. Her father knew that fact well, which meant his protection kept her both safe and away from any alphas.

Emily slid in and to the front of the limo, as far as she could away from them. Levi, Grant and Maddox got in afterward, showing no reaction to her distance. Maddox and Grant had their focus moving from place to place, not darting but a slow perusal. Neither appeared worried, just alert. Meanwhile, Levi had his gaze pinned to his phone, his finger scrolling through whatever he read on his screen.

"I have spin class tonight." Emily crossed her arms and leaned back in the seat. Being ignored never failed to make her want to act out.

Levi lifted his gaze from his phone, a bored expression across his features. "I think we can miss that. The threat against you is credible, and tomorrow we will take you to the airport. At that point—"

"I'll be safe again. Right. Since you're new, I'll let you in on a secret. I'm never safe. After this, Dad will come up with another reason why I'm in danger, another reason why I need an escort." She threw the words out there like bait, waiting for one of the alphas to respond.

That was how it worked. Throw out tiny barbs, little complaints, and play up the "poor girl who just needs a little help" card. One of the alphas would tell her it wasn't so bad, and she'd squeeze out a few tears about how hard it was to be trapped all the time, how she just needed a little freedom, and before she knew it, she'd be off to spin class.

Instead, Levi cocked a dark eyebrow before dismissing her and returning to his phone as if she hadn't spoken.

The gall... Emily's mouth dropped open. She was the only daughter of business mogul Samson Pitch. She was a damn legend. She had mating requests from no less than fifty different alphas, and those were just the ones who had passed the first level of rejections. How dare some hired help ignore her like she were a petulant kid?

"This is all just overreacting," she pressed, wanting him to engage.

Levi placed his phone on his thigh, then set his arm over the back of the seat, finally giving her his full attention. "The threat against you is serious enough for your father to have hired us. You've had too many close calls, recently."

"It's not the first time someone has threatened me. It wasn't the first time my house security was tampered with, or the first time someone thought they could make a few quick bucks by planning to abduct me. You know what, though? Nothing has ever actually happened."

"And it won't happen this time, either." Levi leveled her with a steady gaze, and Emily saw that his eyes were green. Not a light green, but an emerald that didn't seem to fit with his all-work, stick-up-the-ass personality. Eyes like those belonged on writers who recited sweet-but-terrible poetry on the beach. They certainly did not fit on an alpha like Levi.

Worse than those eyes, though? The thing Emily tried her hardest to ignore? The alphas smelled good. No, not just good — they smelled delicious. The scent of all three filled the limo, which suddenly didn't seem nearly large enough. Emily had spent so little time around alphas, she'd never gotten such a powerful whiff of that heavenly scent. She'd had no idea that the potent, masculine smell would have her body reacting, her pussy growing wet without any help from her at all.

So they smell good. So what? They're still assholes. Pizza smells divine, but I'm not about to fuck it.

"Come on. You can't uproot my whole life just because of one little threat." She tried to ignore the effect the small space was having on her, the way her panties had dampened.

Maddox snorted, his gaze out of the window as though he wasn't listening. Still, his curled lips said he'd heard every word.

Grant answered. "Don't tell me that works with the betas?"

"It must, given they did such a terrible job with her protection," Levi said. "Hard to believe some batted eyelashes could sway someone."

Batted eyelashes? Emily sat up straight, feeling the need to defend her skills, skills which went far beyond just some fluttering lashes.

"Betas are easier to manipulate," Levi continued. "They are often looking to prove themselves, and a pretty, bratty omega can get whatever she wants from them."

"She does seem like a brat, doesn't she? Saw that a mile away when we got her files," Grant said.

"Excuse me," Emily interrupted, "but you don't have any idea what you're talking about."

Levi looked in her direction. "So you haven't been manipulating your bodyguards? You haven't been slipping your security details when they can't be manipulated? You haven't been sleeping with them?"

The last accusation hit her the hardest, like a punch to the gut.

She hadn't thought anyone knew about that, at least no one but her father, and he only had suspicions.

I won't feel guilty about it. I have to spend all my time with these bodyguards. I'm never allowed to meet anyone else. Fuck him for trying to make me feel bad for having sex with the only men I'm around. Even as she told herself all the reasons why she shouldn't worry…she did.

Men wanted her for what she could give them, for what a future mating with her could do for them. It meant all those alphas her father had approved, the ones who sent expensive gifts, were the enemy at best. Sleeping with her bodyguards was her *fuck you* to expectations. Even if no one else knew, each was her own little rebellion that made her feel more in control of a life she had no real control over.

"You don't know anything," Emily repeated.

"Of course, Miss Pitch." Levi maintained the uninterested tone which implied he didn't care who she had slept with or why, though in the same breath, he managed to call her a liar. "We will go to your residence for the evening. No spin class, no stops. Maddox can pick up food for us should you have nothing to eat at your home. Tomorrow, you will pack, and we will go to the airstrip. Your plane leaves at four tomorrow afternoon. We'll transfer your protection to the team who will go with you to Europe."

Her father had already said the move was temporary. She'd spend the summer there while those her father had hired worked to ferret out the danger to her. Her father had promised she could come home by winter, that he'd have everything settled.

"So I only have to put up with you for twenty-four hours?"

Grant released a laugh, sitting back. "So, the stories of your brattiness are pretty much on point."

Levi shot him a hard look before returning his gaze to Emily. "Yes. In only twenty-four hours, you will be someone else's problem."

Emily opened her mouth to say something back, something sharp, and to remind them they were not at all on the same level. Instead, a crash silenced her.

As soon as it happened, Levi was beside her, his large, strong hand grasping the back of her neck and pressing her face down near her knees. The limo swerved, but nothing could shake Levi's solid grip.

Another sound, so loud it made her ears ring, filled the space along with something raining down on her. It took a moment for her to realize it was glass.

The alphas shouted, but her ears couldn't make out the words over the ringing in her ears. The limo swerved and shook, like it had gone off the road, and Levi yanked her seatbelt on, managing to hook it before the loud snap of twisting metal filled the limo and everything went black.

Home of Erotic Romance

Sign up for our newsletter and find out about all our romance book releases, eBook sales and promotions, sneak peeks and FREE romance books!

About the Author

Jayce Carter lives in Southern California with her husband and two spawns. She originally wanted to take over the world but realized that would require wearing pants. This led her to choosing writing, a completely pants-free occupation. She has a fear of heights yet rock climbs for fun and enjoys making up excuses for not going out and socializing.

Jayce loves to hear from readers. You can find her contact information, website details and author profile page at https://www.totallybound.com

www.ingramcontent.com/pod-product-compliance
Lightning Source LLC
Chambersburg PA
CBHW020223260626
47156CB00002B/505